THE WARMER

A Novel

Patrick Robbins

ISBN: 978-1-957723-92-1 (hard cover)
       978-1-957723-93-8 (soft cover)

Edited by: Amy Ashby

Published by Pipevine Press
an imprint of Warren Publishing
Charlotte, NC
www.warrenpublishing.net
Printed in the United States

This one's for you, Left Eye.
Love, Schmutzy

PART ONE

Lucy: Why do you think we're put here on Earth, Charlie Brown?
Charlie Brown: To make others happy.
*Lucy: I don't think **I'm** making anyone very happy ...*
*of course, nobody's making **me** very happy either ....*
SOMEBODY'S NOT DOING HIS JOB!

—*Peanuts* by Charles Schulz, **8.16.1961**

1.

In the spring of 2005, I came home from my temp job at the tax bureau to find a note from my mother that read, *The Peppercorn job's yours if you want it*. She had a high school friend who knew the managing editor of Peppercorn Press, a small publishing house in New York City. They were looking for interns, to be paid three hundred dollars a week for twelve weeks of the summer; I mentioned my interest, strings were pulled, and there we were. Things like this have convinced me that 90 percent of life is who you know.

Another connection got me a place to stay, this one with family ties. My mother and her cousin Ruth were born a few months apart and turned out to be best friends. Each was maid of honor at the other's wedding, and one drunken night, they slit their index fingertips, pressed them together, and resolved that their firstborns would have similar names, as a sign of their mothers' special bond. God knows why they kept their drunken word, but they did. Ruth's daughter came first and was called Nadine, so a year and a half later, I was stuck with Ned.

When we were kids and our mothers were visiting each other constantly, Nadine and I would run around and play a lot—we'd go biking, have races, that sort of thing. If it were unpleasant outside, we'd stay in and read to each other or play with my action figures or her Barbies, depending on who was at whose house. Our sensibilities weren't always the same—she'd make G.I. Joe serve tea, I'd have

Skipper throw rocks at Barbie—but we always had fun. Basically, Nadine was the big sister I never had, and I was her little sort-of brother. It was a nice relationship to have, and one I sometimes wish I'd never mislaid.

Once I made a ramp with plywood and milk crates and dared Nadine to try it first. She did, and my excitement turned to horror when the plywood cracked on her and she took a header on the sidewalk. She came out of it with a severe scrape on her forehead; I came out of it with tremendous guilt and a duty to make sure she never got hurt again.

After breakfast the next morning, I called Peppercorn to accept the position. My mother was washing dishes and smiled over her shoulder at me as I gave them the news. "You'll stay with Nadine," she told me after I hung up. "You can work in Manhattan and live there too. She's got a couch that folds out. It'll be perfect." As far as Mom was concerned, the subject was closed.

"She may want a say in this," I said.

"Oh, nonsense." She rinsed off a handful of silverware and put it in the strainer. "She'll be happy to have you."

"She doesn't even know me. We haven't seen each other in ten years."

This was true. The last time I'd seen her was at her eighth-grade graduation, and it took a four-hour drive to do that. While my mother and I stayed in western Massachusetts, Ruth and Nadine had bounced around the Eastern Seaboard until Nadine went to NYU and got caught up in the world of film production. Now she was a lab assistant, which paid enough that she could afford a place on the Upper East Side. Not to mention a couch that folded out.

"She's your cousin—" my mother said.

"Second cousin."

"—so of course she'll be glad to help you. Family takes care of family."

Which turned out to be Nadine's sentiment exactly when we finally got to talk on the phone. "This'll be fun," she said, her voice warm with anticipation. "We can get caught up, you can meet my friends, and there's always something to do."

"And it's okay to take over your couch for the summer?"

She laughed. "It's a great couch. You'll love it." Neither a yes nor a no, I couldn't help noticing, but I kept it to myself.

Something else I kept to myself was my biggest reason for leaving home, and that was Val Whitney. Val had been my girlfriend for the last year and a half of college—more than my girlfriend, I always thought—and her hometown was twenty miles away from mine. This had meant everything to us back in the day. Then Val said how she felt like I was always expecting her to be the one to make the drive down. After a month of my driving up, I felt similarly put-upon. At some point we started caring more about whose turn it was to drive than we did about seeing each other. From there it was just a short step to asking why that might be the case, and the rot spread quickly after that.

I suppose Val and I weren't cut out to be together forever, but that didn't make living with the end of our relationship any more fun. When I'd wake up, I couldn't help reminding myself that I had good cause to be unhappy before I even opened my eyes. Opening them was no help—there wasn't a single noun in western Massachusetts that didn't remind me of Val in one way or another. Towels, streetlights, popcorn, each and every song on the radio—all of them battering my psyche with dull punch after dull punch, chorus after chorus of the Val blues.

I wasn't saddened by the unrelenting lack of Val so much as I was weighed down. Every thought of her made me want to do nothing, say nothing, be nothing. The bad memories slammed my spirit; the good memories crushed it. As she became more abstract, she became more concrete.

Throwing myself into my temp work hadn't been much help; it was too undemanding, gave me too little to think about. I may not have had much time to mope in my workaday world, but in my Val world, time stretched out in infinite loops, and I was dragging myself through every last one of them.

That's why I had to go to New York; I needed to leave my Val world behind, and nothing could do that like going to work in the biggest, the fastest, the most *city* city in America. That little slip of paper my mom had written on would be the first link of the chain that would yank me back to my feet. I was willing to bet my summer on it.

2.

So it was that, one month after reading my mother's note, I hauled a couple of duffel bags out of a cab, pressed the button next to N. WILLIS, and stood in front of apartment 4E as Nadine unlocked the door. I'm not sure what I had expected to see when she opened the door, but I was happy to find she hadn't changed much at all—short but lithe, with small symmetrical features, and still wearing bangs to cover the scar from that biking mishap I'd been at least a little bit responsible for.

Okay, more than a little.

"Neds!" she said, hugging me. As kids, we called each other Neds and Nades, and I knew now that we would be calling each other that all summer. "Oh my God, you got tall," she said. "Come in."

The apartment had high ceilings, with several movie posters on the walls and a couple of framed French ads from the twenties. The furniture was spare and elegant—lots of shelves supported by curved black metal. The couch, bigger than I expected, was in front of the windows. Sitting in the middle of it, looking up from the *Times* in his lap, was a thin man in a black suit, sporting rimless glasses and a severe haircut.

"Tedd," said Nadine, "this is my cousin Ned Alderman. Ned, this is Tedd Long, my boyfriend."

"Tedd with two Ds," he said, rising to his feet and angling over to shake my hand. This was a tall man—a good six and a half feet—made up of sharp corners, from his nose to his knees. His eyes pinned me to the air behind me. "So you're the one who's taking over the couch," he said.

"For the summer, yeah."

"I don't like it. Now when Nadine and I get in an argument, I won't have anywhere to sleep." His lips pulled tight. It was supposed to be a joke, but his cutting delivery sure didn't make it sound like one.

"You don't have to like it," said Nadine. "And you can always go back to your place in Brooklyn. Ned, anything to drink?"

Tedd rolled his eyes. "It's obviously a joke, Nadine."

"Water's fine," I said.

"Regular or seltzer?" she asked, going to the kitchen.

"Regular."

"I'll have seltzer," Tedd called after her. Then, to me, "You knew I was joking." With that, he went back to the couch and returned to the paper. I lowered my duffel bags to the floor, nice and slow.

***

That evening, Nadine cooked a lemon chicken dinner; Tedd, in charge of the music, put on a jazz album. "You like Stan Getz?" he asked. "You have to if you want to live here."

"Don't listen to him, Ned," Nadine said. "Tell me about your mom."

We talked about our mothers, our long-absent fathers, our high school and college years. She was an engaged conversationalist, gesturing with expressive hands, eyes widening and narrowing as she reenacted dialogue. I enjoyed listening to her, and I felt a sense of relief that we still connected so well. I'd say the sense of relief was mutual, only she never seemed to think we wouldn't hit it off. Every now and then I'd look over at Tedd, who listened as he stared heavily at her, the fingers of one hand pushed into his forehead. Something about the force in his expression pulled my protect-Nadine instincts back to the surface, like the skeleton army in *Jason and the Argonauts*.

"Tell me how you guys met," I said.

"Okay," she said, putting down her wine glass. "Picture this. It's winter, six years ago, I'm at NYU, and I'm in the subway. It's rush hour, so we're all packed right in. My stop comes, I force my way out, and I go to take out my wool hat, only it's not in my pocket anymore. And I knew that's where I'd just put it. So I'm annoyed, and then all of a sudden I hear, 'Are you looking for this?' I turned around, and there's this incredibly tall guy in a beautiful coat, and he's got my hat."

"Savior!" said Tedd, raising his fists.

Nadine laughed. "Then he said, 'I'd like to continue this conversation over coffee.' I'm thinking, what conversation? But I figured it was the least I could do—he'd just got me my hat back—so I say yes, and the rest is history. And then, a year later," she opened her mouth wide, conveying *I still can't believe this* far better visually than anyone could verbally, "he tells me that he actually stole my hat right out of my pocket so he'd have something to say to me!"

I turned to Tedd, whose slender fingers slowly wove around in front of him, like a spider's legs.

"I have the touch," he said.

"I mean, Jesus Christ, Ned!"

"Wow," I agreed, watching those fingers undulate. They were hairy and more than a little disconcerting.

"I still can't believe it sometimes," Nadine said, standing up. "But it's not like I dwell on it or anything. Who's ready for dessert?"

We all were, so she took our dirty dishes and retreated to the kitchen. Tedd rubbed his red cloth napkin around his lips, threw it down, and regarded me. I started looking around the room so I wouldn't have to deal with those eyes any more than I had to. Not a judgment—they just weren't friendly eyes. Then I remembered I had a fun fact to share with Tedd, and this looked to be a good time to share it.

"You know," I said, "we've actually got someone else in common besides Nadine."

He lifted his nose. "How do you figure?"

"You work at Lofton-Canova, down on Wall Street."

"That's right."

"So does Siege Brandenburg."

He took a long breath, held it for a moment, then let almost all of it out through his nose before he said, "Who?"

"C.J. Brandenburg. He was my roommate in college. He works there now."

He pulled his lower lip into his mouth for a second, then rejected it for his upper one. Finally, he shook his head. "No bells," he said. "I'm afraid I don't know much about the peons."

If there's one word that never described Siege, it's *peon*. But I decided Tedd should learn that for himself. "Well, you should get to know Siege," I said. "He's a great guy."

"He'd have to be," said Tedd. "If he were going to be your roommate."

I registered this. I took my napkin off my lap and lobbed it onto the table. "What do you mean?" I asked.

"I mean," he said, leaning forward, "that you probably aren't somebody who would choose to live with someone who wasn't a great guy."

I blinked. "Oh."

"Why?" he asked me, a gleam emerging from the back of his eyes. "What did you think I meant?"

Before I could tell him, or figure out a way not to tell him, Nadine returned with three dishes of brownies, topped with French vanilla ice cream that had already started melting. We all made appreciative noises, and the question was set aside, if not forgotten.

3.

The next morning, Nadine walked me to the subway station and showed me how to get to Peppercorn. "Take the six, transfer crosstown, then the A, walk a couple blocks, and you're all set," she said, as waves of humanity poured past us. "You're going to be fine. See you tonight!" She waved and moved into the flow of the downcast and the preoccupied. I watched her being swept away, then went to get a MetroCard so I could start my own journey.

Nadine was right; it was easy enough to get there once you knew how. I couldn't help being a bit saddened by the ride, though. The car was pretty full—both of people and their worlds. Dozens of passengers had emptied out their eyes and flattened their feelings, it seemed to me, making themselves remote and untouchable, held in by the walls of their personal space. We were alone in the crowd, all of us.

At one point a Black man came on board, bone thin, with torn jeans and a stained blue pocket T-shirt hanging on his frame. "I hate that I'm in this situation," he said, in a sad, aggressive whine, just audible over the thunder of the train. "I don't want to take anything from you good people ... but if you could see fit to offer me something ... if you can't give me money, you can give me a smile ...."

Nobody would look at him. A couple of people felt around in their pockets and fished out some change, but they kept their eyes on the floor. Others made themselves statues, frozen in their seats, clinging to poles, posing as drab, lifeless trophies while the train rocked beneath their feet.

I couldn't be part of this expressionlessness. I had no money to give, but as he shuffled close, I put a smile on my face and offered it up to him. He got to me, his hollowed eyes glided over me, and he ghosted on past. Not a pause. No sign that he'd taken my smile. But he must have, because I sure didn't have it anymore. And I knew I wasn't going to get it back. The Val blues couldn't have done a better job at wiping the warmth away.

"Ladies and gentlemen," he said when he reached the car's end, "I thank you for your generosity … and I wish you a lovely New York morning." With that, he pushed the door button at the end of the car, letting the high-speed shrieking and rattling in, and let himself out to talk to the people one car down, rocking to the train's rhythms as the tracks raced beneath his scuffed gray boots. I was the only one to watch him go.

* * *

Peppercorn Press was set up on the eighth floor of an office building on Sixty-Second Street. The elevator was noisy, but not rickety; I felt secure enough in it that I bounced a little on the balls of my feet. I had to—my brain was pumping nervousness and anticipation the way my heart was pumping blood. Even the subway ride couldn't drain those feelings away.

The door opened, and I followed the signs with arrows to a giant curved desk. The receptionist wore thick tinted glasses and a helmet of gray hair. I introduced myself, she picked up the phone, and in a moment, a blur of a man flew out of his office and beelined right up to me. He was short, maybe five and a half feet, with a paunch and the disarrayed makings of a comb-over.

"Ned Alderman!" he said, giving my hand a solid pump. "Son of Rhoda's friend? Right. Jamie Engel, managing editor. Good to have you on board. Follow me. You like New York so far? Oh, greatest city in the world. Listen, we're about to have our meeting, so we'll show you your desk later. It's over there. Here's the conference room. Every morning, quarter of nine? The place to be. Take a minute, get your bearings. Good to have you on board."

He swooped off, leaving me alone in a room with two long tables and eighteen folding chairs, wondering if this was the pace I'd have to get accustomed to. I took a seat and looked around, hoping Jamie Engel would talk from the far end of the room, so I'd be sitting closer to the back than the front.

"Good morning."

I looked up. There was a man in a beautiful suit at the door. He looked about thirty, with a strong build and a great smile. I don't mean *great* as in *very good*; I mean it in the sense that this smile encompassed everything, from the light in his hazel eyes to the couple of cobwebs in the windows to the world beyond. It wasn't fair that nobody could see it besides me.

He walked into the room, slow and smooth, like a rolling wave. "You're just starting today, is that right?"

Transfixed as I was, I couldn't help smiling back. "Yes."

"I thought so, yeah." The fabric of his suit made a slipping sort of noise as he reached out his hand. "I'm Chase," he said. "Chase Becker."

"Ned Alderman," I said, half rising from my chair. His grip was firm; my hand seemed to melt into his.

"Think I'll sit here next to you, Ned Alderman," he said, dropping into the chair on my right. A whiff of cinnamon washed over me, strong enough to almost sting my eyes. "So," he said, turning to face me, "is this your first experience with the publishing world?"

"Well, there was my college … literary magazine, but it …"

I stopped. I could feel ripples of confusion uneasing their way through me. It took an instant to realize why; nobody had ever listened to me quite like this. Chase was sitting there, one arm on the table and the other on his thigh. He leaned forward a little, his eyes holding me in place, much different from the pinning back Tedd's eyes had done the night before. Everything about him was focused on me, not waiting for me to finish or calculating a response to what I'd say, but *listening*. He was forming a connection with me, one that felt tremendously real.

"… wasn't anything next to all this," I managed to say.

"Oh, of *course* it is, Ned," he said, his voice buoyed up by his belief. "Most everyone here was on their college lit mag. That's your experience, and it's good experience. They wouldn't have taken you on if it weren't."

"Well, actually, it's because my mother's friend knows the—"

"Oh, a connection? Well, that'll help you stand out, true, but after they notice you, they've still got to decide if you were worth noticing. And again, if you hadn't been, they wouldn't have taken you on. You've got every right to be here, Ned Alderman," he concluded, dropping a loose fist on the table.

"Oh, good," I said. My face was starting to hurt, and I realized that I hadn't stopped smiling since I'd seen him walk into the room.

Chase glanced over at the door, where people were starting to come in. When they saw him, they offered little grins and waves, which he returned in kind. Everyone brightened up whenever he addressed them. "Rosie, I *love* the hair! … Lee, season finale this week? … Peter, what is going on with the Dodgers?" They all had responses, and they all showed their teeth.

The room was rollicking by the time Jamie came in, a petite young woman trailing hesitantly behind him. "Sit over there next to Chase," he told her, and as she scooted to her seat, he turned and closed the door. "Wow!" he said, turning back. "I feel good! James Brown. Of course I feel good—Chase is back in town!"

People smiled and laughed. Everyone was at ease and very casual. Of all the people in the room, Chase was the only one in a suit. Jamie was the only other one with a tie, and where Chase's was neat and sharp, Jamie's was yanked askew and dotted with what I hoped were coffee stains.

"And joining him," said Jamie, swinging into his seat (at the middle of the table, it turned out), "is a little fresh blood. We've got two editorial assistants for the next twelve weeks, gang. Use 'em well, keep 'em clean, don't you tell 'em what you seen. Ha! Maylene, stand up. Your name, where you're from, a fact about you, one of your opinions. Let's hear it. C'mon, stand."

He was looking at the young woman he'd come in with, who'd just finished settling in on Chase's right. She had a French braid, a gray turtleneck, and eyes as big as could be. It was hard to tell if they were so big because she was petrified, or if they were always that way.

Chase leaned in close to her and murmured something. She flicked a skittish glance at him, bowed her head, and rose, her hands not touching the table. I wondered what a good strong breeze would have done to her. Knock her over? Turn her into a giant goose bump? Cause those eyes to close? I would have liked to see, but with no windows and the door shut, this conference room wasn't letting in a gust of anything.

"Uh, hi," she said. "My name *is* Maylene, Maylene West. I'm, ah, from, from a place called Hexton, in *New* York. And, ah, fact about me is, I just finished my-my junior year at, ah *Yale*. And an opinion: I *really* like the movie *The Princess Bride*, but the book is *so* much better." She said that last part with far more conviction than all the previous truths she'd spoken. People gave her encouraging nods and smiles; she nodded back and sat down, relief washing over her face.

"Thank you, Maylene," said Jamie, throwing his hand in the air. "And in this corner! Come on, Mister Man, let 'em hear you outside. Name, place, fact, opinion. Go."

A gentle weight fell on my shoulder. I looked down at Chase's hand, the wrinkles on his knuckles forming asterisks, and as I did, my peripheral vision saw his face coming close. "You'll be fine," he whispered, with a glint of enamel and the whiff of a cinnamon ocean that lifted me to my feet.

"Hello," I found myself saying to all those upturned eyes. "I'm Ned Alderman, of the Greenfield, Mass. Aldermans. I wear a size ten shoe. And I think the most underrated songwriter of the seventies was John Denver."

The face of the woman across from me shriveled into a lemon-sucking pose. "John Denver?" she asked. "Seriously?"

"Yes!" Chase barked, startling me. "John Denver is the *man*!"

"He is," I said, agreeing with myself.

"Mister 'Rocky Mountain High' guy?" She said it with enough disdain to glaze both conference room tables.

"Let me tell you something," Chase said. He leaned forward, hands out, face alight, sureness coming off him in waves. "You take one of his songs that most people don't know, you get a cool band to record it, I swear to you, those people are going to call it a work of genius, and they're going to be right. Good call, Ned." He leaned back and clapped my upper arm.

"Thanks," I said.

"Whatever," grumbled the woman.

"I like John Denver," piped a little balding guy sitting in the corner.

"Great, terrific," said Jamie. "Have a seat, Ned. And everyone else, we got"—he made rapid-fire, card-dealing gestures around the tables—"Sue, Bill, Anna, Joe, Rosie, Wyatt, Andie, Akari, Other Joe, Lee, Peter, and Caroline. Wonder if I could do that with my eyes closed. Some other time. And behind the desk out front is Louise, master of the phones. Mistress. Queen. There will be a test, hope you were listening. Ha! Okay, serious now, we've got some big issues to talk about this morning, starting with old Mr. McGriff ...."

With that, everyone plunged into talk about contracts and cover art and what was being planned for release the following spring. Since it didn't entirely relate to me, I felt safe giving the talk only half an ear and just watched how people interacted. Jamie's rat-a-tat style may not have been soothing, but it was by no means frantic either—everyone kept pace with their comments and ideas. They all addressed each other by name, so it became easy for me to keep track of who was who. Wyatt referred to charts and statistics and exuded calmness and control. Akari asked a lot of questions and answered most of them herself. Lee may not have been a John Denver fan, but she sure seemed to know her stuff otherwise.

As for Chase, he just sat in his chair, saying very little, nodding and laughing if someone said something funny. He was the only non-intern in the room who didn't have a tablet or notebook or something in front of him. I couldn't believe how much he was storing away as we all went back and forth—the focus he had must have been unbelievable. Behind him, I could see Maylene giving him sidelong glances. Since her moment of panic had long passed, I could now safely say her eyes were always that big.

"And that's all she wrote!" said Jamie, dropping his pen on the table and letting it rattle-dance to a halt. "Ned, Maylene, we got some ropes here and we're gonna show 'em to you. Lee, take Maylene. Ned, why don't you go with Bill? Chase, come with me. Everyone else, be great!"

We all stood up. I turned to Chase to thank him for his support, but he was already halfway around the table to join up with Jamie. I went to follow him, but bumped into Maylene, almost having to catch her so she wouldn't fall backward.

"Oh, sorry," I said.

"Rocky Mountain hi, guy," she said, with the barest hint of a smile.

"Oh, that was good," I said. "Excuse me." I got around her and looked for Chase, but he was gone. I shrugged and worked my way over to Bill, who turned out to be the little balding guy in the corner.

"Nice to meet you, Ned," he said, shaking my hand. "Think you'll enjoy working here?"

"I think so," I said, following close behind as we left the room. "I mean, with people like Chase here, I can't imagine—"

"Oh, Chase doesn't work here," Bill said over his shoulder.

"He—what?"

"Chase doesn't work for Peppercorn Publishing," Bill repeated. "This isn't what he does."

I looked behind me at all the people going back to their desks. Chase wasn't one of them.

"He only comes in for meetings every now and then," Bill went on. "When Jamie thinks things might be tense, he brings in Chase. Like today, with that whole McGriff contract fiasco."

"But he knew everybody," I said. "He seemed like he was a part of the place—why doesn't he work here?"

Bill stopped next to a desk. He turned to smile at me. "Want to know the truth?" he said. "We can't afford him. With what he makes, we're lucky if we can get him twice a month. So this is your desk. Now, have you ever formatted anything?"

* * *

Bill turned out to be a good, patient teacher, taking me from awareness to understanding in less than an hour. He let me have a couple of cheat sheets and told me that if I needed any more help, he'd be right at his desk, which, as it turned out, was in the back corner.

Once he left, I set about my first real order of business—writing an email to Siege.

5/31/05, 10:23 AM
From: nalderman@peppercornpub.com
To: cjbrande@loftoncanova.com
Subject: Look who's here

Siege—This is my first email on the job, and really, it had to go to you. (You're honored, I can feel it from here.) So far, so good, though the guy I was sure would be my favorite coworker turned out not to work here. I guess he's just some kind of consultant. Say—is there anywhere to get a drink in this town? – Ned

Within an hour:

5/31/05, 11:14 AM
From: cjbrande@loftoncanova.com
To: nalderman@peppercornpub.com
Subject: Re: Look who's here

Hey Rooms, good to hear you made it in okay. Look forward to your stories. Not tonight, though—making up for having Memorial Day off yesterday. Tomorrow, come down to 4th Street—I'll meet you at the station (let me know what line you're on) and take you somewhere cool and tell you all about my hot date with a wad of toilet paper. We're talking double-ply here, my friend. – Siege

4.

"Hey!" said Nadine, waving as I came into the apartment. She was sitting on the couch, her legs curled up under her, a cell phone pressed to her ear. There was another phone, a landline, next to her computer. I'd have to ask her about that.

"No," she said as I closed the door, "that's Ned, my second cousin. He's staying here this summer …. Shut up, I totally told you about him!" She rolled her eyes. A moment later she snorted a laugh. "I don't know, I'll ask him," she said. Holding the phone out so the person on the other end could hear, she said, "Ned, do you have a girlfriend?"

It was all I could do not to wince. "No."

A tinny voice blasted from the phone. "He's not gay, is he?"

"You're not gay, are you?" Nadine asked, using the voice of an unctuous game-show host.

"No, I'm not," I said, raising my voice so the person on the other end could hear me.

"What's he look like?" said the tinny voice.

"I'll just put him on," said Nadine. She covered the mouthpiece with her thumb. "This is my friend Alexa. She's kind of a party girl, but she's not an airhead."

"That's a rare combo," I said, taking the phone. "Hello?"

"Hi, Ned, my name's Alexa Pine." Her voice was much less tinny now, much nicer to listen to. "I was just trying to get your cousin there to come to my party on Saturday, and she won't do it, even though it's going to be awesome. Hey, why don't you come? I can say it's a welcome-to-New York party, and you'll get to meet a whole bunch of new people. You should come. You've got to try my pasta salad."

I couldn't believe how fast this was all moving. I hadn't even taken off my shoes yet. I just accepted that this was how things were done in the big city and rolled with it.

"Please don't make it in my honor," I said. "If you don't, then I'll come."

The first part of her response was lost behind a beep. "—an't wait to meet you!" went the tail end.

"Uh, Alexa, there's another call coming in," I said. "I'm passing you back to Nadine." I handed off the phone and went to the kitchen.

"I'll call you right back," she said, and she pressed a couple of buttons. "Hello? … Hey, Tedd … No, I was just talking with Alexa … No, I told her we couldn't go, don't worry … Okay, fine, you're not worried."

I turned on the cold water and let it run for a bit as I picked out a good-sized tumbler. I filled it up and shut off the tap in time to hear Nadine say, "That's not fair," in a considerably harder voice than she'd been using. I decided against returning to the living room for the moment.

"You're the one choosing to look at it that way," she said. She'd gotten to her feet; I could hear her footsteps padding around as she paced the room. "I do not," she said. "I do *not!* … Tedd, that is so not fair… When I *what?* Excuse me, that was not … Would you … Tedd, remember when you asked me to let you know when you were being a jerk? … I am not going to stand here and listen to you talk to me like this, I'm just not … Fuck you, Tedd."

I almost gasped. It was the first time I'd ever heard Nadine swear. I could never have imagined that sentence coming out of that mouth. But it had, and her delivery of those cold, iron words made hanging up redundant. I waited a bit, took a sip of water, and went back to the living room. Nadine was standing next to the bookshelf, rubbing her lips and staring down at the floor.

"Nades?"

"Sorry you had to hear that," she said, not looking up. She sounded like she'd taken fifty pounds off her back and looked angry that she'd had to.

I went into the kitchen again and returned with a diet soda, which she took gratefully. "Tedd can be an asshole sometimes," she said as she opened it. "He wants me to get rid of this place and live with him in Brooklyn, and I don't want to. And sometimes it's hard for him to accept that." She took a sip and kind of laughed. "And this was one of those times."

"Well, it sounded like you gave as good as you got," I said, sitting down.

She shook her head. "No, I didn't. But at least I'll have less to apologize for." She took another sip and sighed. "Tedd gives really good apologies," she said.

The landline phone rang. She looked at it, reached down, and pressed a button. The light on the phone blinked out.

"But I've got to be in the mood to hear them," she concluded, sitting back down at the other end of the couch. "Anyway! What'd you think of Alexa? Oh, and tell me about your first day!"

I told her about the depressing subway ride, the tasks I did at work, the people there, the charisma of Chase Becker. She listened, nodding, smiling, managing to keep the sparkle in her eye from trickling down the side of her face. It saddened me to see her hurt like this, and as I spoke to her, I was once again reminded of *Jason and the Argonauts* as I mentally assembled my army of skeleton protectors and resolved to do everything I could to help keep her from feeling this way again.

5.

Siege Brandenburg was a man who filled his space. He had a big solid physique and a slow, rumbling voice that could steamroll other people's conversations into dust. He also had a sense of mischief, a knack for debate, and an acidic wit, usually turned on himself. We had hit it off my freshman year; a shared affinity for heckling bad movies on cable TV and an argument about JFK that went on for three nights sealed our bond, and we roomed together the next three years. He went straight to New York after graduation, landing at Lofton-Canova and getting promoted before the year was out. Now we were sitting across from each other, working on emptying a pitcher of the finest ale Nelson's Tavern had to offer.

"What kind of a party?" Siege asked.

"I don't know," I said, putting my glass down. "The latest in a long line, from the sound of it. Wanna come with?"

He snorted. "Pass. I got less important things to do."

"Lucky man. Hey, tell me a little about Tedd."

Siege poured himself another pint and topped off mine. "Ted-duh," he said. "I like to say that the extra D is for 'douchebag.' I suppose this'd be a good time for me to ask if you like the guy."

"I only just met him," I said. "The jury's still out."

"First impressions?"

I took a drink. "Douchebag."

Siege held up a there-you-go hand.

"No, that's not quite right," I amended. "He seems like a smart guy, but it's a dangerous smart. He's not going to ask if you're with him or against him—he'll decide for himself which one of those two slots he wants you in, and he'll put you there."

"Which slot are you in?" Siege asked, wiping some foam off his lip.

"I think I'm in his 'for' slot. I'm Nadine's second cousin; I might be of some use to him."

Somebody played Neil Diamond's "America" on the jukebox, which caused half of Nelson's patrons to groan out loud. Siege's voice rose over it with little to no effort.

"Okay," he said. "I wasn't going to tell you this. But Tedd came up to me yesterday. He said, 'I understand Ned Alderman was your roommate.' I said, 'Yeah.' He said, 'Why?' you know, like, why would anyone in their right mind, et cetera. He said, 'Nadine can't pick who she's related to, but you could pick out who you were gonna live with—why'd you pick him?'"

I didn't say anything.

"That sound you hear is the jury coming back in," Siege said, looking over at the bar.

"What'd you tell him?"

"What'd I tell him?" He turned back to me and shrugged. "I said, 'He's a good guy.'"

"What else?"

"Nothing else. 'He's a good guy.' It's true—what else am I supposed to say?" He took a long swig.

I was torn between being annoyed at Siege for not using more vitriol to defend me and moved that he considered my goodness all that needed to be said. While I weighed the annoyed side of the argument, I blurted out, "He called you a peon."

Siege let out a giant, rattling belch. "Well, he's probably right about that," he said.

We finished off the pitcher inside of half an hour, and Siege went to the bar to order another one. When he came back, he said, "Don't stare. The girl at the bar in the green T-shirt."

I put my left temple in my palm, nonchalant as could be, and looked askance. There was a woman sitting alone at the bar, working on a colorful blender drink of some kind. She had on a tight little military T-shirt and tan shorts that showed an awful lot of leg.

"What are my chances?" Siege asked as he poured.

"Right now?"

"Right now."

"She's got a froufrou drink. She's dressed up tough but sexy. She's mixing her signals, and you're not going to be able to read them, on account of you've got half a pitcher of beer in you. I don't like your chances."

"Fine. You go talk to her."

"I'm not the one who's interested."

He grumbled at the lip of his glass and drank. I risked another look at the bar girl and gave the equation some more thought, but the answer remained the same. It wasn't that Siege didn't have appeal to girls—they enjoyed his company and were often surprised at the tenderness under his brusque exterior. Siege's problem, I always thought, lay in his having kept his high school girlfriend for the first three years of college. When she dropped him before our senior year, I had rejoiced, but his skills were so stunted that he never got back in the saddle all year, not even during Senior Week. Now, a year later, he was still struggling—not so desperate that his struggling had become flailing, but I had to wonder if he were headed that way. Me, I looked forward to the day when I had energy enough to flail.

"Fuck it," he said. "I'm going in."

Experience had taught me that there wasn't any point in arguing. "Let the record show I don't support this," I said.

"Noted." He slid out of his chair and moved toward the bar. I took the opportunity to get up and use the restroom, rocking back on my heels to read the graffiti as I peed. When I came out, I saw Siege was already back at the table, and his face told me all I needed to know.

"Sorry, man," I said as I settled into my chair.

"Ahhhh." He waved a dismissive hand and topped off both our pints. The jukebox started playing "Black Velvet." It was official: I despised this jukebox.

"Here's to you," he said, raising his glass, "for a great New York City summer. And here's to me, the last in a long line of Brandenburgs."

"Oh, don't say that," I said as he drank. "You're going to be passing down wisdom for generations of Brandenburgs to come."

He put down his glass. "Not unless tissues develop ovaries, I won't," he said.

6.

The first week of work was pretty good, overall. I got the hang of formatting documents fairly quickly; it was tedious as hell, but it needed doing. I also learned how to create invoices and where to record the sales data. By Friday I truly believed I had every right to be there, just like Chase had said.

Sometimes while I worked, Jamie Engel would go striding past me, talking a mile a minute on his phone. Sometimes he'd point at the phone as he spoke, or he'd pull it away and stare at it, incredulous, before yanking it back to his mouth and hollering at it as he stalked away.

"What do I look like, an idiot?" he'd ask. "Do I look like an idiot? Well, if you *could* see me!"

Jamie in action was far more entertaining than menacing. I had to wonder how much he gave these performances for our enjoyment, how much to make himself feel like the Man in Charge, and how much because the call needed to be made. I'd put the ratio at thirty-sixty-ten.

The other employees were good people. They smiled at me when I walked by, addressing me by my name. Everyone at Peppercorn was good about calling each other by name and not by "Hey, um," or "Dude," or the like; somewhere along the way it had been ingrained, and as a person who's bad with names, I was grateful.

Almost all of them, though, were a good ten-to-twenty years older than me, some with kids, a couple with grandkids. We didn't share much common ground beyond work. Bill, for instance, was twice my age, and after a Y chromosome and a respect for John Denver, our similarities petered out. I resigned myself to the fact that any friendships I made on the job would be site-specific.

The only regular staffer under thirty was Lee, and she'd taken Maylene under her wing. Besides teaching the intern all the duties of an editorial assistant, she talked to her about boys, her apartment, her cat, boys, various TV shows, and boys. Not to mention boys.

I know all this because, being birds of a youngish feather, the three of us would take lunch at the same time and go to various delis and food carts and park benches in the area. Lee would talk, Maylene would listen, and I'd tune in and out and marvel at the taste of souvlaki or the degree to which delis overstuffed their sandwiches. For me, these lunch breaks were like picnicking alone on a raft; you get away from the life you know, take in a little nourishment, and pay silent witness to the sights and sounds and actions of the world as they pass you by.

Sometimes Lee would ask me a question—usually something like "Don't you think so, Ned?"— and I'd be so zoned out I'd miss it completely. "Huh? What?" I'd say when I realized they were both looking at me, and Lee would get annoyed and Maylene would turn away and I'd go back to my food.

Maylene was a better audience than I was—she'd make suitable noises or ask a leading question, and she knew better than to change the subject. Over the week, as her comfort level increased, she lost some of the tics in her speech, no longer repeating words or emphasizing them at random. That was nice to hear, but I didn't hear anywhere near as much of it as I could have on account of Lee dominating our discussions.

The few times Maylene and I got to interact alone were pleasant enough. Her desk was right near the reception area, so when Louise would say good morning to me, Maylene would hear and greet me as well. She also had a good sense of humor—once I told Louise a shaggy-dog joke about the Pope, and when I finally got to the punchline, Maylene laughed before Louise did. She wasn't going to have a starring role in the movie about this summer in my life, but she was better than an extra.

One more thing about Maylene: she had a tendency to buy herself a big cookie for dessert, usually oatmeal, and then only break off a piece of it and give the rest to me. To my mind, it seemed a waste of a dollar fifty, but the cookies were always good, so I wasn't about to complain.

***

I was also getting to know Nadine again and really enjoying the whole reconnecting process. She knew more about movies than anyone I'd ever met, and she had a collection of videotapes and DVDs that filled a cabinet and a half, with trash and treasures equally well represented. "Some people like the movies, and some people like the movies they like," she told me. "I'm psyched that you're in that first category." We resolved to screen at least one movie a week on her huge TV, talking at it just as much as we pleased.

I told her about my Val blues, and she expressed her sympathies and assured me that a summer in the city was just what I needed. "Pain does fade, Neds," she said. "Especially if you stop inflicting it on yourself." I shrugged and sort of agreed. I knew she was right, but it was going to take a while before I could believe it.

She told me her phone by the computer doubled as a fax machine (she'd rescued it from her lab's dumpster), but I could still use it if I needed to make or receive any calls. She told me that she wouldn't think of taking a cent more than fifty dollars a week for rent, which was very generous of her. She also told me a little more about Alexa. "Alexa Pine is the kind of girl who signs her name with an exclamation point," she said. "She comes from big money—I think she's worth more than all our parents and stepparents combined. She likes attention, but she doesn't crave it or anything. She uses the party girl side of her as kind of a guard for the quiet side of her. But the thing is, everybody loves the guard. So there's no need for her to let it down."

"Has she got a boyfriend?" I asked.

"She's still looking for someone who can keep pace, she says. Let me show you her MySpace page. Feel free to use this computer, by the way."

We looked at her pictures, which showed her and various friends (Nadine among them) in various states of celebration. She was blond, with eyes like a cat's, and she could open her mouth awfully wide. There was an announcement about the upcoming party, "with a very special guest!"

"That'd be me, wouldn't it?"

She smiled. "I'm guessing so. It's not me, anyway."

"Yeah, why aren't you going?"

"Tedd's taking me out to Whittaker's. It's a really fancy restaurant. You need to book two months in advance if you want to go on a Saturday."

"So everything's copacetic with you guys."

I said that very carefully. Since the phone incident, she hadn't said a word about Tedd, and I wasn't about to bring him up. She hadn't been moping around the apartment or anything, but she could have been putting on a brave face for my benefit. Now, at last, a chance to find out.

She moved her mouse on the pad, clicking it, closing all the windows and revealing her screen wallpaper. It was a picture of her and Tedd in formal wear, standing side by side in front of a dark dance floor. There was barely enough light to see the people behind them, in their tuxedos and strapless blue dresses and a swirling bridal gown. Tedd was bending down to kiss the top of Nadine's head. Nadine's arms were wrapped around him, her ear pressed against his chest. She looked very happy.

"Everything's back to normal," said Nadine, studying the monitor.

"And that's good," I said.

"And that is good," she agreed, shutting the computer off with a few final clicks.

"So I shouldn't worry?"

She gave it some thought, then turned back to look at me with kind of a wistful smile. "I'd rather you didn't," she said.

7.

Alexa lived about six blocks away, close enough to walk there on an agreeable night. I found a bar along the way and used a couple of their gin and tonics to lower my inhibitions, so I was ready to roll by the time I got to her apartment building. She lived in a place that had a green awning out front with the address on it and an old-fashioned doorman, complete with white gloves. He gave me directions to Alexa's place on the fifth floor, but I would have had no trouble figuring out which one was hers; if I couldn't have heard (and felt) the muffled beats coming through the door, the construction paper arrows pointing to the doorknob would have been the giveaway. I guessed nobody would hear me if I knocked, so I steeled myself and went inside.

The room was lit with strands of Christmas lights, electric candles, and not much else. The thick red carpet muffled the samba music and multiple conversations going on around me to a level that I could handle. There were fewer people than I expected; of course, it was only eight thirty, and the real action likely wouldn't be starting for a while longer. I moved farther into the room, nudging my way past several full-body silhouettes, and wondered if those were my inhibitions I could feel creeping back into place. They pushed my shoulders up toward my ears as if I were walking down a narrow hallway. They lined my tongue with thick quilts, making it soft, heavy, useless. Speaking for myself, if anyone puts me in a big shadowy room full of bad music and complete strangers, I'm going to clam up, and I can't imagine how anyone in his right mind can do otherwise. That's got to be the reason drugs are so integral to raves and discos.

I turned a corner and found myself facing the kitchen, where someone was replacing a regular light bulb with one that had been tinted red. I figured this had to be Alexa. She wore a clingy yellow dress, bright red lipstick, and styled her hair into thick waves. She looked like a pinup girl from the forties, where the boys knew she was unattainable but she didn't, and it took an effort not to fall half in love with her right there.

The new bulb lit her with a soft rosy glow, and she turned toward me. She stopped, squinting in the dim light, and leaned toward me. "You," she said, "have got to be Nadine's cousin." Her voice was lower than it had been on Nadine's cell, rounder in tone.

"Second cousin," I corrected her, offering a little wave and resisting the fall-half-in-love urge again.

She came up to me in a wash of muted meadow lilacs, put her hand on the back of my neck, and pulled me down until her lips came to rest on my cheek. At that point I gave up. What the hell, I figured; it's only half in love.

"Don't take offense—I kiss everybody," she said as she released me, apologizing but not really. "I'm Alexa Pine—hi. Tell Nadine I hate her for not coming. No, that's not true, I totally understand." She took a step back and looked at me head to toe. "Still straight and single?" she asked.

"Y-es," I said. My voice was like melted glass: clear but different, with no tensile strength of its own.

"We'll have to talk about that." Her eyebrows did a bewitching little dance, and then my hand was in hers. "Come on," she said. "I want you to meet the very special guest."

"I thought I was the very special guest."

"Attitude. I like that. Come on."

"Oh," I said as she pulled me along behind her. We slalomed around corners and guests; for a moment I felt exactly like a water-skier. Then we careened up to the refreshment table, where two men were talking next to the punch bowl, their backs to us. Alexa stopped short, nearly pulling me right into her.

"Ned—" She pivoted to face me, confused. "Alderman?" I nodded, and she grinned and spun back. "Ned Alderman, I'd like you to meet Chase Becker."

And there was Chase, turning around, smiling, hitting me with a whiff of cinnamon beach and a wave of positive energy as he reached for my hand. Then he recognized me, and the flash of realization pushed his eyebrows up an extra few millimeters, as the light in his eyes flared just a little bit more brilliantly.

"Ned!" he exclaimed, as our hands briefly melded together. "Hey! How was your first week at Peppercorn Publishing?"

This threw me. Not that he remembered me—somehow, he made that feel like no surprise at all—but that he didn't just call the place "Peppercorn." For someone to be as familiar with the company and its people as he was, and then to call it by two names instead of one, gave it a tiny note of formality that didn't belong. Like if someone wore a bow tie to a pool party.

"It was great," I said. "Good people, and it turns out I can handle the work."

He punched my shoulder, not so hard that I had to take a step back to regain my balance. "I told you!" he said.

"You guys already know each other?" Alexa asked. She sounded disappointed. Maybe she wanted to watch the rapture move across my face as Chase worked his magic. I was sorry to let her down.

"We met earlier this week," I said. "We bonded over John Denver."

"We did, didn't we?" said Chase, smiling.

Another odd moment. He'd been so adamant in his support for John Denver that I didn't think he'd have to be reminded. I was beginning to question his sincerity, and I really didn't want to do that.

"Well, I'll go find you some more people you don't know yet," said Alexa. "Ned, to be continued." She turned and sauntered off, stopping to twitch her hips at a particular drum rhythm playing just then.

"Ned," said Chase, half turning. "I was just telling Bryan—"

But the man Chase had been talking with had skulked off. Chase turned back, looking sheepish. "Well, I was telling Bryan that if Alexa brings someone over, don't be offended if I stop talking to you and pay all kinds of attention to them. She says she wants me to meet as many of her friends as possible."

"How do you know her?" I asked.

"I met her last week." He picked a single corn chip out of a bowl. "I was at her friend Julie's party, we talked a bit, she asked me to this one, and here I am."

This was heartening news. Chase wasn't her boyfriend; if he were, my chances would have been cooked. I got a cup to fill with punch and said, "She seems like a special person."

"She does. She does." He popped the corn chip into his mouth and crunched.

She does. Not *She is.* Another good sign.

"I love some of this artwork," he said, pointing to a print on the wall across from us. "You can't see it very well from here, but you should check—"

"Chase!" Alexa was bearing down on us, followed by a short redhead with a Vandyke beard. He had bright red lipstick on his cheek, but I took some small pleasure that she hadn't taken him by the hand to bring him over. "Chase, this is Aaron Brown, my dentist. He lives downstairs."

"Aaron Brown!" Chase repeated, swinging away from me and locking onto Aaron. "Aaron Brown, you're her dentist? Well, listen, I have to tell you, if Alexa's teeth are any indication …"

Aaron Brown stared up at him, dazzled, agog. I could see justifiable pride welling up inside him as Chase expounded on the gifts Aaron had to offer. That pride was tinged with an unfillable wish to possess Chase's kind of command, his magnetism. I recognized those feelings, as they were mine too. I took my drink and decided to start mingling.

"It's a genuine honor to shake this hand," floated Chase's voice behind me.

***

As the night went on and more and more people came in, I spent my time walking through the room, doing my best to convert strangers into friends. A number of would-be—excuse me, *aspiring*—models and actors told me some horror stories about the job, and a ruddy standup comic in a green suit did a two-minute bit for me on men's soap versus women's. One girl showed me some of the jewelry she'd made. Another wanted to know if Peppercorn might publish her children's book.

I got to spend a little more time with Alexa too. I asked her to tell me about some of the artwork on her walls, and she confessed that she mostly got them based on other people's recommendations or as gifts. "Over the years I've really come to appreciate them, though," she said, scooping up some dip with her carrot.

"What's your take on Tedd?" I asked her.

She studied the ceiling and thought. "Tedd with two Ds," she finally said, "is not a bad person deep down."

I laughed. "That's a ringing endorsement."

"Hey," she said, more serious than I'd seen her all night. "He doesn't raise a hand in anger. He's been with Nadine a long time. She's a smart girl—if he were bad news, he would be gone. They've gone through a lot—more than Tedd and I have gone through, right?—and that makes a real connection. I might question Tedd, but I will never question their connection."

"All right," I said. She'd kind of ducked the real question, but she'd still given me a good enough answer.

But she wasn't done yet. "I'll tell you something else," she said, more aggressive than I expected. "She cares. Your cousin cares so much for people."

"Second cousin."

"Last winter I had pneumonia," she went on, "and she took time off from work to take care of me. She told me she had to use her sick days anyway, but after I got better, I found out she'd already used them up. So she got a smaller paycheck for two weeks and she never said a word about it to me. She cares for Tedd, probably more than anybody else in the world. I may not be crazy about the guy, but I wouldn't tell Nadine to stop giving him that kind of care for anything."

I raised my punch cup. "Respect."

"Yeah." She smiled at me, a smaller smile than she'd given everyone else that night, maybe a little embarrassed, maybe more tender. It reminded me a little of Val's smile when she'd just paid me a quiet compliment. But this night, for the first time in months, that was a thought that didn't bother me.

Alexa's gaze slipped to her feet. I took a step closer and she looked back up. Her smile grew wider, and mine began to grow as well. Then she pointed behind me and said, "Look at Chase."

I turned around. A girl had started dancing the samba with Chase, keeping hold of one of his hands at all times as she shimmied and spun around in front of him, fell against him, bounced away. Chase didn't have to do much following for a dance like this, so he just kept on smiling at her, expressing his approval, catching and releasing her when called to. The dancing girl was giving her all, and as she danced, the look of concentration on her face was gradually replaced by the awareness of how well she was doing, how much we were all enjoying it. Somebody boosted the volume, and we all began to move to the song, to the dancer. Heads bobbed, bodies swayed, arms swung, and bodies surged onto what had finally become a dance floor. Alexa was one of those bodies; I hadn't felt her steal away from me. She had her fists in the air, the left one over the right one, both over her head, her mouth opening as wide as it was in the pictures I'd seen, her body pulsing inside her beautiful dress. The room temperature was rising, and the scent of sweat began to mingle with the colognes and perfumes already in the air. People raised their voices to be heard above the excitement. And it *was* excitement, not some contrived imitation. Everyone in that room, at that moment, was stirred up inside, whether by their own actions or the actions of those around them; whether they were like Chase, at the epicenter of it all, or like me, standing by a Wyeth print, tapping my foot, taking it all in.

* * *

Alexa turned on the overhead lights, and their brightness caused people to moan and turn away, like wretched old vampires caught in the sun.

"Everyone!" she said, squinting. "We've got a great crowd here tonight, we've got a great atmosphere, but we've also got some neighbors who want their sleep." After a round of good-natured booing, she continued, "So we're going to move on over to Take Two. It's just down the street. It's a great place; they're expecting us, no lines, we'll just go right in. So I hope to see all of you there in a few minutes. You don't have to go home, but you can't stay here."

I glanced at my watch; it was a little before eleven. People started filtering past me, a couple of them wishing me a good night. I thanked them and started looking around for Chase. He turned out to be at the snack table, eating the last of the cucumber sticks.

"Chase," I said, approaching him. "Coming out?"

He shook his head. "No, I'm calling it a night." His smile was simple, apologetic.

"Aw, c'mon."

"I can't," he said, a little firmer. "I need to take my notes."

"Notes?"

"Chase?" We turned to see Alexa coming toward us. She had a piece of paper between her fingers—a check.

"Job well done," she said, passing it to Chase. "Thank you very much. Seriously."

"Sure," he said, making the check vanish in an instant. "You ever need me again, you have my info." He looked a touch uncomfortable, a little furtive with his motions. I looked at the pocket that had the check in it and wondered what the story was.

"Ned, we'll talk more," she said. For the second time she pulled me down so she could kiss my cheek. As she did, I sensed Chase withdrawing, like the tide going out. I had to stop him.

"You too," I said to Alexa, rather nonsensically, and as she smirked I went to the door, catching Chase as he entered the hallway. "Chase," I said, "I really want to talk to you."

"Ned," he said, turning to me and walking backward. He kept his voice low, in deference to the other tenants. "Try to understand."

"Let's go to a bar someplace," I hurried on. "You can take notes at a table there. I won't interrupt."

"I wouldn't be very good company."

"*I* would."

He stopped at that. He put his hands on his hips and regarded me. There was still a light in his eyes, but it was a different light now. Not the bright spark that went along with his smile, but a low gleam, one that tapped into something deeper inside of him.

"Would you now," he said.

8.

Sweethaven was an underground tavern where everything was made of wood. There were no tiles on the floor, no metal in the table legs, no foam cushioning on the chairs and the benches. There wasn't even a jukebox or a television. This was an establishment that catered to people who wanted to do only two things—drink and talk. I felt at home right away.

"This was an off night," said Chase, writing in a medium-sized notepad and squinting to read what he'd just written in the dim light. An untouched glass of ginger ale was on the (wooden) coaster next to him. My coaster held a half-empty glass of Belgian white ale.

"A night off from what?" I asked.

"No, an off night. That dancing part saved it, but I've done much better work."

"Work at what? What were you doing?"

He shot a glance at me. "You don't know?"

"Know what?" I was getting exasperated. "What is going on?"

He took a small silver box out of his pocket and popped it open with a twitch of his thumb. There were some bone-white business cards inside. He took one out and passed it to me.

CHASE BECKER
JOY FACILITATOR
CHASE@JOYFACILITATOR.COM

"Joy facilitator?" I asked, staring at the card like it was in a foreign language I vaguely knew.

"I'm also called a warmer. The opposite of a cooler. But that sounds more like slang than an actual job title, doesn't it?"

I shook my head. "Joy facilitator," I said.

He anticipated my next question. "What I do," he said, "is hire myself out to gatherings. Could be a meeting, a party, a benefit, a seminar, anything with people. I go there and I work the room, talking to everyone, putting them at ease. By the end of the shift, if I've done my job, people will come out feeling better than they did going in. And if people come out happy, ipso facto, the gathering's a success."

"Thanks to you," I said.

"In part," he said, sipping his ginger ale. "I'm like the oil in the machine. The machine is what does the work, but the oil is what keeps it running smooth."

"And there's a market for this?" I asked. It sounded kind of crass when I heard myself say it out loud, but I truly couldn't imagine such a thing.

Fortunately, Chase took the question in the spirit of puzzlement, rather than eye-rolling disbelief. "Ned," he said, "this is New York City. People pay good money for their pets to see psychiatrists. Of *course* there's a market for this. I couldn't do this for a living if so many people didn't feel the need for it.

"Look at Jamie Engel," he went on. "He's a guy who likes to call me if there's a specific tension bomb that needs defusing. Like if the staff is divided on a matter and he needs to cast the tiebreaking vote. Or when there's a couple of new interns coming in and he doesn't want them to be anxious."

I jerked my head up. "He did that? He hired you for me and Maylene?"

"That's why I sat next to you guys."

Part of me wanted to appreciate Jamie for looking after his newest workers, but another part of me felt manipulated. "I think we would have been okay without you, Chase," I said.

He shrugged. "Jamie's the kind of guy who'd rather know than think."

I found I couldn't disagree with that. I also found myself wondering if my half-love for Alexa may have been untrue, artificially engineered by Chase's sheer presence. Not a pleasant thought to dwell on, so I didn't. Instead, I drank the last of my Belgian white, leaving the chunk of orange at the bottom of the glass. "So," I said, "how does one become a joy facilitator?"

Chase folded his hands and rested his chin atop them. That was when I realized how big his head was. Sitting only a few feet away, leaning in close, his body in the background behind his arms, Chase presented this enormous orb of a head to me. His face, proportionate in size, was like a giant playground for all his emotions to run across. I wondered if the fact that it took so much happiness to fill his face made it easier for him to beam it out to the world, like a giant searchlight. Could physical appearance be directly connected to the sharing of emotions?

"One has a mother and dad who give a lot of parties," Chase said, startling me back to the moment. "One grows up watching these parties from the upstairs, looking forward to the day when he's old enough to walk around with a tray full of drinks. One learns body language well enough that he can see a guest arrive at seven and know what that guest's state of mind will be by midnight. One practices at these parties. One gathers as much knowledge about social interaction as he can, from books and films and articles and life. Especially life. Then one takes this knowledge out into the field and finds it consistently works. And then one goes into business as a joy facilitator."

"And how much does one charge?" I asked. Very gauche, but I felt it was an important brushstroke on the way to getting the full picture.

Chase leaned back. "Well, I can only speak for myself," he said, as though he'd just spent the last minute doing otherwise. "I use a sliding scale based on number of hours and number of people. For one to twenty-four people, a one-hour block costs three hundred dollars. That's good for those staff meetings, or for a one-on-one with a chief executive who needs a boost of self-confidence before a big speech. A three-hour block goes for seven hundred fifty. That's long enough to get a party's momentum going in the right direction, or to ensure that bad feelings have the time to get dismantled and stay that way. Anything after that, it's two hundred an hour. And as the crowds get bigger—fifty, a hundred, five hundred—so's the pay."

"Holy ..." I said, searching for a suitable noun to go with that adjective. *Cow? Crap? Mother of God?*

"But here's an important part—they don't pay me until the end, after I've delivered the goods. If the customers aren't satisfied, they don't have to pay. But they're always satisfied. I stumbled a couple times at the beginning, but in the past nine years, I've never once finished an assignment without getting paid. Not once."

"You get a lot of assignments?"

"I've done book signings and baptisms," he said, pinching a fingertip at a time. "I've done interventions and wakes. I just finished up a very busy prom season. So yeah, right now I'm in pretty good shape."

"And you write about them in that book?" I asked, pointing at the notepad on the table.

"Oh, this?" he said, picking it up. "Actually, this is where I record the mistakes I made. Then I write what I would have done if I'd thought about it. Writing it down, actually handwriting it, it's that much more tangible. I study it, I process it, and when the situation comes up again, I can do the right thing without even thinking about it. Like tonight," he said, touching a page, "there were a couple of times when I ended conversations too early. You were one of those, you may have noticed."

"That and a couple other things," I agreed.

His head snapped back, his face suddenly alert. "What couple other things?" he asked, picking up his pen.

I told Chase about the "Peppercorn Publishing" and "We did, didn't we?" hiccups. He wrote them down, nodding rapidly. "That's true," he said as he wrote. "Those are very good points. I can't believe I introduced uncertainty with a negative—wow. I *knew* it was an off night." His pen danced over the page, his concentration fierce. I was relieved that he didn't get defensive about my critical nitpicks but chose to see them as an opportunity to learn.

"Well, these are easy fixes," he said, writing as fast as he could. "Just say 'Peppercorn.' Use the familiarity you already have. And a better phrase … 'We sure did. We sure did.' How's that?"

"Perfect."

He wrote it down. "'We sure did. We sure did.' Say it twice. Extra affirmation. And the second time slower."

"It's so clinical," I said.

"It's work," he said, recapping his pen. "This isn't a ten-hour workweek. I'm doing research on human interaction every day. I go to the gym every other day. Dance and guitar lessons every week. I never stop training. And the more work I do, the shorter these entries get." He gave the notepad two firm pats. "When I first started keeping this, one entry could be three pages long," he said. "Now they're down to half a page. When I'm down to one line, that's when I'll know I'm doing something right."

I sat back in my chair, looking at Chase Becker with new eyes. He had found an incredibly esoteric need and filled it. He was good at what he did, and he was working hard to get better. He'd just spent three hours making more money than I would take home over three weeks. And it was all designed for the purpose of improving people's outlook on life. Everybody won.

"Look at you," I said. "You've got to be the happiest guy in the world."

There was a distinct energy to Chase Becker that I hadn't encountered in another person before. When he was "on," interacting with people, smiling and sharing, it was at its most palpable. But even in his downtime, when there wasn't a crowd around to fire him up, he still had a buzz to him, a low background hum that settled into you and didn't turn off.

I mention all this because my little comment turned it off.

He blinked a couple of times, and his eyes, darker now, went from my eyes to my chest, my chest to the table. The muscles in his face slackened his expression into plainness. He picked up his notepad and pen. "All set?" he said, pocketing them.

"What?" I asked. "Did I say something?"

"I'm all set," he said, standing up.

"You're not done with your ginger ale, though."

"I am, actually." He didn't say this with any malice or regret or sarcasm; it was just the way things happened to be. He went over to the exit; I followed him, and whether out of force of habit or not, he held the door open for me.

"I'm going up Fifth Avenue," he said, when we were both outside. "I'll have better luck getting a cab there."

"More cabs around than subways," I added.

"I don't ride in the subway." He was walking at a good clip now, and I hastened to keep up. "It saps me if I'm not careful."

"Hey, me too!"

He said nothing. Just kept walking.

"Are you not the happiest guy in the world? That was just a figure of speech, Chase, I didn't—"

"I provide happiness for others, Ned," he said. "I'm not selfish enough to waste it on myself." His words were flat with no force behind them.

"Waste?"

"I'm a carrier. I give. I don't hoard."

"Are you *kidding*?" I managed to say. "It's happiness! It's good for you—you of all people ought to know that!"

"It's good for others," he said. "I'll give you that. I just don't feel the need to experience it myself."

"How are you going to know happiness if you don't experience it?"

"I've managed pretty well so far, I would say."

We reached the curb; he looked left and started crossing without one hitch in his stride. I looked both ways and followed. There were more people around us now, more New York nightlife. Cars purred and rumbled by; angry obscenities mixed with cheerful ones. Somewhere close by, Alexa was having fun without us.

"What if you were your own client?" I asked as we reached the other side. "You've got this great talent, and you're a great cause—why not put it to use on yourself?"

Chase shook his head. "It's not personal, Sonny," he said. "It's strictly business."

"*Godfather*," I said automatically.

"Hey, right on, you know your movies. Anyway, you know it's bad business to dip into private stock. What if I try a little of it and I like it so much I decide to keep it all for myself? Not cool."

"Chase …" I was going to get winded if we kept up this pace much longer. "Chase, I don't want to think of you being miserable while everyone you talk to is happy."

"Oh, I'm not *miserable*, Ned," said Chase, sounding surprised. "Don't get me wrong. I'm not sad or depressed. I just don't happen to be able to possess the feeling of happiness. That's all." He looked left and held out his hand; half a block up, I saw a cab lurch a little as the driver hit the brakes.

"Chase," I said. "Tell me something."

"I think I have," he said, as the cab pulled up next to him. "I think I may have told you too much."

"Just one more thing," I said. "What happens when you do get sad? What do you do then?"

He opened the door and climbed in to tell the driver the address. He shut the door and rolled down the window before I could knock on it. He looked up at me, and ever so slowly, his smile eased back onto his face. I smiled to see it, to feel the energy between us thrum back to life.

"You've seen *Sound of Music*, right?" he asked me.

"Yeah?"

"Well, I simply remember my favorite things. And then I don't feel."

I waited for him to finish the line, and as I waited, he sat back and the driver put the cab in gear and they started down Fifth Avenue.

"Hey!" I yelled. "Finish that! Finish that line, Chase!"

But he was gone.

9.

"Will you be eating outdoors this morning?" the waitress asked.

"Well, let's see," said Siege, rubbing his chin. "Blue skies, nice breeze, the promise of a new day—you know, I'm going to leave it up to you."

She laughed—polite? Hard to tell—and led us over to a table by the door. "She loves me and doesn't know it yet," said Siege, swatting his napkin open on his lap. "Poor kid. Now let's hear about this incredible night."

I told him about Alexa's appearance in my life, the way her party moved into higher gears, and the entire account of Chase Becker—as a party guest, as a business entrepreneur, and as an emotional iceman. "So you can imagine how bad I feel," I concluded, stirring my Bloody Mary with a dewy stalk of celery that was still nice and rigid. "He's done his job, he's unwinding, talking about it, and I have to go and wreck it."

"Yeah," Siege agreed. "It's all your fault. 'You're awesome, you must be really happy.' What kind of fuckin' idiot says something that stupid?" he said, adding a "Sorry" for the benefit of the two old ladies in sweaters and berets glaring at us from the next table over.

"Okay, I take your point," I said, stopping him with a policeman's *halt* gesture. "But you've got to admit that it would have been better not to rile him up like that."

"No, I don't think I do," said Siege, putting down his Bloody Mary. "You're on his radar now in a way you weren't before. You got him talking about himself in a way that I'm willing to bet nobody else has in forever. And you know what you did best?"

"What?"

"You demonstrated value. You pointed out a couple mistakes he made that he knew were mistakes and didn't know he made. And you picked up on a good *Godfather* reference. I'm serious," he insisted, catching my skeptical look. "You see if that doesn't make a difference somewhere down the road. Anyway, now he knows you have something to offer. You're bringing something to the game that he can use. He's not about to let that go."

This sounded good to me, both in its plausibility and in its reassurance. I hated to think a slip of the tongue could mean the complete end of a relationship, and Siege's pronouncing this not to be the case was something I had hoped to hear this morning. He'd usually been right when he gave me advice back in the dorm; I wanted to start testing his track record in the real world.

Our waitress came back with our omelets, wheat toast, and a smile. As she weaved her way back to the kitchen, Siege continued, raising his voice so the waitress would hear him. "Speaking of beautiful women ..."

The sweater ladies glared over again.

This time, Siege turned to address them directly. "What?" he said. "You are! Don't let anybody tell you different."

They tittered and went back to their tea. Siege leaned over his omelet and said, "Seriously, speaking of that, what's the story with this Alexa? You gonna see her again?"

"I hadn't thought about it that way," I muttered to the piece of toast I was holding.

"Well, think about it that way for a second."

"Siege, I'm not like you. I don't go right to 'happily ever after.' I need time to think about what all's happened and what could happen. I mean, from what I gather, she's good at being single, and maybe there's a reason for that. Or maybe she's looking for someone with an

actual bank account, or someone who can get her places she's looking
to go. I can't give her that kind of stuff—I'm just a guy with a summer
job who's sleeping on a couch. And let's not forget, I had a relationship
shrivel up and die on me not that long ago."

Siege drained his Bloody Mary and put the glass down. "Four
questions," he said, holding up his hand and ticking them off on each
finger. "Yeah? And? So? What?"

I considered this. Someone in the background clanked their
silverware on their plate once, very loudly.

"Dude, if you're going to get shot down, at least let somebody else
do the shooting," he went on. "The game's there to be played, and
you won't be getting anywhere just looking at the board, or thinking
about moves you would make if you were playing, or deciding why it
is you're going to lose. Just play the game."

"Well, you may be right," I said, and I ate a forkful of omelet.

Siege frowned. He knew full well that this was my way of closing
the subject. It left my opponent with an empty victory and nothing
more to discuss. He didn't like it, but he knew not to take it to heart,
and for the time being, he would let the matter drop.

"I need a refill," he said, looking around. "Where's the future
Mrs. Brandenburg?"

* * *

When I got back to the apartment, Nadine was sitting on her swivel
stool in front of the computer, still wearing her blue plaid pajamas.
"Hey, sleepyhead," I said.

"This is a pajamas-all-day kind of day," she said. "Hey, Neds, give
me your work email for my address book."

I did, and she clickety-clicked it in and took a sip from a small glass
of orange juice. Somehow she was pulling off the feat of looking tired
and refreshed, both at once.

"You went to quite a party last night," she said, spinning to face me.

"And you went to quite a fancy restaurant," I countered.

"And I got a call from Alexa this morning asking all about you,"
she fired back.

The first thing I noticed was that my heart didn't leap to hear this, or swell, or skip a beat, or any of those things that hearts do. Right now, it was the *idea* of Alexa that was interesting me, the head that was being appealed to. This was one of the hazards of my falling half in love with someone; it never lasted for long, and it was more involved with the rational thought process than the irrational world of emotions. *Too bad*, I thought; *Alexa would be a nice girl to dream about.* But hey, just thinking about her was something I felt more than prepared to do.

"Really? What'd she say?"

"She wanted to know why you didn't go to Take Two with everybody else. She thought you were smart, and she's worried that you're too smart for her and that you thought the party was boring."

"No, I just got sidetracked," I said. I'd tell Nadine about Chase later. "I'm not that smart—she doesn't have to worry. She's on the ball herself. And she's way prettier than her pictures."

Nadine grinned. "Sparks?"

I paused. "Could be. I'd like it if there were. I'm still kind of finding out, though, and I don't want to say there are if I'm not really sure yet."

"But there's potential."

"There is potential," I agreed. "I'll go that far. Now what about you? How was Whittaker's?"

"Ahhh, Whittaker's," she said. She hunched over and looked off to the side. "There is a lot of money there," she said. "The place is full of money. The butter pats were shaped like little crowns. I didn't even want to use them, they were so perfect. I felt so self-conscious the whole time. Tedd was in his element."

"What'd you guys eat?"

"He had steak; I had duck something or other. It was good—at those prices it'd have to be. But the whole thing was too much for me, and I was freaking out a bit. Not the screaming and running around kind of freaking out, just like sitting there in my seat, in this really nice black dress I got last month just for this dinner, and feeling more and more like *nothing*."

I felt a huge wave of compassion wash out of me toward Nadine. Of all the words in the world that could have been used to describe her, I didn't want her to latch on to *nothing*. I wanted to protect her from the sting of that word. Or, if I couldn't do it, I wanted to know that somebody else had tried.

"Did Tedd say anything?" I asked, sitting down in the corner of the couch.

She nodded. "He did. He said, 'You know, considering how long it took to get a reservation here, and considering how much it costs, the least you can do is pretend you're glad to be here.'"

More waves. A wave of anger at Tedd for daring to belittle her like that. A wave of my skeleton army to guard and protect her from those who hoped to tear her down. And another wave of compassion.

"Oh, Nades," I whispered.

"I said a few things, he said a few things, and I wound up leaving before he did." She pushed her lips hard together for a moment. "Kind of a waste of a nice dress," she said, with a half-giggle, half-sob. "But I told him I needed to take a break from him. I don't know if it's going to be for a long time or what, but I have to think."

I didn't say anything.

"The thing is," she went on, "you're seeing him at this bad point, and this is all you know him by, so this is all you have to judge him by. But I've known him for more than six years, Neds. That's a quarter of my life. There's a lot of history between us, and that means something. He's done a lot of great things for me, and I know how important we are for each other. But it's just as important for us to take a break right now so I can figure things out."

We sat there in the late morning sunlight, neither one of us looking at the other as we thought about this turn of events. The city rambled along outside, paying oblivious witness.

"Say something, Neds," she said.

I sighed. "I won't ask if you love him," I said. "Because you obviously do. But I do have to ask—does he make you happy?"

She shook her head, but not as an answer. "It's not a question of happiness," she said.

"Well, maybe it should be."

She shrugged, her shoulders staying up for a good four or five seconds before she let them drop. In the kitchen, the refrigerator began to hum.

"You're too good a person to believe it when somebody says something like that about you, Nadine," I said. "Don't listen to him. There's no reason to listen to him if he's going to say something like that."

She sat there for a few moments, and then she looked at me, her eyes shining bright, the workings of an actual smile coming together. "Tell you what," she said. "Today's the day we start our movie watching."

"All right," I said. "You got a deal. You have something in mind?"

"Well, it should be a comedy to help cheer me up a little. It should be New York-related, to welcome you. It should be at the start of the alphabet, because it's the beginning of our watching movies. It should be something about romance, to give us both something to shoot for. And it should be something we've seen before, just for the comfort of familiarity."

"That narrows it down considerably," I said, as she went over to her cabinet and opened it up. The movies weren't in any order that I could figure, but in seconds she had picked out the one she'd been looking for. "Ta-da!" she said, whipping around to hold up a copy of *Annie Hall*.

"Not *The Apartment*?" I asked.

"Hey, wow!" she said. "That fits the rules perfect too, doesn't it? Wow, I'm impressed."

That made me feel pretty good. I was glad to know I was demonstrating value.

"But no, this is an *Annie Hall* kind of day," she decided. So we got sodas and made popcorn, Nadine got a blanket for herself, and we settled in front of the huge TV. She brushed at her eyes with the side of her index finger and chuckled, preparing her laugh for the movie. I felt an overwhelming urge to take her from her pain, to keep her from being hurt again, to bring her something better. She was worth so much more than she knew, and as the FBI warned us about the dangers of piracy, I resolved to do away with her troubles any way I could.

"You may already know this," she said as the opening credits silently went by. "But the original name for *Annie Hall* was *Anhedonia*. Woody Allen changed it when he realized that nobody knew what the word meant."

"I didn't know that," I said. "What's 'anhedonia' mean?"

"That's a condition where you're incapable of experiencing happiness."

"Really? Hey, that reminds me—"

"Shhhh," she said, touching her lips. "Let's just watch the movie."

10.

When I got to work the next morning, trying my best to shake off a particularly depressing subway ride (an old woman had spent the entire time crying into a filthy handkerchief), Louise the receptionist offered me an open box. Inside were a batch of the best peanut butter cookies I'd ever tasted. "Maylene made these for everyone," she said. "So make sure you leave enough," she added as I reached back into the box. I got the message and didn't take any more.

After our morning meeting, I went to my desk, fired up my computer, and found this:

6/4/05, 3:10 PM
From: alpinegal@gmail.com
To: nalderman@peppercornpub.com
Subject: Hi!

Hi, Ned! Nadine sent me your email address so I could let you know what a good time I had meeting you on Saturday. Hope you had a great time! Next time don't leave the party just when it's getting started—you'll have fun, I swear! Keep me updated on stuff with Nadine & Ted, and I'll see you soon!

Alexa!

PS – I know it's "Tedd"—sometimes I spell it "Ted" because I like thinking how much it'd piss him off! (Don't tell Nadine?)

PPS – You wouldn't believe how many people look at my email address and think I'm a skier!

It was a nice little note. I made a quick promise to myself not to go reading too much into it—that had been a big problem of mine in the past. If anything were to grow out of this, I wanted to be sure it would grow organically, without my forcing things along. So, I wrote a nice little response to her nice little note.

6/5/05, 9:14 AM
From: nalderman@peppercornpub.com
To: alpinegal@gmail.com
Subject: Re: Hi!

Alexa – Thanks both for writing to me and for throwing a good party; next time maybe I'll have more staying power. I'll give you Tedd updates as I see them (though I suspect you'll get them from Nadine first). Hope it's a good week for you – Ned

Then I set about writing the email I really wanted to write.

6/5/05, 9:14 AM
From: nalderman@peppercornpub.com
To: chase@joyfacilitator.com
Subject: Saturday

Chase – I just wanted to let you know how much I enjoyed talking with you this past Saturday. It was fascinating learning about joy facilitation, and I truly appreciate you letting me into that world. I hope you're not upset or offended by any of my uninformed talk; I never meant to cause discomfort, and if I did, I apologize. Anyway, I'd like to hang out some more (at

Sweethaven? I really liked it there). You've got my email now,
so if you're ever interested, let me know – Ned

As I clicked on "send," Maylene walked by my desk. "Hey,
Maylene," I said. "You make great cookies."

"Oh, thanks," she murmured, looking down and not breaking
stride. She was still pretty shy.

* * *

Nadine's break from Tedd didn't last forty-eight hours. On Monday
morning, a large bouquet arrived at the film lab where she worked;
she was making up with him on the phone when I came home that
evening, and by Friday, they were dating again. It wasn't something
I really understood, and I felt like any attempt to understand through
talking with Nadine would be prying. I also didn't really like talking
about it with Alexa. She may have been closer to Nadine than I'd
been over the last few years, but she was still on the friend side of the
family/friend divide, and I couldn't shake the feeling that it wasn't
right to air out the dirty laundry for the neighbors to see.

Siege and I talked about it, but only long enough to dismiss it and
file in the "women—who can figure 'em?" file. Besides, we were
having too much fun talking about things that were more our speed,
like stories about growing up, and the people we knew in high school,
and observations and arguments. ("Give me one good reason why that
statue sucks." "Whattaya on—crack or something? *Look* at it!") We
were already good friends, but the fact that we had parallel lives now,
not overlapping ones, added a new dimension to our relationship, and
I for one was really enjoying the strengthening of our bond.

I didn't have much of a bond to strengthen with Chase, and
whatever bond I did have wasn't doing anything. He never responded
to my first email. My second one, a more direct request to meet up
after work, got a brief, friendly reply—he was tied up, but a meeting
would be something to do, and we should play it by ear. After that—

nothing. I got no emails, and things were going well enough at work that Jamie Engel didn't need to bring him in for any joy injections.

As for me, I was making all kinds of adjustments in my life. I developed a kind of protective shell that helped me get through my subway rides without any more troubling to my psyche. I was doing good work (grunt work, maybe, but it needed doing) and getting along fine with everybody there. I got regular emails from Alexa and an occasional fun forward from Nadine. My paycheck, while small, kept me solvent. Siege showed me some random stores in the Village that were a wonder to walk through. I was eating more worldwide cuisine than I'd ever imagined, and I was walking around to such an extent that I was losing weight involuntarily (which I submit was not a bad thing).

Finally, I was having a great time with Nadine. We liked our movie time so much, we started doing it twice a week—she'd pick the Sunday movie, and I got to choose on Thursdays. We caught each other up on our pasts, and we talked more about the present day and the things we'd done with our friends the night before. And, as it turned out, the couch was so soft and comfortable that I never bothered unfolding it when it was time to go to sleep.

One night, as I was about to cross into the fog between awake and half-asleep, I realized something that opened my eyes: I hadn't thought of Val once all day. She had been in my head for so long— never mind renting space in it; she'd owned it—and now she was an afterthought. What's more, the realization didn't sadden me. I had moved past the sorrows and regret, moved away from the anger and the hurt. I had moved on. I had done what I had come to New York to do, and now I could see what it was like to wander through the world truly unencumbered. The idea made the short trip to unconsciousness a very pleasant one. Life, I thought, as I rested my head back on the cushion and closed my eyes, was good.

11.

Nadine was involved with postproduction work on *Enough*, a documentary about starvation across the globe. "They show people who live in deserts and the war-torn countries, all the places you'd expect," she told me, "and then they turn around and show you homeless people in America. And then they interview the ones who are 'hungry by choice,' an anorexic lady and a guy on a hunger strike. It's supposed to make you think," she said in a deep, sonorous voice that gave her words not-quite-mock gravitas.

On the 24th, the first Friday of summer, an organization called FAMINE (Feed All Mankind In Nations Everywhere) was holding a one-hundred-dollar-a-plate benefit dinner to help support soup kitchens throughout the city and to help defray the costs of making the documentary. They had worked very closely with the filmmakers, and so it was that Nadine came home with an invite to attend.

"Nadine Willis and guest," I read aloud. "So you and Tedd."

She grinned. "Nope. You and me."

"What? What about Tedd?"

"Oh, Tedd's coming too. But he told me he wants to pay for his ticket. He can afford it, and he can write it off on his taxes at the end of the year. And it's good karma for him. Plus, this may be the only chance you'll ever get to attend a dinner like this, right?"

My one concern was that I didn't have a suit for the occasion, but Siege took care of that. "We're off to my pal Sal's!" he said, and within an hour we were at a Salvation Army, rummaging through racks of used suits that, to my growing amazement, were in perfectly good condition.

"When I first moved here," said Siege, "back before I could afford anything, all my suits were Salvation Armani."

"Look at these," I said, running my fingers down a coat sleeve. "No stains, no rips, nothing wrong with them at all. Why would anyone get rid of these? Who would donate suits this nice when they could keep them in their closets?"

"Widows," Siege said.

My face fell. "Oh, right."

"Wearing the clothes of the dead," Siege half-sang, sliding the hangers down the pole in rhythm. "Hey, here's a good one."

I wound up buying a dark gray suit with narrow lapels and a *that's-not-toxic-is-it?* smell that dry cleaning hadn't eliminated so much as replaced. The waist was a little snug, but nothing that good posture wouldn't fix. Besides, what do you want for thirty bucks?

"It's the very definition of a cheap suit," I told Lee and Maylene at lunch the day before the dinner. "But it does its job."

"What's a suit's job?" Maylene asked, pushing most of her oatmeal cookie toward me.

I finished my pickle and raised a finger. "A good suit does three things," I said. "It makes the wearer look handsome, smart, and three inches taller."

"I can see why you'd want all three," Lee muttered.

"I love you too, Duchess," I said. This was a line Siege and I had picked up from our bad cable TV movie watching, which the actor delivered to the girl playing his daughter with an unintentionally comic lack of conviction. We loved that line more than I can say. We said it whenever we wanted to crush the other one with insincerity. We said it enough that it sometimes popped up in front of the wrong audience. This was one of those times.

The three of us finished our lunch in silence.

**

So the stage was set for Friday night, the first Friday of summer and the first time I'd be seeing Tedd since my arrival. He'd come by the apartment a couple of times since the so-called break, but I happened to be out both times. I hoped I could maintain a good frame of mind in his presence. *Water under the bridge*, I thought as I checked out my reflection in the bathroom mirror. *Water under the bridge.* Hopefully it wouldn't stay under the bridge and turn stale and brackish on me.

When I emerged, Nadine was standing there with a digital camera. "Look at you," she said, and the flashbulb went off and left me blinking. "I'm so sending this to Alexa," she said. "One look at you in a suit and she's going to go nuts."

"It's just a suit," I mumbled as she took another picture. But I'll confess that the idea of a girl being attracted to me just by looking at a photograph of me was an idea I liked.

"I'm going to get ready now," she said, handing me the camera. "Can you work this? Take a picture of Tedd when he comes in, take one of me when I come out, and then take one of us together." With that, she whisked off to her room.

I didn't want to sit down at first, for fear of messing up the crease in my pants, until I remembered we were taking a cab there anyway. So I parked it on the recliner and passed the time reading an old issue of *Film Comment* that Nadine had brought home. It's not a good magazine for a light, casual read; the articles are very involving. I was caught up in a piece on Hal Ashby when I heard the knock at the door.

"Come on in," I called, picking up the camera and twisting around in my seat.

The door opened, and as Tedd leaned in, I snapped his picture. The flash startled him enough that he took a step back. When he recovered, he lasered a look at me and wagged a finger. "Not cool, Alderman," he said, slow and chilly. "Not cool."

"Sorry," I muttered, feeling a lot more guilt than I deserved to feel.

Tedd closed the door behind him and composed himself. "Now you can take one," he said. He was wearing a black pinstripe suit, set off with a dark purple necktie and handkerchief. The cut and the creases emphasized all but one of his angles, and he took care of that final angle himself when he tilted his head back just so. A good sketch artist could have drawn an accurate likeness with just ten or twelve straight lines.

I stood up, put him in frame, and clicked. That taken care of, I called, "Nadine! Tedd's here!"

"Be out in a minute!" she called back.

Tedd slid closer to me, eyeing my suit. "Where did you ever find something like this?" he asked, fingering my sleeve.

I suppressed my impulse to yank it away. "Siege took me to a Salvation Army downtown," I said.

"Is that right." He landed equal emphasis on all three syllables. Each word was spoken in a lower tone than the one before; it was a question that didn't sound like a question. He was keeping his approval or disapproval well hidden, or maybe he was still making up his mind. I braced myself for a final judgment, but before he could deliver it, there was a sound of rustling and footsteps, and Nadine appeared.

She was breathtaking. Her hair was swept back and pinned into an intricate knot. Her dress was a shimmering black, with bare shoulders and a burgundy sash across her chest. She had made up her eyes to look wider, and her smile was lovely, if far more tentative than it had any right to be. The camera floated up to my eyes, and I captured the way she looked for all time.

"You *had* to wear *that* dress," said Tedd.

Through the viewfinder I watched her smile fade to nothing. She made two small fists and then released them.

"I think it's a beautiful dress," I said, half defending Nadine and half expressing myself.

"I'm not saying it isn't," said Tedd. "She has great taste and she wears it beautifully. It's just that that dress has a history."

"This is the dress I wore to Whittaker's," Nadine explained, her voice weary.

"And you had to wear it tonight." He shook his head, disappointed.

"It's a beautiful dress," I repeated, with all the conviction I could muster.

She looked down and murmured, "Thank you, Ned," in a blank voice. She still looked lovely, but she'd changed inside, and the effect was painful to see and feel. I was glad I'd gotten the picture of her before Tedd had said anything. Oh, right—the picture.

"Let me take one of you together," I said, holding up the camera.

For a moment, neither one moved. Then Nadine slipped across the room and came to a halt by Tedd's side. He put his hand down on her far shoulder and stared out at me.

"Okay," I said, stepping back a couple steps to get as much of Tedd in the frame as I could. "Say 'hungry.'"

"Hungry," Nadine echoed. Tedd said nothing. In the resulting picture, Nadine's mouth is slightly open and stretched out to say the syllable -gry. Her mouth has been tricked into a smile, one that doesn't mean a thing. And Tedd, who stayed silent, isn't smiling at all.

***

The benefit was held in a grand old ballroom, with the tables set up at one end and a bar at the other. A scattered few were already sitting at tables here and there, but most of them were mingling around the alcohol. I went right to the bar and ordered up a scotch and soda. It would look classier than a beer, I figured, even one in a pilsner glass.

The people milling around were a bigger mix than I expected; I thought the place would be filled with retirees, but that wasn't so. Mostly, it was beefy middle-aged men with graying crew cuts and sharp chins and aggressive smiles that emphasized their crow's feet. These were men who'd been jocks in school, made their fortunes with any number of steely handshakes, and now were learning how to share the wealth—and learning well. Not my crowd, I guess is what I'm saying.

These men had brought their wives, some by their sides, but most off in their own little groups, both hands wrapped around the stems of their wine glasses as they talked and listened. Not a gray hair among these women, they glittered back and forth, telling some secrets and hiding others as best they could. They showed no tarnish, and I'm sure they stood for a lot of great things.

Other ages were represented too—people in their twenties, most of them more chiseled and less wide-eyed than me, and people in their twilight years, plump dowagers in light pink, old men with hearing aids tucked into ears the size of dollar bills. All of them were at ease with one another, gladly learning, gladly teaching, finding common bonds. It was exactly the kind of atmosphere you'd want at a benefit.

I began to circulate, walking around with little purpose. I saw Nadine talking to a man in black who had a shaved head and his hands up high on his hips. I saw the back of Tedd's head, higher up than anybody else's. And off toward a wall, halfway between the bar and the tables, I saw Chase Becker.

Of course. I don't know why it hadn't occurred to me before that he might be here.

Tonight his suit and shoes were chocolate brown, classy and warm. He'd gotten a haircut since I'd last seen him; it was too long to bristle and too short to flop about. He was smiling at a woman who was in her final days of being able to carry off wearing a strapless gown. She made a lot of two-handed gestures, her fingers spread wide apart. As I came closer, I could hear her voice, a giddy near-screech that made me wince. If I hadn't known him, I wouldn't have believed how Chase could keep that welcoming warmth on his face. It was, I knew, something that was beyond me.

"And she landed on all fours *again!*" the woman said as I reached them. "Just like a cat!"

"Chase?" I asked.

He saw me, and once again I felt the thrum of good vibrations as his face lit up. "Ned!" he said. Then, quickly, "Mrs. Hanover, I'd like you to meet my friend, Ned Alderman. Ned, this is Thelma Hanover." After we'd how-do-you-doed and she'd twittered a laugh, he said, "Mrs. Hanover, I need to talk to a few other people, but I would love to continue this conversation later. Would that be all right?"

She said it would, and Chase walked off with me. I was about to ask him about his lack of contact, but before I could, he asked, "How are things at Peppercorn?"

"Ah-ha," I said, pointing at him. "I see what you did there. You've been learning from your mistakes."

"I sure have," he agreed. "I sure have."

That was the first time I'd ever heard Chase use his sense of humor, and I liked how smart it was. It was also fun in its self-deprecation. I was growing more convinced that the only person who could take Chase Becker down a notch or two was Chase Becker.

"Can I get you a ginger ale?" I asked.

"Great," he said, and we walked over to the bar. "Glad I could rescue you from that lady," I said as we bellied up.

"Who? Thelma Hanover? Oh, that wasn't a rescue, Ned. I was really enjoying her."

"Even with that voice?"

"That's just how she talks," he said. "You know? Hey, that suit looks great on you, by the way."

I basked in that compliment as the bartender came over and fixed up a ginger ale. "This is a good gig for you," I said. "Lots of people."

"It's true," he said. "It's an interesting crowd—most of them are already in a pretty happy place, mentally, so I'm focusing a little more on the altruistic side, how so much good comes out of donating to such a worthy cause. That way, they realize—" He stopped and shook his head. "I'm sorry," he said. "I always seem to wind up talking shop with you."

"No, don't worry about it," I said, happy just to be talking. As we sipped our drinks, a man stepped aside to reveal Nadine saying goodbye to the bald guy and watching him walk off toward the tables. "Hey, Chase, I'd like you to meet somebody," I said.

"Sure," Chase agreed, and we worked our way through the crowd. A couple people called out to Chase as we walked, and he turned to call back to them. When we reached Nadine, he was twisted almost completely around to finish acknowledging someone, and she was still looking in the other direction.

"Nadine," I said. "This is Chase Becker."

And they turned to face each other, forming their smiles as they did.

12.

There's the *snap* when two jigsaw puzzle pieces fit together. There's the *clunk* of two railroad cars coupling, the *crack* when a baseball hits the bat right at the sweet spot, the *rip* when a basketball hits nothing but net. There's the *chunk* when you plug a good guitar into a good amp, the *smack* of a perfect high five.

These are sounds that you hear when a connection is made, and each one is quite satisfying in its own way. But those are all objects. Until the 24th of June, during my summer in New York City, I had never witnessed the power of two *people* connecting who are meant to connect. I had the privilege of witnessing it that night when Chase locked eyes with Nadine.

I'd like to ascribe a crackle-popping noise to it, like a loose wire spitting out sparks, or a log burning in the fireplace. But that's not true—there was nothing between them but the silence of outer space. I'd also like to say that the rings of amicable energy coming from Chase shorted out, or maybe doubled in voltage, but if either one happened, I didn't realize it. All I can honestly pay witness to is what I saw and heard and felt, not what I wanted to see and hear and feel. So bear with me while I stick to the facts and leave my flights of fancy for another day.

***

"Chase," I said, "this is Nadine Willis, my second cousin."

Both of them had stopped cold, and they were staring at each other with some kind of wonder. After a moment their right hands, acting independently of the rest of them, completed the meeting cycle and took hold of each other. Once they did that, they didn't move.

Their hands may not have been shaking, but the rest of them seemed to be. Chase's broad shoulders squared with an involuntary twitch, and his foot tapped twice. And I could feel Nadine trembling from where I stood, a foot away. "I think you got hit by the thunderbolt," I said.

"*Godfather,*" they both said. And with that, the shock of the moment passed, and they were able to complete their handshake and let their natural smiles replace their official ones as they murmured their intimate hellos. I took a step or two back, giving them their space, but I had no intention of looking away. They were entrancing to see together. Chase may have just discovered a connection to his heart. And Nadine may have just found someone who could give her the love and respect she should be getting, someone who would be good for her, not someone who took—

"Hello?"

Speak of the goddamn devil.

Tedd glided past me and loomed up beside Nadine. "We should think about getting a table," he said.

"Oh, right," she agreed. "Tedd, I'd like you to meet someone."

"We don't really have the—"

"This is Chase Becker," she said. "Chase, this is Tedd Long."

"Tedd with two Ds," he added, shaking Chase's hand distractedly. It seemed to me he pulled his shoulders back to stand up straighter and taller. "What do you do, Becker?"

Somebody walked between me and the three of them to get to the tables. I took a few baby steps closer so that wouldn't happen again. I didn't want to miss any of this.

"I'm a joy facilitator," said Chase, sliding a casual hand into his pocket.

"Oh, a warmer. I've heard of you guys. You get people to believe you can just stand around them and all of a sudden they're going to feel great. Did I get that right?" The question was caked with insouciance—he didn't care if he got it right or not; that's what Chase was in his mind, and that's what he would stay.

"I completely understand why you'd be skeptical," said Chase, just as calm and as warm as could be. "It's a pretty unbelievable thing—if you try to analyze it." He sipped his ginger ale.

Tedd sniffed. "What a racket," he said. "And people actually think it works?"

I had to jump in. Not that Chase needed my help, but I didn't like seeing his livelihood attacked. "That's why he's here tonight, Tedd," I said. "The FAMINE people hired him to help with the atmosphere."

"Well, bang-up job so far," said Tedd. I think he meant it to be sarcastic, but in the brief silence that followed, we all had time to reflect on how well the evening had been going, and we couldn't help thinking that Chase may indeed have played a part in that. Nadine looked over at Chase and tried to suppress a smile.

Then Tedd said, "I bet you can't make me happy."

Chase lowered his ginger ale from his lips. "Excuse me?"

"That's your job tonight, isn't it? Making people happy? Well, let's see you do your job."

More people were walking past us to their tables. "Tedd," said Nadine, touching his sleeve. "Maybe we should—"

"Hold on, hold on," said Tedd, waving her away, not taking his eyes off Chase, probably fighting the urge to circle him. "Okay. Let's say my girlfriend and I"—he snapped his head at Nadine—"have been in an argument. I'm all sad, and I'm walking around, and I run into you." He folded his arms and raised himself to his full height. "Try and make me happy," he said.

Chase stood there, regarding Tedd. He had a different look than I'd ever seen him have, one of thoughtful curiosity. I caught eyes with Nadine; she looked as anxious as I felt. Tedd stood there, ramrod tall, staring down at Chase. Waiting.

Finally, Chase gave his head two or three tiny shakes. "I don't know if I can," he said.

My heart sank.

A mean barracuda smile broke out on Tedd's face. "I knew it," he said. "I knew the whole thing was a sham."

"And how does that make you feel?" Chase asked.

Tedd started to answer, then stopped. He started to answer a couple more times and stopped. Watching his face struggle against itself, my mental skeleton army cheered, and my heart shot back to the surface and took a whooping gasp of triumph. Tedd couldn't deny it—for a few seconds there, Chase had made him happy. It may have been done by trickery, but by God it was done. There was now no doubt in my mind that Chase could have turned the Gobi Desert into a rainforest if he so chose.

"We should take our seats," said Chase, looking over at the tables. Two business cards materialized between his fingers, and he pressed one into Tedd's hand and one into Nadine's. "If I can do anything more for you, *please* be in touch," he said. "I'm really glad to have met you both. Take care." With that, he was off to the tables.

The three of us watched him go. I looked up at Tedd, expecting him to say something. But he didn't. He just kept his eyes on Chase, watching him choose a place to sit. Once he'd sat down, Tedd started off to a table on the opposite side of the room. He never looked at Nadine or me.

"Ned," Nadine whispered. She slipped Chase's business card into my coat pocket. "Hold this for me."

* * *

That was the last thing I heard her say all night. She didn't say anything while we ate. She didn't say anything while the FAMINE people made their presentation to a representative of New York's soup kitchens, or while her colleagues introduced and showed a brief clip from *Enough*. She didn't say anything during the cab ride home. (Tedd was strangely quiet too; I wondered if he was still trying to figure out how Chase had caught him so neatly in the happiness trap.) When we got back to the apartment, I wished Tedd a quick goodnight, then hopped out and went on upstairs; if she said something then, I didn't hear it. She didn't say anything when she came into the apartment—she just went right to her room and closed the door behind her.

The next morning, Saturday the 25th, I woke up with my face planted deep enough in the sofa cushion to make a ribbed pattern on my cheek. I rolled over, shaking off the last few tendrils of sleep, and saw Nadine in the recliner. She wore a white T-shirt, jeans, and no shoes; her bare toes picked gently at the floor. My suit coat lay crumpled in front of her; in her hands, undergoing careful analysis, was Chase's business card, freshly fished out from one of my coat pockets. She looked over at me, and at long last she spoke.

"Neds," she said, holding up the card. "You have *got* to tell me more about this guy."

13.

I'd told her about Chase before, but I'd never gone into any real detail—just a few of the things I'd seen him do and say, enough to give a general idea. Now, with Nadine eager to hear everything she could, I unloaded. I told her about our first meeting, about Alexa's party and the long talk afterward, about my take on what had happened between the two of them last night. She listened and listened, rapt in my words.

"That's amazing," she said, once I'd finished. "I know exactly what you mean about that energy vibe thing. The second I saw him, I felt like someone had blown a hole in my stomach. And the handshake—well, you called it with that 'thunderbolt' line."

"You don't understand it, but you want to."

She nodded, more to herself than to me. "Yeah," she said. "I do."

"So you like him?" More than anything, I wanted the answer to be yes. No, scratch that – more than anything, I wanted her to see that Chase Becker was the Answer.

"Like him? I don't even know the guy, Neds, come on. I'm just saying I never reacted to anybody like that before, not even … not even …" She looked down and busied her hands in her lap.

"You think you could like him, though?" I prodded.

"I have a boyfriend."

"That wasn't my question."

She continued to look down at her hands. After a minute, still looking down, she said, "What was it you said about him not knowing how to be happy himself?"

I refused to remember my words. "That was before," I said. "From what I saw last night, I think you could have changed all that. I think he's the perfect man for you."

She looked up at me. She ached to believe me, I knew. But there was a lot of baggage holding her back. At least six and a half feet's worth, as far as I could tell.

"I don't want the perfect man," she said. "I want the right man."

"There's no reason he can't be both," I said.

She didn't say anything.

"Okay, so I'm not his best friend and I don't know everything about him. But I know chemistry when I see it, and last night I saw it between you two. You totally have to give this a chance—both of you. You might be the best thing that ever happened to each other."

She remained silent. Any emotions she felt were getting lost before they reached her face. Clearly she was going to need more convincing, and not just from me.

"Look," I told her. "You should call up Alexa. She's a girl, she's met him, she can probably tell you more than I can. Whatever she says, I can go along with."

Would I have said that if I thought Alexa was a big fan of Tedd's? Maybe not. But the girl talk part was true, at least; I felt sure that the two of them would have a lot more to say than the two of us.

"That's a good idea," she said, getting up. "Don't go far, though." She got her cell phone and nipped off to her room.

I figured this was going to be a while, so I got up off the couch and fixed myself some breakfast. Then I brushed and flossed, showered and shaved. By the time I'd gotten dressed, fixed up my suit, and folded my blankets, she still wasn't off the phone. I shifted into time-killing mode and opened up her movie cabinet to look for potential movie-night selections. The first couple Sergio Leone movies ... *Down by Law* ... oh, we *had* to see *Sweet Smell of Success* ...

Finally, I heard Nadine winding up her call, her voice sounding lighter than I would have guessed. She came out, marched up to me, and slugged me on the arm.

"Ow!"

"*That's* for not telling me you and Alexa have been emailing each other every day," she said. Then she popped me one on the other arm. "And *that's* for not asking her out yet."

"Ask her out?" I folded my arms so I could rub the sting out of both my biceps. "She doesn't want to go out with me."

"Well, nobody told *her* that."

"You're joking, right?" That was the only explanation I could come up with. These weren't deep, exploratory emails we'd been sending each other, all of them from my work email address. She would just tell me what was up with her, and I'd respond (all I ever did was respond—never initiated a single volley) and tell her what was up with me. And she still signed her name with an exclamation point. No big deal. Or so I had always thought.

"Neds," she said, going over to the computer, "think about it. Is Alexa Pine really the kind of girl who would write to someone every day if she wasn't a little bit interested in him?"

"Sure?" The fact that a question mark showed up unbidden at the end of the word was a good indicator of my dawning realization that things weren't the way I thought they were.

"No," said Nadine. "She isn't. She's someone who knows what she wants and who works to make it a part of her life. And I think you ought to help move that process along. You've recovered enough from Val—you're ready. Here," she said, getting up off the stool. "Log on to your email account."

"What for?"

"So you can send her an email inviting her to Sunday brunch."

"What, the three of us?"

She shook her head. "You *are* oblivious, aren't you?"

I shrugged. "I don't know. I guess." I pulled up the Peppercorn site. "You think she'll see it in time?"

"She should," Nadine said, walking toward the kitchen. "I told her you were about to send it."

"What if I don't want to?" I called to her.

Her response arced back, laden with finality. "You do."

Well. Apparently I did. Guess that took care of that. But to be honest, I still didn't know what my thoughts were about Alexa. Sure, I was half in love with her that night at the party, but that's only half in love; that doesn't really count. I was open to the idea of things going further, but I hadn't been moved to further those things myself. Val may have been in my rearview mirror, but that didn't mean I was looking down the road. Maybe all I needed was a good kick in the pants. Well, Nadine had given me one, and now here I was acting on it. Maybe this would be the start of something real and good and true. The only way to know was to press on.

I logged in to my account. "Hey," I said, "did you guys spend any time at all talking about Chase?"

She came back to the living room, holding a bowl of cereal near her chin as she ate from it. "Obviously," she said.

"Can you tell me anything about that?"

She smiled sweetly. "Nope. Just for us girls."

"Well then," I said, studying the screen. "I guess I can't tell you anything about the email Chase sent me last night."

"What??" She ran over so quickly I barely had time to minimize the screen. "What's he say? What's he say? Is it about me?"

"Sorry. Just for us boys."

She didn't like that.

"Nice sneer. Hey, you mess with the bull, you get the horns."

"Hey. When *I* mess with the bull, I get a steer." She polished off a spoonful of cereal, mushmouthed "So watch it." at me, and went back to the kitchen.

I maximized the screen again and wrote that invite to Alexa, suggesting the place where Siege and I had had our Bloody Marys. Then I went back and reread the first non-response email Chase had ever sent me.

6/24/05, 11:13 PM
To: nalderman@peppercornpub.com
From: chase@joyfacilitator.com
Subject: (No Subject)

I don't know whether you check this account on Saturday mornings or not. If you do, meet me for lunch at Mister C's on 68th and 3rd at noon. I have some things I need to ask you.

Best, Chase

14.

"Tell me about Tedd Long," Chase said.

I spluttered a bit and put down my beige plastic water glass. "That is so not what I thought you were going to say."

"Tedd Long," he repeated. "What can you tell me about him?"

He was different today than I'd ever seen him. His eyes didn't have that warm, open light to them—they were pressing me, insistent, almost urgent. There was no sense of threat from them, nor from the rest of Chase—he wore a casual shirt and slacks, and as he talked he kept his back resting against the vinyl of our booth. But these were the eyes of a man who wanted answers.

I told him what I could, which admittedly wasn't very much—after all, I'd only met him twice myself. Chase pressed me for facts, and once I'd run out of those, he let me give him my impressions. Those took a while longer to tell, and my finishing with them coincided with the arrival of our food.

"All right," Chase said. "Now tell me about Nadine Willis."

We'd both ordered mushroom burgers—half-pound angus burgers, mine with cheese—and fries. By the time I'd finished talking, Chase's burger was three-quarters gone and mine hadn't been touched. I had more to say about her, obviously. I'd expected this lunch to be more about her than about Tedd, so I had a number of semi-prepared lines, like "It's been a real treat getting to know her again." and "She doesn't know what she needs in her life." and "After you guys met, she didn't say a word the rest of the night." If someone had accused me of painting her in a desirable light and painting Tedd in an unflattering one, I wouldn't have denied it.

Chase sat there, taking it all in, waiting for pauses before he asked me questions (fewer than he'd asked about Tedd), panning for truth amidst all the exaggeration and hyperbole I'm sure I was offering. He asked about her parents, her job, her friendships. He asked about her attitudes toward each of them. He asked what I thought was her greatest accomplishment, and whether she would agree with me. I answered as best and as fully as I could, hoping what I said would be something he could return to, something he could bring forward when they met again.

After I finished, he thought for a minute, moving his thumbnail to and fro across his lips. Then he gestured at my plate. "Eat, eat," he said. "I'm sorry—I made you talk all this time and now your food's getting cold."

The food may not have been hot anymore, but it was still delicious. It came as no surprise that Chase knew where to find the best burger in town. While I consumed mine, he finished his, played with the straw wrapper, exchanged brief pleasantries with the very attentive waitress. He was preoccupied with his thoughts and words, and I didn't want to run his chariots of higher thinking off the road. So I savored my food in silence and waited.

When I was down to my last three fries, Chase finally spoke, and the words fairly flew out of his mouth. "Your second cousin did something to me last night, Ned," he said. "And it wasn't her beauty that did it, though she *is* a beautiful woman. It wasn't what she said— we just talked about *The Godfather*. Neat as that was, it's not enough to alter someone at their core."

"Oh, I don't know," I demurred.

Chase paid me no mind. "What she did was stop me. Right in my tracks. I was going along just fine, understanding my place in the world, and then there's something saying, *No, this is your place in the world.* And it's a place I have to know better. That's all there is to it."

He rubbed his eyes, his hair. "You know, I haven't slept since yesterday morning," he said. This wasn't the least bit obvious—as always, he looked impeccable. "And a night of work like last night's usually wipes me out for the rest of the weekend. But I'm not wiped out. Everything inside me is running in a higher gear now. And that's because your second cousin did something to me last night."

He picked up his water glass and sucked on his straw until the ice cubes touched bottom. He put it down and said, "You're the only one who can help me, Ned."

"Help you? How?"

Rather than answer me, Chase rested his cheek on his palm and looked off to the end of the table, where the napkin dispenser was. His countenance took on a gentle air, and as the gentility spread across his face, it grew in strength. I never knew about the way peacefulness generates power until the morning I saw it move across the great half-asleep face of Chase Becker. That was when I suddenly understood why the waitress was being so attentive, why people kept glancing over at our booth, why I myself wanted so badly to know how I could help him. He wasn't taking us into his world—he was bringing us in. Not with commands or orders, but with offers and invitations and requests. His door was open to us all, and while everyone else may have been content to crane their heads and look around a little, I was ready to step inside.

"How can I help you?" I asked.

"Ned," said Chase, turning his eyes back to mine, "Do you believe in love?"

"Love? Sure. Sure I do."

"But it's brought you pain."

A weak stab of Val got me in the chest. I paid it as little mind as I could. "It has, yes," I said.

"But you still believe in it."

I nodded. "Yes."

Chase turned up a palm. "Because?"

This was a test, I knew, and I also knew I couldn't pass it. Any answer I gave was bound to turn into platitudes before I got halfway through. To buy myself some time, I ate one fry. Then I shrugged and said, "Nothing's ever been strong enough to turn me against it, I guess."

He mulled this over, the fingers of one hand tapping the table one after another, too slowly to be called drumming. Then he asked me, "Do you think Nadine believes in love?"

"I'm sure she does," I said, without hesitation.

"All right," he said, leaning forward. "What I need for you to do, Ned, is to believe in love for me. For a while. Until I'm ready to pick it up. Because I want to believe in love; I want the *belief*"—the word fairly exploded from his lips—"that you have. Meeting Nadine's given me the sense that having that belief could save me someday. So do that for me, if you would. And ask Nadine to do it too. I want to get my future in as many good hands as I can. And I think it's good to have it in your hands ... but I think I may need it to be in hers."

* * *

On my way back to the apartment, I thought about the awesome responsibility that Chase had just given me, that I had leaped to take on. It wasn't a very clear-cut responsibility; I couldn't give Nadine his contact info, as he'd already taken care of that, and it wasn't my place to put them together. Really, my role seemed to be confined to rooting the two of them on.

And it was kind of a mean thing to do in that I would be rooting for another relationship to be torn asunder. Not that Chase had told me to in so many words, but come on, right? For Nadine and Chase to come together, Nadine and Tedd would have to come apart. I had no problem with that, of course—I still wanted to protect her from harm, after all these years, and I felt she'd be much safer with Chase than Tedd. Maybe neither one of them felt especially happy, but I felt sure Chase could outdo Tedd in making Nadine happy, and that was what mattered to me.

There was one thing about our lunch that I couldn't figure out— besides the tip, which Chase calculated in a flash. Chase had said that everything inside him was running in a higher gear. I'd been around him enough now that I could pick up on his energy and know it for what it was. But today, I didn't feel a thing from him. Not an amp, a volt, a watt, an erg. Nothing.

Here's what I couldn't figure out: Was this higher gear turning all his energy inward? Or was he just deluding himself?

15.

Sunday brunch with Alexa was different from Sunday brunch with Siege or Saturday lunch with Chase. For one thing, with Siege and Chase, I didn't put on cologne. For another, this time I wanted to be the one to steer the conversation. So, after I got the inevitable slow kiss hello on the cheek (I gave her one back, just to be polite), I said, "We have got to talk about Nadine."

"Oh," she said. "I wanted to talk about us."

"Not after you hear this, you won't."

I knew it was true, and I was right. She went from miffed to gleeful in under a minute. Her laugh wasn't the frothy giggle I had expected; it was a cackle, bringing verve and kick to go with its contagion. She looked really good—a white tank top, khaki shorts, and sandals showed her fitness in a way that her yellow dress couldn't do, lovely though it was—and she liked a good Bloody Mary for Sunday brunch too. Darn it, there I went falling half in love again. At least now I knew it wasn't due to Chase affecting the ambiance of the room.

"How much of this did you tell Nadine?" she asked.

"None of the super-personal stuff. I made a promise to myself that from now on, anything one of them tells me in confidence, I won't tell the other. I want to feel like I deserve the trust they have in me."

"But you're telling me all this," she said. "And you know I'm just going to turn around and blab it all to Nadine."

I pulled a *well, maybe* face. "All I can say is, family takes care of family."

"I see." She smiled and did that devilish thing with her eyebrows. "So this channel doesn't go both ways?"

"Chase doesn't need my help to get in close with Nadine," I said. "The more she knows, the better she'll do. I don't think it makes a difference how much Chase knows going in."

"So how will you be helping him?"

"I'm still a little unclear on that myself."

She swizzled her drink around with her celery stalk, and the ice cubes rang gently against the glass. Then she raised it and said, "Well, here's to clarity. May it strike us all one day."

"To clarity," I said, meeting her eyes, and our Bloody Marys sang one pearl of a note to each other as they touched.

***

This, sad to say, was probably the high point of our time together.

Once we got away from the topic of Chase and Nadine and moved on to Ned and Alexa, things began faltering. It started when she said, "You know I think you're cute, right?" Before I could get past my disbelief and tell her I hadn't known that, she added, "People have gotten together for a lot more superficial reasons."

"Yeah, and look what happened to them," I said. Don't ask me why; I just said it.

Alexa supposed this was true in some cases, and that conversational thread ended, hopelessly frayed. I never even thought to thank her for saying I was cute.

Then I wondered aloud if people ever got together who weren't meant to be together just because a joy facilitator was in the room when they met. Not necessarily Chase, I hastened to clarify, but any joy facilitator anywhere. She found that hard to believe, and since I couldn't name any other joy facilitators ("Mister Rogers doesn't count."), I guess I can't blame her. Topping it off, she never answered the question.

I tried to make up for it by telling her I thought she was cool.

"I was starting to wonder what you thought," she said.

My first reaction—*What's that supposed to mean?*—I managed to stifle verbally, but I imagine my raising one eyebrow as I recoiled kind of gave it away. I certainly picked up on her unspoken response—I didn't get it all, but profanities and a verb were involved.

Throughout all this, I was dismayed to see her own inner light fading out on me. I kept trying to bring it back up with compliments ("I like that little chip in your tooth."), conversation starters ("How'd you get it, anyway?"), and encouragement ("Well, you shouldn't give up on rollerblading completely."), and nothing worked. I was blowing it—or I would have been if I'd known what I was trying for.

When we got up to leave, both of us were a little downcast, wondering in our own worlds. We exchanged niceties about what we could do to help Nadine and a promise to keep emailing, but that just felt like chatter to keep us busy until we got outside. Once there, I was about to give her a so-long wave when she stepped up close, reached for the back of my neck, and pulled me down for the familiar kiss on the cheek. She let me go, and I found myself staring into her eyes, blue eyes, ocean blue, deep ocean, diving deeper, *my God how could I have never noticed her eyes?*

"Don't forget," she said. "I kiss everybody." And she turned to go.

"Hey."

She turned back to me as I approached her. I leaned down, grazed her cheek with my hand, and kissed the other cheek, even softer and slower than she'd done. I moved back enough so I could get one last look at those eyes.

"Don't forget," I told her. "I don't kiss everybody."

With that, the light inside her came back to life again. She smiled at me—not a happy smile, but one of renewed interest. "Okay," she said. "I'll remember that."

Rather than screw things up again with a misspeaking of some kind or other, I gave her a half-wave, half-salute, mouthed the word "bye," and went on my way. I thought it best not to look back.

***

"Doesn't sound like you screwed up to me," said Siege when I called him to talk about it. "You talked, some things went good, some didn't, you ended on an up note. I'm not seeing the problem here. Course, maybe she just wants the rugged good looks of a young professional from the Financial District who can hold his liquor and who got a merit badge for tying knots. Can't say as I blame her. Let her know I can pencil her in for next Wednesday."

"Manipulative? God, no!" said Nadine, her back to me as she went through her movies. "All you said was 'look what happened to them.' You didn't say that to make her feel a certain way; you said it because it's what you were thinking. You're putting too much into this. This date was for getting to know someone better, not something that needed to be perfect. Which it didn't. Hey, you've seen *Some Came Running*, right? You *haven't*?"

"Oh, stop your nonsense," said my mother. I'm surprised she didn't hang up on me.

I appreciated the support, but I knew what I knew. I didn't like who I was at that brunch. Half the things I said were whiny little dribblings, and I didn't even know why I said them. When she wanted to talk, I'd dismiss her. ("Not after you hear this, you won't."—what was I thinking?) Sure, that was a nice moment at the end, but I'd lucked into it; what if I hadn't been in such a contrary frame of mind?

What I needed was some of that clarity we'd toasted to with our Bloody Marys. Not just in this relationship, but in my life. Clarity might get me to recognize my faults better, and then I could deal with them. It could help me make my post-Val life the best life possible— the wounds wouldn't just be distant, they'd be healed. It could help me see the good I could do out there and the ways to do it. It could only do me good. And I wanted it to start as soon as possible so I could get rid of the bad before it got too deeply entrenched and became an incontrovertible part of my life for the next fifty or sixty years.

I had to do it.

And I knew how.

**

That evening I found Chase's card and dialed his number. As the phone rang, I took a cautious glance over my shoulder. Nadine was in the kitchen, washing dishes. This was good; I didn't want her privy to our conversation. If I had been on a cell phone, I would've taken it into the bathroom and locked the door behind me.

"Hello-o." He said it not as a question but as a statement it gave him great pleasure to make. His voice dropped in tone on the O.

I took a beat. "Chase," I said, "I want you to teach me how to be a joy facilitator."

"All right, tell me why. Without thinking, right now—go."

"I want to be a person who does greater things," I said. "And if I can help make the world a greater place, maybe that can make me a greater man."

There was a pause. It went off an electrical ramp and hung in the space between us. I feared for its landing safely, and I awaited the inevitable click of Chase hanging up. I was in the middle of wondering what made me think this was such a good idea when I heard Chase laugh. It was a warm chuckle, almost fatherly.

"You know," he said, "over the past few years, a lot of people have asked me to make them my projects, or my protégés. But they always had some kind of ulterior motive—they wanted to get the job, or the part, or the girl. They weren't aware that this wasn't about them. You're the first person who ever realized that what's done for you is the by-product of what you've done for others. You get it. I'm impressed, truly."

"So you'll do it?" I couldn't help blurting.

"Now hold on. This is *work*, you understand. This is a job, and you shouldn't come to it lightly."

"I understand," I said. "I won't."

Another death-defying leap of a pause. And then he said, "All right, yes. Yes, I'd be glad to."

"Great!" I said, and let out a little whoop.

"All right. May I ask who's calling?"

The sincerity of his question should have deflated me in a matter of seconds, but I was filling up with too much excitement for it to have much of an effect. "Chase, it's Ned," I said. "Ned Alderman."

"Ned?" he asked in what sounded like genuine surprise. "Ned, you've got a terrific phone voice. Peppercorn should put you in their sales department."

"Oh, thanks." Nobody had ever complimented me on my phone voice before.

"I'm twice as impressed now. You really put a lot of thought into this. Great potential. I'm looking forward to working with you. On both our projects."

I looked over at Nadine, who was cleaning a wine glass with a sponge bent in half, to get both the inside and the outside at once. She hummed a melody, one I didn't recognize. I thought of her and Chase together, him discovering a belief in love, her discovering a truly deserving partner, both of them discovering what it meant to be happy. I thought of Alexa and me, finding out that the way forward was indeed in each other's presence. I was filled to near bursting now with anticipation, more than is healthy for any man. But I hold it to be true that there is no greater feeling than anticipation justified and fulfilled. I had true justification to become a joy facilitator; the fulfillment was sure to take me over the moon.

"Oh, Chase," I said. "This is going to be great."

"It is great, Ned," he corrected me. "It's just up to you to find out how."

But I *had* found out how. I would deliver my second cousin from Tedd's clutches, bring her to see the value of a life with Chase, and discover in myself the extra 1 percent that would allow me to be more than half in love with Alexa. It was as simple as that.

PART TWO

*Lucy: Charlie Brown says that we're put here on
Earth to make others happy.
Linus: Is that why we're here? I guess I'd better
start doing a better job ... I'd hate to be shipped back!*

—*PEANUTS* BY CHARLES SCHULZ, 8.18.1961

1.

6/27/05, 12:11 AM
To: nalderman@peppercornpub.com
From: chase@joyfacilitator.com

Subject: Lesson One

I've attached a list of joy facilitation-related books to this email. You'll find the books cover a wide range—memorization, body language, fashion, self-expression, personality types, conflict resolution, marketing, and so on. I'm not asking you to read them all word for word (great though that would be), but I do expect you to gain familiarity with them and become well-versed enough that you can apply their lessons in everyday life. I know you're on a budget, so I recommend used bookstores and libraries; most of the books will be there, filed under self-help. Don't read any intermediate books before beginner books, nor advanced before intermediate.

I propose we meet every Wednesday at six, so we can discuss what you've read and experienced. And make sure you come in with some good notes—writing down the lessons you've read and learned after, or even as, you've read and learned them will impress the knowledge deeper into your mind.

In the meantime, here are some basics you can start using this morning.

- Smile. Smile when you walk into a room. Smile when you talk to people. Smile when you listen. It may feel phony at first, but keep it up. People will smile back, which will make yours feel all the stronger.
- Use their names. When I'm first meeting someone, I fit their name into the conversation (their full name, if I can) as many times as possible, to help me remember it. At subsequent meetings, I use their name to reaffirm our connection and to provide a sense of security. It works, Ned. See?
- Open your posture. Basically, you should never fold your arms again. You'll not only look more receptive if you're not hunched over and half turned away, you'll feel that way, and then you'll be that way.
- Listen with your body. By this, I mean don't just have one ear turned toward them, literally or figuratively. Give them the respect of your undivided attention. Think of your body as a satellite dish, picking up as much of a signal as it can.
- Don't judge. This may be the hardest to do, but I assure you it's the most important. If you can listen to people without judging them by things like their voice, their choice of words, even their opinions, they'll feel they're in a safety zone and open up even more. You'll be surprised at how much accepting people for who they are allows them to express themselves freely.

Before our first meeting, I want you to practice some of these actions. Initiate conversations at work. Write emails to your friends. Tell them that they matter, and then tell them why. Pay them genuine compliments. Be somebody they look forward to seeing. We'll discuss the results on Wednesday at six.

Best, Chase

* * *

"Hey, Bill."

"Hey, Ned, how's everything?"

"Great. Bill, I was thinking—I never took the time to thank you for training me and getting me started. I'm feeling really good about the work I'm doing here, and a lot of that is due to you. So here's a long-delayed and heartfelt thank you."

"Well. Well, thank you, Ned. And thanks for keeping up the good work. Put 'er there."

* * *

6/27/05, 10:47 AM
To: alpinegal@gmail.com
From: nalderman@peppercornpub.com
Subject: This is just to say

Alexa – I enjoyed being with you at brunch yesterday. It's good to know somebody who can put away her Bloody Marys with zest and never lose her inner sweetness. I'm looking forward to sharing updates about Nadine and Chase with you, and I hope you can make time in your social whirl to hang out with me some more. I'd like that – Ned

6/27/05, 11:25 AM
To: nalderman@peppercornpub.com
From: alpinegal@gmail.com
Subject: Re: This is just to say

For the first time you email me before I email you, and it's not just a polite response, but it's full of the sweetest little things— who are you, and how did you hijack Ned Alderman's account?

Seriously, I love it—keep it up!
Alexa!

* * *

"Maylene! Do you have a second?"

"Umm ... yeah, sure."

"Maylene, I don't think I've let you know that I really appreciate working with you. It's good to have another intern who's going through the same things I'm going through at the same time. Just knowing I'm not alone is a big help. So thanks for being there, and thanks for having lunch with me every day. It really makes a difference."

"Well that's, um, I'm, that's really nice of you, Ned. You're sweet. It's, I mean—I like—it's ah, good working with you too. Oh, and I'm glad you liked the cookies."

* * *

6/28/05, 11:01 AM
To: nadine@cellulab.com
From: nalderman@peppercornpub.com
Subject: Quick note

Nades – I was just sitting here at work thinking how I wouldn't be here if it weren't for your generosity in taking me in and letting me hog your couch all summer. I'm fast becoming a movie snob (but in a good way), and I've attended more expensive charity dinners than any of my friends back home—all thanks to you. Add to that getting to know family again, and really enjoying the process of doing so, and I'm so glad I took this job. So, thank you – Neds

6/28/05, 11:08 AM
To: nalderman@peppercornpub.com
From: nadine@cellulab.com
Subject: Re: Quick note

Dear Neds,
Thank you for coming down—I've loved having you in the building from day one. You're a good listener when I have to vent (and I have to vent a lot, did you notice?), and it's been great watching movies with you and talking about them. I still can't agree that Duel is the best thing Spielberg ever did, but it was fun to hear you explain why you thought it was. (Next up—underrated Altman!)

See you tonight – Nades

* * *

"Hey, Lee."

"Hey, Ned, what's up."

"Can I just say, I like what you're wearing today."

"What, this?"

"Yeah. Golden brown is your color."

"It's actually copper."

"Well, it looks great. You've got a really good eye for clothes. The designs, colors ... and you wear them well."

"Well. Glad you think so. Listen, Ned, I've got to get these invoices done."

"Oh, sure. Go ahead. I just thought I'd let you know."

"Yeah, thanks."

* * *

6/29/05, 9:50 AM
To: cjbrande@loftoncanova.com
From: nalderman@peppercornpub.com
Subject: Not to get sappy, but…

Siege – It's funny, but after three years of rooming with you, I feel like this is the summer that I'm getting to know you best. It's meant a lot to me to have a friend already here in New York to help me be less lonely, and the fact that you've become an even better friend has meant even more. So thanks for being you, and for being here when I needed you the most – Ned

6/30/05, 12:58 PM
To: nalderman@peppercornpub.com
From: cjbrande@loftoncanova.com
Subject: Re: Not to get sappy, but…

I love you too, Duchess. – Siege

2.

I like seeing my worlds collide every now and then. When a coworker helped an old teacher of mine, or a friend met my mother, the way they interacted often threw new light on them for me, even as it emphasized the things I'd known about them before. The experience was edifying all the way around. So when Chase and I decided to make Sweethaven our regular meeting spot, I had to invite Siege to come along as well. He'd heard a lot about Chase from me over the past month, and it was high time they crossed paths.

"Sounds great," said Siege. "But let him know I'm coming. I don't want to be an unpleasant surprise."

"I'd like to meet your friends," said Chase. "They will need to understand that you and I are going to be conducting a class and not socializing. If they're okay with that, then it's fine."

"Will there be beer?" Siege asked. "Then I'm okay with that."

And so it was that Chase entered Sweethaven and found me and Siege starting our first beers (Belgian white for me, stout for Siege).

Savoring the moment, I said, "Chase Becker, this is C.J. Brandenburg."

"C.J. Brandenburg," Chase repeated, smiling and rising to shake his hand. "Like the Brandenburg concertos?"

"Hey, you're the first person who's ever said that," said Siege, his overly bright voice making it clear that (a) this was something he heard all the time, and (b) it didn't bother him at all. "Question for you," he went on as they sat down. "How is it I've lived in New York for over a year and I've never heard of this place?"

"You like it?" asked Chase.

"It's great. It's so quiet I can hear myself getting drunk."

Chase laughed that warm chuckle. Then he turned to me and said, "You got your notebook, Ned?"

I brought out my composition notebook, the sort that has Rorschach blots all over the covers, and I turned to page one. For the next three-quarters of an hour, we discussed what differences I'd seen in my few days of opening up more and why some people may not have reacted as positively as others. Chase explained how to manage emotions—both on and beneath the surface. He talked about awareness of my own energy and how to raise or lower it to match that of my audience. He had an "instant lab," where I talked with a stranger at the bar, then discussed our body language with Chase. The whole process exhilarated me. I felt like I was back in college, and some dynamic new professor had just awoken me with a lecture that made me realize what all the fuss was about.

Siege kept quiet the entire time. I expected him to pepper the lecture with comments and wisecracks, but he never made a single interruption. In fact, he was getting caught up in the lesson himself; when he finished his stout, he didn't get up for another one. Let me say that again: Siege Brandenburg didn't get up for a second beer. If that doesn't testify to the power of Chase's presentation, nothing will.

Other laws of nature, of course, could not be ignored so easily, and at the forty-five minute mark, Siege announced, "I gotta drain the dragon," and headed off to the restroom. I was glad for the break in the action, as it gave me the opportunity to say, "Chase, is there anything I can tell you about Nadine?"

He looked up from his fingernails. "Nadine? No, not yet."

"Anything?" I repeated. Never mind my earlier promise to only pass things along to Nadine; I wanted to repay Chase for taking me on as a pupil, and the only thing of equal or greater value that I could offer was information about her.

"For now," he said, "just keep being there for her. If she wants to talk, you need to listen. Not for my sake, but for hers. Right now, that's the best way you can help me." He looked at his watch. "I have to wind this up a little early," he said. "I've got a bat mitzvah party to get ready for."

"Bat mitzvah, huh?"

"It's one of the easier gigs I get," he said. "Next to quinceañera parties. It's next to impossible to find anybody who isn't all festive at one of those."

We wound things up, and I was promising to have at least one book read by next week when Siege returned. "What'd I miss?" he asked as he sat back down.

"We're just closing up shop," I told him.

"Aw, all right. Hey Chase, let me ask you something—you think a guy could learn how to pick up girls with this joy facilitating business?"

Chase turned to me. "Ned?"

"This isn't a means to an end, Siege," I said. "You can't play the game if you're only in it for the trophy. Your motives have to be noble." Chase nodded as I spoke; what I had said was the truth. I was happy to have tapped into that truth so early in my apprenticeship.

"Ah, fine," said Siege. "Okay, I got one more for you. Kind of a hypothetical."

"All right," said Chase, settling in.

"Let's say there's this guy. To protect his identity, we're going to call him, ah, Todd Lang."

I shot Siege a look. He ignored it.

"Now Todd's kind of a douche—pardon my French. Hey, that *is* French. Anywho, how do you handle a guy who's smug and condescending and raises himself up by putting others down? 'Cause speaking for myself, I figure there's got to be an answer somewhere between smacking the guy and walking away."

Chase raised his eyebrows, amused. "Todd Lang, eh?"

"Yeah, just to pick a name at random."

We all knew, and we all knew that we all knew. But Chase accepted the case as it was laid before him. "Mmm. Well, C.J.—"

"Come on, call me Siege."

"All right, Siege. When I'm facing a predator, my goal is not to be the prey. I don't let myself get pushed around or devoured. I make sure I understand what he's saying. And vice versa—very important. Put yourself in his shoes. Give him the gift of your understanding and your goodwill and your love. And give it honestly."

"Uh huh," said Siege. His face didn't give away how much he was buying this. "And what if all that doesn't work? You realize he's out to hurt you—what then?"

Chase stood up. "Well," he said, moving behind his chair, "remember that it's not a fight to the death. And if Todd—or whoever—is superior to you, and he's going to do some real damage, there's nothing wrong with walking away."

That wasn't what Siege wanted to hear. It was as though he'd just been told that not only was there no Santa Claus, but it had been a real pleasure tricking him into thinking otherwise. "So you just quit and that's it?" he asked.

"You don't quit. You disengage. You choose to preserve yourself. If you take yourself out of a potentially fatal equation, then you'll still be here and still be capable. And there will always be a next day." He pushed in his chair. "I'll see you here next week, Ned. Siege, it was a real pleasure to meet you. Take care." He waved and went out the door.

Siege rubbed his chin. "Who—mind you, who—was that masked man?"

"What'd you think?" I asked. "Or is the jury still out?"

"He's an odd egg," Siege said. "Not judging; just saying. He smells like that chewing gum that burns your eyes when you chew it. I don't dislike him. Don't know him enough to like him. Like him better than Ted-duh, but that's not saying a whole hell of a lot. But he's got a lot to offer. Hey, speaking of offering, you think you could forward me that reading list he sent you?"

"Yeah, no sweat."

Siege picked up his glass and reached for mine. "Great. Then this next round's on me."

3.

The next day, on the dollar carts outside the Strand bookstore, I found three of the books Chase had assigned me. I spent every spare moment of the following week learning how to say what I meant, how to listen to the unspoken words, and how to make way for my heart. The best time for reading turned out to be on the subway; finally, I had a way to shut out all the sullen androids and their unpleasantness, and it was for a worthy cause. I brought my books into work and read them during my lunch breaks.

"What's that?" asked Maylene, gesturing at me. She had a chicken fajita wrap and corn chips in front of her; I was eating leftover mac and cheese with salsa, and Lee was working her way through an enormous salad.

"I'm learning how to win friends and influence people," I said, holding up Dale Carnegie's book. "I've been reading a lot of self-improvement lately."

"You don't need to improve yourself, Ned," she said. "We like you just the way you are."

"You and Billy Joel both," I said, and she laughed. She laughed at a lot of my jokes, even the stupid ones. "Anyway," I went on, "I like to think I can help make the world a better place. And charity begins at home."

"Hold on a second," said Lee, pointing the three plastic tines of her fork at my head. "Those compliments you've been handing out left and right—was that something these books told you to do?"

"They made me more aware of how important it was to express honest appreciation," I said.

She smirked. "I knew those weren't real compliments."

"No, I meant every word. You do look good in copper."

"Well, thanks, but if you're told to compliment someone and you do, the compliment doesn't mean as much. It's got to come up unbidden if it's going to mean anything."

I shrugged. "Well, you may be right," I said.

My default argument ender with Siege turned out to be an oft-recommended little trick in my reading: give your opponents the acknowledgment they crave, and you remove a major source of conflict; then, more often than not, they'll subside. Besides, that simple acknowledgement is the truth—they may be right, they may be wrong; that's why you're debating.

Sure enough, Lee sat back in uncertain triumph, and we all kept eating. Maylene unwrapped her cookie, and as she broke off her own little piece, I held out my hand. She gave me a curious look, and I found myself feeling embarrassed. "Pavlov," I muttered, and she smiled and handed me the rest of the cookie, just like always.

Lee finished her lunch first, despite the fact that she had more food than either Maylene or I did. She picked the final tiny pieces of olive out of her plastic tray with thumb and forefinger, popped them into her mouth like aspirin, and then rested her hands on her stomach. "Ohhh, I feel like I'm about to give birth to a salad," she moaned, and Maylene giggled.

"Well," I said, "you'd better have it done by Caesarian section."

Judging by the ensuing silence, neither one of them found that even remotely funny. Oh, well—they may be right.

* * *

I have to admit that I was as interested as Siege in seeing the extent to which joy facilitating would affect the way one related to women.

That wasn't my sole focus, of course, but having an interesting girl be maybe interested in me gave me added incentive to create a newer, stronger self. Also, I thought my progress with Alexa might be a good way to gauge my progress with my studies.

It helped that Alexa was easy to make progress with. She was more than happy to extend her emails and talk over the phone, and when she told me her stories and her dreams, I didn't have to pretend I was interested. Nadine was right; Alexa wasn't just a rich little party girl in the big city. She was someone I enjoyed spending time with, and I got the impression she was starting to feel the same way about me.

The turning point in our relationship came on the Fourth of July. It was on a Monday that year, which I'm guessing dialed the citywide celebrating down a notch from a Friday Fourth, but this being New York City, there was still a lot of celebrating to be done. Offices were closed, flags were out in force, Nadine and I had a matinee movie showing (we watched *Yankee Doodle Dandy*), and Alexa was throwing a rooftop party. Chase wasn't going to be there—"I'd be hiring him in an official capacity and he wouldn't get any quality time with Nadine," she explained in an email. "Besides, I think he's booked."— but Tedd was on the list. I guess you can't really take ten couples and invite nine and a half of them.

Tedd almost didn't go. He had told Nadine he'd been planning to surprise her with reservations at a restaurant one of his work colleagues had invested in, so new that it had opened but not yet had its *grand* opening. She said no, that she wanted to celebrate by watching fireworks with a bunch of people, not by eating dinner with one. This did not go down well with Tedd, who wanted nothing to do with "rooftop riffraff," but Nadine stuck to her guns with greater tenacity than I knew she had. And so it was that come sundown, the three of us were in an elevator going up. She had on a chartreuse summer dress; I went with cheerily obnoxious Hawaiian tourist garb (my reading had taught me that loud clothes get attention and make a great conversation starter), and Tedd wore a black silk shirt, black linen pants, and a big scowl.

"Take off your dink suit, Tedd," said Nadine. "We're almost there." He grumbled back something unintelligible. I feigned deep interest in the numbers above the door.

Alexa greeted us at the rooftop door in shades, a modest bikini, and flip-flops. She kissed us all on the cheek (even Tedd—she really does kiss everybody) and announced us to the ones already there. I recognized Aaron Brown, the dentist at the last party, but everyone else was new to or unrecognized by me. I went to the ice bucket, grabbed myself a beer, and set out to change that.

The sky was as clear as a New York City sky can be, and with no breeze and a grill cooking up some hamburgers and hot dogs—"For any vegetarians out there, there's pasta salad!" Alexa reminded us—it was a very comfortable temperature to socialize in. I practiced all my newfound skills, watching people's faces as they grew more interested in what I had to tell them, and as they grew more *aware* of their growing interest. I rephrased what people said, then complemented them for saying it so well. I brought out the disposable camera I was using for a prop and asked for a good "loving gaze" pose. Before long I felt that positive vibration moving through the party, taking it to another level, and I knew with no small pleasure that the wave had originated with me.

The only person immune to my charms was Tedd. He hung around the edge of the roof, looking down, fading into the darkness as the night moved in. Some people did go over to him with a bottle of beer or an offer to converse—I heard him say "Tedd with two Ds" several times—but they didn't stay for long. If he ever ate or drank anything, I didn't see it happen. He seemed to be subsisting on his own isolation, gaining strength by being remote. I could have tried to bring him into the fold, but I didn't yet have the confidence I needed; I couldn't risk watching all the goodwill I'd built up being torn down by one big outburst. I thought of Luke in *The Empire Strikes Back*, going up against Vader before he'd finished his training and getting his Jedi clock cleaned. More importantly, I thought of Chase telling Siege and me that there was nothing wrong with walking away. So, I picked my battle, and that battle wouldn't be tonight.

Nadine broke off the conversation she was having with Alexa and someone else and went over to Tedd, who stared across the flickering lights and noises of the city. She put a hand on his arm and said something; he responded without looking at her. I didn't think she was in any danger from Tedd tonight, but I still thought I should look after her in case she needed a guard or a witness. I'd gotten very protective of Nadine over the past six or so weeks, and any dealings she had with Tedd tended to put me on full alert. Sure, she could take care of herself, but I would have preferred a scenario where she had a boyfriend who wasn't constantly making her prove that.

I was in the process of edging closer to them when Alexa sidled up to me. She had made a couple of concessions to the night, propping up her sunglasses in her hair and wearing a white lab coat over her bikini to keep her from getting too cold. It was unbuttoned—far more suggestive than the bikini alone.

"Hey, you," she said, stepping up close and giving me a poke in the ribs. "Everyone's talking about you, you know," she said. "So far I've had three people ask me if you were single."

"How many asked if I was gay?"

She laughed. "With that outfit, everyone knows you're straight. Trust me."

I looked down at my rayon and polyester, my paisley and madras. "Fair enough."

She smiled and looked off toward Central Park. Down on the street, some kids set off a string of firecrackers, popcorn bursts mixed with delighted shrieks.

"Beautiful day for a Fourth of July," I said.

She nodded. "Kinda hazy," she said, "but not a cloud in the sky."

"Yeah. Sort of like our future."

Something inside her paused. Even with her facing away, I could feel it inside. I summoned up all my positive energy and projected it as she turned to face me.

"Our future?" she asked, in a seedling of a voice.

"It's what came to mind," I said. A note of apology wanted to be in the words, but I refused to let it out.

Alexa stood there, looking up at me. All signs of her party-girl persona were gone, dissolved into the warm night air. Never before had she been so vulnerable around me. A part of me didn't recognize her, wanted to find out more about this girl, much more.

"I like that," she said.

There was a soft *whump* in the distance. A few seconds later, a loud *pop* overhead, and Alexa's face was bathed in yellow light.

"Hey, the fireworks are starting!" someone on the roof shouted.

"Valedictorian," muttered Tedd, a few feet away.

My hand was in Alexa's. "You know, Ned, I've never been kissed during a fireworks display."

"Never?"

"Never. And I've always wanted to be."

Whump. Pop.

"Well, I can fix that," I said.

She closed her eyes, and I was about to lean in, but at the last second, I remembered my training: for every two steps forward, one step back. I pulled away and said, "But not yet. Not during these one-at-a-time fireworks. Wait until they send up three at once."

She nodded and squeezed my hand. She'd waited all these years; she could wait a few more minutes.

Whump. Pop.

Red streams of light umbrellaed over the city. Behind me, a couple of *ooohs* and *ahhhs*, weighed down with irony. One guy wailed off-key about the rockets' red glare.

Whump. Pop.

Nadine stood in front of Tedd, both of them facing out. His hands were locked in front of her, just under her throat. Without looking back, she reached up, unlocked his hands, and guided them to her shoulders. He began massaging them, and she leaned back into him a little.

Whump whump. Pop pop.

Two sprays of aquamarine, very pretty.

Whump. BOOM!

"Whoa!" went the rooftop. I heard similar commotions from the people on nearby rooftops, from the families on their decks and their fire escapes.

Alexa, so close.

Whump whump. Pop BOOM!

Car alarms were going off everywhere. I imagined millions of dogs quivering under their masters' beds.

Whu-whump. BA-BOOM!

She wasn't looking at the sky anymore. She was turning to face me, the front of her flip-flops bumping my sandals, her hand letting go of mine to touch my arm, the light from the fireworks diminishing as it sank into her hair. Any shields she may have had, any defenses, had been banished. She stood before me, radiant and intoxicatingly open.

Whump whump whump.

I fell in.

The sky exploded around us as we kissed, our eyes shut to its sights. Our front teeth knocked against each other, and the click they made resonated far more deeply than any fireworks, which, after all, were hundreds and hundreds of yards away. More cheering, as we explored each other's lips and what lay behind them. Another triple shot of fireworks burst onto the scene, the last of their sparks crackling as they fell to earth.

The kiss ended, and I opened my eyes before she did. I'll always be grateful for that second of Alexa with her eyes closed, her lips half-parted, her cheeks pink with heat, a combination of peace and excitement coursing through her face. It's a second I've thought about many times since, whenever I want to think about that summer and the happiness I was able to bring into being. It's the second I realized what I could now provide for other people, and what a power I had. In the final fraction of a moment that her eyes were closed, I resolved to use that power as wisely as I could.

Then she opened her eyes.

Oh, her eyes.

"I don't kiss everybody," she said.

"I know," I told her, and we were kissing again, as the fireworks came faster. I reached inside her lab coat and pressed the small of her bare back. Her hands found my hips and dug in. Only our awareness of those around us kept things from going further.

There were cheers, piercing whistles, an electric *whooooo-haaaaaa* from the streets below. I could see the flashes of light with my eyes closed, but only as flashes—the spectacle of the colors was lost on me.

They were really coming now, the *whumps* of the launchings obliterated by the *pops* and the *BOOMS*. We were jammed together, not wanting to stop, and I felt happy and lucky and thrilled and different and—at the very end—a little twinge of sorrow that after all this, I was still only half in love with her.

4.

The first half of July absolutely flew past. I found more ultracheap copies of books on the reading list, and even with the note-taking slowing me up, I was still moving through them at the rate of one every three days. Chase and I kept up with our meetings; he used lectures and playacting to teach me how to recognize and counteract certain emotions, how to give and receive feedback, how to listen with everything I've got. He was what I'd call a very good, steady teacher, not one to get excited—he taught straight from the books and never used any personal anecdotes for illustrations, rather to my disappointment. Whenever I showed that I had grasped and understood a concept, he would say, "Right, good," and move on to the next topic. On those rare occasions when I made great leaps and connections—"So the extent to which you can enter someone's personal space has to depend on their rapport with you and not vice versa?"—he'd take one extra step: "Right, very good."

Siege didn't join us after that first meeting, but he and I continued to have our nights out two or three times a week, where we'd talk about joy as well as the Red Sox and blockbuster movies. Siege took a different approach from mine; he was just as likely to read a book from the advanced list as one from the beginner list, and he was glad to share what wisdom he could glean with me. We hashed out the works and methods of Harry Lorayne, Suzette Haden Elgin, and Robert Greene, our voices growing more rambunctious as the drinks added up.

"Y'know, all this book learning's well and good," Siege said one night, "but a fat lot of good it'll do us if it doesn't work in the field."

"You aren't getting results at work?"

"Who said anything about work? I'm talking about stepping out. Walking into a bar alone and walking out with some company."

"You're not supposed to apply it to just one facet of your life, Siege."

"Hey—you play in your field. I'll play in mine."

* * *

My field was my life, and it just kept getting greener and greener. Everybody was responding to my flow of positive energy, from Jamie Engel—"Moxie on the *ball*! I *love* this guy!"—right down to Claude the cleaning man—"You know, that's all I ask, is that people notice." Even Lee started to loosen up a bit, partly due to Maylene continuing to laugh at my jokes, and partly because of my regular assurances that she may be right. I asked for and got the chance to make a few telephone sales calls, and I turned out to have a knack for it. Maybe Chase had been right about the voice being an integral part of the process. Anyway, it was another skill I was happy to develop.

My time with Alexa continued to improve too; by now the awkward parts of that Sunday brunch were a distant memory, their faint hum receding in my mind. We had a couple of dinners together, one of which she cooked—stuffed mushrooms and pasta salad, both catching me off guard with their excellence—and we continued to learn about each other. I told her about the Val blues, and she said she would eradicate the last traces of those blues for me. Her use of the word *eradicate* surprised me. Her ability to wash my blues away didn't.

One night she came over to Nadine's, and the three of us ordered in Chinese food and played Scattergories. After seeing Alexa to her taxi, I came back upstairs to find Nadine studying me. "That was really interesting, watching you two interact," she said. "She's not on autopilot around you the way she is around other guys. You engage with her at a different level, somehow."

"You think it's love?"

"No, not love. But I think you both want to get to the bottom of this."

* * *

On Wednesday, the 20th of July, about a month before my internship was due to end, Chase sat down across from me and my Belgian white.

"Hello, Ned," he said. "Ready for lesson four?"

"Chase, what's wrong?" I asked.

His eyebrows perked up. "Tell me why you say that."

"Well," I said, "you dropped eye contact almost instantly. You looked down and to your left. You're sitting in a closed position; your shoulder's down like you're about to block somebody. You did away with pleasantries entirely. And to top it off," I concluded, checking my watch, "you're ten minutes late. You. Ten minutes late. Taken all together, I've got to think something's not right."

There may have been a touch of consternation in Chase's expression, but far more than that, he looked pleased and proud. "I'm very impressed," he said. "Look at this—the egg teaches the chicken. Well done."

"Thanks." I took a swig of beer so the glass could hide my face.

"Okay. Lesson four. The importance—"

"Way-way-wait," I said. "Hold on. You never answered my question."

"Hm."

"Hey, if you'd rather not, I totally understand," I hastened to assure him. "Totally. But just tell me—can I do anything to help?"

He shook his head no. I was convinced now that whatever was bothering him was personal and I wasn't going to pry it out of him. After that night when he told me how "one" got into the joy facilitation business, he'd been a lot more circumspect about his past. There weren't going to be any authorized biographies about Chase Becker.

"How about with Nadine? Is there anything I can tell her for you?"

He breathed in, expanding his chest, and looked up. "To answer your first question," he said, "my streak is over. I did poorly enough on a job that my client chose not to pay."

"Oh."

"It was a salary negotiation," Chase went on. "One of the New York Giants. They hadn't agreed on a salary, and I guess the general manager thought that if I were in the room, I'd mollify the guy and he'd accept the terms he'd been offered. Well, things didn't work out that way. The player and his agent—real shark, this guy—had done their work. They *proved* he deserved what they were asking and that there were three other teams who were very willing to pay it. The GM caved inside of an hour. At the end, he pulled out his wallet and took out three hundreds. He gave me a good look at them, and then he handed them to the player. 'Have lunch on me,' he said. And the player smiled and said thanks and took my money out the door."

"Well," I said, "you made *him* happy."

Chase smiled. "Too bad he wasn't the one who hired me."

"I guess. Geez, I'm sorry, Chase."

He waved it off. "No need to be. Really. That's an occupational hazard when your work is guaranteed to satisfy and it doesn't." He drummed out the Lone Ranger theme on the tabletop, his four fingers the only part of him moving. "What bothers me," he went on, "is that I didn't pick up on this. I should have made the GM understand that I'm not a weapon, and I didn't. I've got to figure out why that is."

I moved back to my chair. "We could postpone the lesson today," I said. "If you needed the time."

He took a breath to answer, and then held it as he gave the question some thought.

"It's not a problem for me," I said. "There's a lot of reading I can do." I felt like I was back in college, trying to persuade our professor to have class outdoors on a gorgeous day.

Chase regarded me. "You'd be okay with that?"

"Oh, sure."

"What are you reading right now?"

"I just started some Deborah Tannen."

"All right, good. Next week we'll talk about the importance of compassion." He took out his notepad and pen as I finished my Belgian white and stood up, wondering what to do with my next hour. Pick up some groceries, maybe.

"Oh, and Ned? About your last question. Tell Nadine I said she could be a giant. She could be a giant. Tell her that." He gave me one last warm smile, and then he submerged himself deep into his notes. From where I stood, I could see that one page of his notepad had a loose drawing on it. It was a drawing of Nadine. I recognized the hair and the eyes in an instant. The nose and lips were ghostlier, but even the faintest lines had a distinct character. Before I could open my mouth to comment, Chase very casually, without looking up at me, moved his arm forward and covered the drawing with his wrist.

***

The hell with groceries—I was going right home. I had a message for Nadine from Chase, and by God I couldn't wait to deliver it. I took the winding stairs two at a time, using the banister to pull myself along a little faster. I pulled out my key as I approached 4E, barely breaking stride as I unlocked the door and entered.

Nadine was embedded deep in the recliner, a box of tissues in her lap, looking up at me with a startled, tear-stained face. She made a move to get up, then decided against it and slumped deeper into her chair. "Hey, Neds," she said, her voice wet and clogged. "You're early."

"Nades, what's wrong?" I asked.

She blew her nose and dropped the tissue on the floor, next to a few other crumpled wads. "I just had a fight with Tedd. He left maybe five minutes ago." She sniffled.

I sat down at the end of the couch nearest her and gave her all my focus. I wanted to put her in as safe a space as I could. I put my hand on her shoulder; human contact in these circumstances is reassuring. I kept quiet and paid attention.

She took another tissue and brushed her eyes. "Tedd's going to the West Coast on business for a couple weeks," she said. "He leaves Saturday."

"Really?" My mind started to race with possibilities; it was all I could do to rein it back in.

"And he asked me tonight if I'd go with him. I told him no; I needed a lot more notice than that, and besides, we're in the middle of processing half a million feet of film. Well, he didn't like that, and things were said that shouldn't have been said, and it all kind of escalated. And now here I am telling you about it." She took another tissue and blew her nose again.

"So you're taking another break?"

"Mm-hm." The sounds were sad and gummy. "A real one this time. The last thing he said to me was, 'I'm coming back to LaGuardia at quarter of five on Sunday the seventh of August on American Airlines flight 24. I'll see you then.'" Fresh tears streamed down her face; one landed on the arm of the recliner with a soft tap.

"Part of it was my fault," she said.

"Oh, come on, Nades."

"No, it's true. If I hadn't said half the things I said, we would never have taken it as far as we did." She blinked at me a couple of times. "I do love him, Neds," she said. "He means a lot to me. But I hate it so much when he makes me feel so small."

I saw my chance and dove at it. "It's funny you should say that," I said. "I was talking with Chase today and he said to pass on a message to you."

Her face changed. The muscles beneath it stopped twisting. Her eyes glimmered, and it wasn't her tears making them do it. "He did?"

"He said, and this is a direct quote, he said, 'Tell Nadine I said she could be a giant.'"

She sniffled, more briskly than before. "Did he say that?" she asked, inner sunshine breaking through. "Did he really say that?"

"Swear to God. And right when you needed to hear it. I have to say, nothing about that guy surprises me anymore."

"That was really sweet," she said. "Next time you see him, tell him thanks." She took one more tissue and touched the last of the tears off her face.

"Hey," I said, standing up. "Grilled cheese and tomato sandwiches, with tomato soup. How does that sound?"

She shifted around in her chair; she wasn't sucked into it so deeply now. "Can you cook?"

"No, I can't, but I know my way around grilled cheese sandwiches."

Twenty minutes later, we were getting our paper plates greasy and watching *A Hard Day's Night*. I defy anybody to watch that movie without singing or humming along at some point. Plus, no romantic subplots to watch out for.

"This was a good choice," said Nadine, as we watched the Fab Four cavorting to "Can't Buy Me Love." "But we're still watching *Double Indemnity* tomorrow."

"Oh totally, sure."

"You know, Ned," she said. "You're really good at cheering people up."

"I'm pretty good," I said. "But I'm getting better."

* * *

The next morning, I found three emails of significance in my inbox. The first was from Alexa.

7/20/05, 10:38 PM
To: nalderman@peppercornpub.com
From: alpinegal@gmail.com
Subject: What a sweetie

I just got off the phone with Nadine, and she told me what you did. Fair's fair—if I get into a fight with Tedd, will you fix me grilled cheese sandwiches too?

Alexa!

The second one was from Siege.

7/21/05, 8:47 AM
To: nalderman@peppercornpub.com
From: cjbrande@loftoncanova.com
Subject: Sorry

Dude, there wasn't anything I could do. Love the sinner, hate
the sin. – Siege

It didn't make sense until after I'd read the third one.

7/21/05, 8:53 AM
To: nalderman@peppercornpub.com
From: eslong@loftoncanova.com
Subject: (No Subject)

Your friend C.J. Brandenburg was good enough to give me your
email address. I need to talk to you about an important matter.
Meet me at Shadows Restaurant tomorrow (Friday) at noon.
And for now, let's keep this between you and me.

Tedd.

5.

Shadows Restaurant was only a block and a half from Peppercorn. It had a pomegranate-red awning, with the word SHADOWS painted on it in fat capital letters, with enough of a shadow to give them a 3-D effect. Inside, it was dark. There were plenty of lights, but they all had forty-watt bulbs or were tinted red or orange. The lower level, where Tedd had insisted we sit, had a low ceiling, ornate booths, and a thick black carpet. There were small colorful bottles of various ages, shapes, and sizes on the window sills; they had once held inks, perfumes, and medicines, and now the foggy greens and icy blues served as decoration. There were also chessboards set up in all the luxuriant booths around us. Most of the boards were made of soft canvas, and they all had four neat rows of black pieces, white pieces, red pieces. I had never seen red chess pieces before.

"They have tournaments here some weekends," Tedd told me as the waiters whisked away one of the boards and its pieces. "But they'll still make room for you if you ask." He slid into one side of the booth and I took the other.

Tedd was in his usual Wall Street finery; he looked rich, capable, and sharp enough to cut you in half. I was in a denim shirt and khakis, not rich but not a disgrace. I went over a few of the principles I'd learned: hold my center; respond, don't react; turn into a push, don't push back. Tedd removed his glasses and squinted at the lenses. The waiter spirited up to us with menus, laid them down, and vanished into the gloom.

"I'll get right to the point, Alderman," Tedd said, rubbing his glasses on his napkin. "You may already know that I'll be away on business for a couple weeks."

"Yeah, Nadine told me."

"Of course. Well, I arranged for another man to take care of my apartment while I was away. Unfortunately, there's a medical crisis in his family, and he's no longer in a position to help. I'd like to know if you could take his place."

Of all the things I expected to hear from Tedd Long at this lunch, a request for help was near the bottom of the list, somewhere below bird calls and above a fertility chant. "That's it?" I asked. "You just wanted to ask me to house-sit?"

He turned his head so that he was looking at me out of the corners of his eyes. "Why would you think it would be something else?" he asked.

If he'd asked me that back in May, I probably would have clutched and started babbling. But I'd learned an awful lot since then, and I had no trouble keeping cool and saying what I meant. "Your email was pretty cloak-and-dagger," I told him. "Important matter, keep it between us, everything but 'come alone.' I expected something more than asking a favor."

Tedd relaxed, as much as someone like him could relax. "Point taken," he said. "And you didn't tell anyone, did you?"

"No." I knew he would ask me that, so I made sure to keep it quiet. I had a feeling he'd know if I were lying, and I didn't want to give him the satisfaction of finding his mistrust in me was well-placed. The only person who knew I'd be at Shadows was Maylene; she'd asked me that morning what I would be ordering for lunch, and I told her I actually had a lunch date but I'd be glad to take her cookie off her hands later. She did her best to feign disappointment, which was really quite decent of her, I thought.

"So what do you say?" Tedd asked. "You'd be living in Brooklyn Heights for two weeks and taking care of a dog and two fish. The dog doesn't handle kennels very well, and he needs a full-time presence. I can offer you three hundred dollars. Twenty dollars a day for fifteen days. I think that's fair."

"When to when?"

"You'll start tomorrow and end when I come back on the seventh."

"Tomorrow? That's kind of last minute."

"The man who begged off was kind of last minute too," he pointed out. "If you need to think about it until the end of the meal, go ahead."

"No, I'll do it."

He nodded. "Good. One less worry."

Water glasses were brought out and filled. I listened to the water gurgle and the ice crackle and hiss, and I thought how harmless this had turned out to be. I'd have the opportunity to explore Brooklyn, a borough that, rather to my chagrin, I'd not yet been to. And after all, three hundred bucks was three hundred bucks.

"Incidentally ..." said Tedd.

Uh-oh. I'd read more than one language book that told me this was a word to watch out for.

"... you're friends with the warmer, Becker. Correct?"

I nodded. "Correct."

"How long has he been corresponding with Nadine?"

It's a wonder that the chess pieces in the next booth over didn't rattle. That's how hard my jaw slammed into the glass tabletop. (Okay, not literally true, but it might as well have been.) *"What?"* I near-shrieked in a piercing falsetto.

Tedd recoiled. I knew instantly that I'd never see him look this surprised again. Not that he looked all that different; his eyes got wide and his jaw muscles grew tighter. That was really about it.

"You didn't know?" His surprised voice was no higher than his regular one.

"No, and I'd like to know why not, too!"

He looked away. "Nadine said you wouldn't. No," he added, louder, "give us a few more minutes." I turned around in time to see another waiter fade to black.

"We should really look at our menus," Tedd said and reached for one. Then he stopped. "Can I confide in you, Ned?" he asked. It was the first time he'd ever called me Ned.

I knew that a good joy facilitator would say yes and mean it, that he could project the necessary trust without reservation. Now I also knew that I wasn't yet a good joy facilitator. I was too wary of deception, of a double cross, an ulterior motive. At this moment, I could not say yes and mean it.

"Yes," I said.

Tedd leaned in, so far that he was half a head lower than me, looking up. "Nadine is someone very special to me," he said. "I love her. I love who she is and what she does for me, and I don't want to lose her. Now, I don't know what she and that warmer are writing to each other, but I don't want them making plans to get together while I'm gone. I don't want to lose her, Ned. I need you to promise me you'll keep that from happening."

Inside, I was aghast. The fact that I didn't show it is concrete evidence of how far I'd come in so short a time. "I can't make that promise, Tedd," I said. "I'll be an hour away by subway. More to the point, I can't control someone else's life. It's their life, and they'll do with it whatever they want."

"Okay," said Tedd, holding up a hand. "Okay. I didn't phrase that well. At least promise me you'll keep me appraised if anything develops."

"That I can do," I said.

"Good." He picked up his menu and opened it. "Order anything you like," he said. "It's on me."

As I opened my own menu, a thought came to me. Had Tedd just tasked me to do something totally unreasonable simply to make something borderline unreasonable sound acceptable? Had I just agreed to spy on my second cousin? Or did he just want me to keep an eye out for her, to protect her, to make sure she was okay? Was I seeing things that weren't there? Was I deluding myself into thinking they weren't there? Was I thinking about it too much altogether?

I looked out at all the chessboards, the games not yet played, the pieces centered on their squares waiting for someone to make a move. I'd walked into this room thinking I knew my stuff, and now I didn't even know which end was up anymore. I'd just been manipulated by a master. If Chase had been here instead of me, I don't know if the outcome would have been any different. And that didn't make me feel too good.

"Ready?" said Tedd, looking up from his menu.

Not even close, I thought, looking down at mine. "How are the fried clams here?" I asked.

Tedd considered this with a thoughtful grimace. "They can be trusted," he said.

6.

When I got back to work, the first thing I did was write Chase an email telling him everything and wanting to know why he'd never told me about his correspondence with Nadine—hard to say without sounding petulant, but I think I managed. I sent a similar email to Nadine. Then, almost as an afterthought, I let Siege and Alexa know I'd be spending the next couple weeks in Brooklyn.

Siege wrote back first, demanding to be invited over on Sunday so he could drink Tedd's booze and piss in his sink. Alexa wrote to point out that this would be my first time living by myself all summer and that she hated to think of me in that big bad house all by my lonesome. She had to go see friends in the Hamptons that weekend, but when she got back, she'd fix it so I wouldn't feel so abandoned. For the first time, she closed without putting an exclamation point after her name—instead, she used an ellipsis.

I kept checking back over the course of the afternoon, between pages of sales data entry. But neither Chase nor Nadine ever wrote back.

***

"Don't do it," said Nadine.

I was taken aback, to say the least. I'd just walked in—hadn't even closed the door yet—and here she was, hands on hips, not hostile but ready to be, ordering me not to do it.

"Do what?" I said, closing the door. "House-sit for Tedd? Why not?"

"You'll hate it. I don't want to think of you stuck in that house with that dog. It's not a good environment for someone like you."

I went to the kitchen. "I'll be fine," I said, taking a bottle of water out of the fridge. "I'd think you'd be happy. You get your couch back for a couple weeks. You can stay up all hours watching movies now. You can have friends come over and talk about all the things you did that you wouldn't want your dorky second cousin hearing about."

"Don't do it," she repeated.

I shrugged as I opened the bottle. "I already gave my word, Nadine. It's too late for him to find anyone else now, anyway."

"We won't be able to have movie nights."

"I guess that's true."

"What if I need you to be here?"

"For what? Do you need me to move the furniture?"

"No, to talk to!"

"Hmm. I really do need to get my own cell phone, I guess. I was going to wait till I got home. Well, hey—there's always smoke signals." I raised my bottle to her and then tipped it back.

"Ned, what if something happens with me and Chase?"

Water cascaded down my windpipe. I coughed violently, doubling over, not even bothering to cover my mouth as tears swam across my eyes. I cupped my knee and coughed a few more times, getting myself to breathe clearly. Once I could, I steeled myself for a moment, then straightened up, slow and careful, to look at Nadine. She was no longer ready to be hostile; she was vulnerable now, her ankles crossed, her hands back behind her, her head down, eyes not meeting mine.

"When you say 'if something happens,'" I asked, "what do you mean by 'something'?"

She rocked around a little. "I think you know what I mean," she said.

I thought so too. "And this has something to do with the secret emails you guys have been sending each other?"

She didn't say anything, but the growing redness in her face was answer enough.

I summoned up all my good energy for her. "You want to talk?" I asked.

She nodded, sat in the recliner, and the floodgates opened. She said she'd emailed him the day after the benefit, saying she wished they'd had more time to talk. He'd written right back, asking her to tell him everything.

Everything about myself? She'd asked.

Tell me everything, he replied.

This started an ongoing exchange, up to six emails a day, all of them original content. She'd tell him about her situation; he'd write back and say what it sounded like to him, the way she described it. As the weeks went by, she'd grown more and more self-confident, and Chase picked up on it, pointing out how she was no longer filling her writing with qualifiers like "I guess maybe" and "I'm not sure, but," going instead with assertions like "no question" and "this has got to be," and evolving from "I think I should do this" to "I should do this" to "I'll do this."

"One time," she said, "I told him that after spending time with Tedd, I felt like he was the smartest man in New York City. But after spending time with Chase—or with his emails, anyway—I felt like *I* was the smartest woman in New York City. And he wrote back, and all he said was, 'Why shouldn't you be?' And reading it, it was like a light went off, and I thought, *Hey, yeah, why shouldn't I be?* But Ned, nobody's ever said that to me—not even my mom! To see it, and to know he was right, really know, deep down ... well, it was a revelation."

"Speaking of revelations," I said, "how did Tedd find out about all this?"

She nodded, smirking a little; she must have known the question was coming. "When I told him that I wouldn't just drop everything and run off to California with him, he couldn't believe it. Even after I told him why. Finally, he started to come around, and he said, 'Well, it's not like you're carrying on with someone I don't know about.' And for just a second, I thought of Chase. And he spotted it instantly. Just like that, he figured something was up. I knew it, and he knew that I knew it.

"So I told him I'd been emailing Chase. He tried to tell me I had to stop."

"Which isn't true," I said.

"I know!" she said, in the tone of someone who'd just discovered this herself. "And I let him know it. He just stared at me, and it turned into one of those thousand-yard stares. And then he said, 'Maybe we shouldn't see each other for a while.' I said, 'Yeah, what with our being on different coasts and all.' And he said, 'I'm serious.'"

"Wait—the break was his idea?"

"This one was. So he said he'd be back on the seventh and he left. Then you came home and cheered me up—thank you very much. The next morning, I emailed Chase and told him what happened. About ten minutes later, he wrote back and said, 'Does that mean you're free this Saturday?'"

I nearly dropped my bottle. "Holy shit," I said.

"So tomorrow I'm going to see Chase for the second time. And I'm doing my best not to be scared shitless." She showed her teeth for a terrified one-second smile. "Do you disapprove?" she asked.

Disapprove? I was already picturing having Chase Becker as a second-cousin-in-law. "Hardly," I said. "I think this'll be great for you. I think it's just what you need."

She nodded for a long time, more to herself than to me. I finished my water and tossed the bottle. "I'll tell you," I said. "Now I really want to stay here. But I can't. I made a promise. I'm committed."

She pressed her head back against the recliner. "And I probably ought to be," she said.

7.

~~Hamilton~~ Ned:

Welcome to the Long House. Thank you in advance for a job well done.

I have ten commandments:

1. *By the time you read this, you'll probably have encountered the dog. His name is Nido (God : Dog :: Odin : Nido); he's a Brittany spaniel and he's almost a year old. He needs to be walked once before you go to work and once when you get home (weekends too, of course). The leash is hanging in the kitchen closet, where you'll also find plastic bags for the inevitable BMs. His food is under the kitchen counter—keep one dish full of dry food and give him half a can of wet food in the morning, half at night, in the other dish, after the walk. The water dish, obviously, should also remain full.*

2. *The goldfish are named Tristan and Esau (née Isolde; I was misinformed as to his gender at purchase). Give them no more than six flakes total once a day.*

3. *You'll want to put the garbage out before 6 a.m. this coming Tuesday. You'll want to put the garbage and the recycling out before 6 a.m. the Tuesday after that. I recommend putting it all out on Monday night.*

4. *My bedroom computer is 100 percent off limits. You can use my office computer if need be. Please don't delete the browsing history (mine or yours).*

5. *I watered the cacti before I left. Pay them no mind.*

6. *There's a washer and dryer in the bathroom. If something happens to them, there's a 24-hour laundromat just down the hill. Stay away after midnight.*

7. *There are four remotes on the coffee table. The Samsung one turns on the TV. The Emerson one changes the channel. The Hitachi one is for the DVD player. The Sony one controls the sound system. Don't touch the bass, treble, volume, etc. They're all right where I want them.*

8. *You're welcome to eat and drink anything in the house, particularly if it has an expiration date.*

9. *You'll be sleeping in the guest bedroom, off the kitchen. The door sometimes sticks, just so you know.*

10. *I can't stop you from snooping. All I ask is that you make sure you close any closet, cabinet, or cupboard doors you open. And leave things as you found them.*

If there are any house issues (plumbing, electrical, etc.), the super lives downstairs. You have my email address if there are any questions. Good luck, and I'll see you on the seventh.

Tedd.

***

The greatest impression I got as I wandered through the house late that Saturday morning was how dirty it was. I don't mean dusty, although that was in evidence to some degree. I don't mean cluttered either—there were a few stacks of old *Business Week* and *Wired* magazines in the corners, but for the most part there was a place for everything, and everything was in its place. What I mean is, there was a sort-of gray film over the furniture, the floor, the rugs, the curtains (all of them drawn), the fixtures. Even the dog hairs were off-white. The cleanest part of the place was the aquarium; the water was crystal clear, and Tristan and Esau (the smaller one was Esau, I guessed) looked happy to be there. I erred on the side of caution and fed them nothing.

As I continued exploring, Nido jumped all around me, putting his front paws on every part of my torso that he could reach. He was white with butterscotch markings, a long narrow build, and had a tail that hung between his back legs, wagging like it was attached to a motor.

His toenails clicked and skittered across the wood and the tile, but he didn't do any barking. I wondered if it had been trained out of him.

The bathroom, the office, the den, the kitchen—all of them dingier than I'd like. I didn't want to be Tedd's cleaning person, but if I were going to be living here for two weeks, I had to do something. I looked at the wall decorations, which were limited and consisted entirely of portraits—both paintings and photographs—of men in suits. They all looked past me, with varying degrees of severity. Half of them had one hand on the back of a chair. There was one sepia-toned picture of a boy in a suit; the jacket cuffs hung over most of his hands, and the pant cuffs bunched on the floor. He wore a derby and a fearful expression. It could have been a young Tedd if it weren't for the 1800s feel of it. Only the guest room had some clutter to it—boxes, file cabinets, old exercise equipment—but it was marginally cleaner, due to its lack of use.

I went around opening all the windows to chase out the stale air, with Nido bounding alongside me. I thought of raising my energy level to match his, but I wasn't sure how long either one of us could handle that. I also felt funny about the idea of saying "down" or "sit" or "stay" to him. He wasn't mine to command—there was no real reason for him to obey me.

Tedd's office was cramped and poorly lit, with a gray steel desk pressed up against the wall. He'd loaded it down with all kinds of envelopes and a sleek black computer that looked as much out of place as the monolith in *2001*. Next to that was an old desk phone, with a two-tone pattern of cream and grime. I just knew Tedd would be checking his phone records to see whether I'd used it, but I wasn't going to let that stop me.

"Hello?"

"Hey, Nades."

"Neds!"

"Hey, I'm just getting settled in here."

"Cool. Listen, what are you doing tonight?"

"Uh, walking the dog," I said, watching Nido scrabble around the place at high speed.

"Can you do me a favor? Could you come with me and Chase?"

I sat down in a wooden chair in the corner; being wooden, it was less likely to be dirty, I figured. "Come with you where?" I asked.

"Wherever we go." Her voice was quiet and furtive, like she was making plans to sneak out after dark. "I just want everything to be casual, and I thought a good way to do that would be to have you come along."

Nido took a corner too fast, bounced off the wall, and sped down the hall with no ill effects. "How does Chase feel about this?" I asked, watching him go.

She hesitated. "I … was going to ask you first, and then I would ask him."

"Huh," I said. "Well, I'll tell you what. If it's okay with Chase, it's okay with me."

"Oh, I knew you were going to say that!" She sounded agitated. "C'mon, Neds, you're supposed to want to help me here."

"You don't need my help. You'll be fine."

"It would really help me, Ned."

"Call me back," I said, in a big, reassuring voice, "and let me know what he says."

Silence.

"Nades?"

"Hmpf," she grumbled. "Some second cousin you are."

By now I knew her well enough to know she wasn't as ticked off as she made herself out to be. "I'll talk to you soon," I said. "Bye-bye."

After we disconnected, I thought that I might as well check my email as long as I had the computer in front of me. Good thing I did too.

7/22/05, 10:02 PM
To: nalderman@peppercornpub.com
From: chase@joyfacilitator.com
Subject: Busy Saturday?

I hope your second cousin has grown into giant status. If you're both available tomorrow (Saturday), I'd like to offer you a fun evening in New York with me as a guide of sorts. I'm sure Nadine would love it. Let's see if we can get her wearing size 22 pumps before the night is through.

Best, Chase

How interesting. It seemed Chase had arrived at the same conclusion as Nadine—namely, that they could use a good fifth wheel like me. I took a moment to note his technique, the way he brought up Nadine first, the way he worked to make himself the chaperone and me the one that needed guiding instead of the other way around. I'll confess, I didn't expect to see the low-level manipulation so clearly. I wondered if it was because I now knew the magician's secrets, or if Chase was getting careless. I mean, he'd just gotten stiffed for doing a bad job—could lightning strike twice in the same week?

I didn't like the thought of Chase's performance slipping. So I pushed that thought out of my mind, concentrating instead on the thought of letting Nadine know that I'd be glad to join her and Chase tonight. It was a much happier thought to entertain.

8.

Nido's leash was a retractable leash, and he used every inch of it on our first walk that evening. He ran as far ahead of me as he could, and when he came to the end of the leash's reach, he turned around and ran as far as he could behind me. I didn't even bother trying to keep up with him; I think if I'd started running, it would've been the equivalent of the jockey using his whip. All Tedd had hired me to do was to be a full-time presence for Nido, get him his food and his exercise, and wait for him to take a dump so I could pick it up. If he wanted more, he should have said so.

Maybe Nido picked up on this. At any rate, I soon found out why Tedd was so adamant that I keep his closet door shut. I came out from a post-walk, pre-fifth-wheel-date shower and shave to find that Nido had abandoned his dinner, taken my left shoe, and done unspeakable things to it. It was yanked open at the seams, a hole had been gnawed into the toe, the tongue was a fibrous mess, and it was covered in drool (I chose to believe it was drool). I stood there in my towel, staring at my poor helpless shoe, and Nido sat back on his haunches and panted gratefully at me. He was even more grateful when I kicked my right shoe over to him and went to get dressed.

Once I was clothed, the first thing I did was open my temporary closet door, toss my duffel bag inside, and close it. Any other things Nido decided to rip up weren't going to be mine. The next thing I did was open up Tedd's closet in the hopes that he might have some footwear I could borrow. Most of his shoes were Wall Street shoes, black and glossy, housing way more shoe trees than any one man should have. But in the back, I found some Weejuns that suited me perfectly. They were comfortably worn, they went with my outfit (you can't go wrong with jeans and a black polo), and best of all, Tedd also took a size ten. After all these weeks, it was great to have something nice to say about Tedd Long.

***

"How do I look?" Nadine asked me. She had on a pink cotton blouse, white jeans, and whiter tennis shoes.

"Good," I said. "Casual, but classy."

"Hair up or down?"

"Down. He's seen it up."

"What about the earrings?" She brushed her hair back to show me the half-dollar-sized hoops. "Too much?"

"Guys don't care about earrings, Nades. You're fine."

"Ohhhh." She gave me a disappointed smile. "You have much to learn, Grasshopper."

I was all set to acknowledge the truth of that, but before I could, there was a knock at the door. Nadine made a little hop and waved her hands in front of her like she was drying her nail polish. I gave her a double thumbs-up for assurance and went to let Chase in.

It had been only three days since I'd seen him, but I wasn't prepared for what a change he'd undergone. The man standing at the door was everything I knew about Chase, only more so. He wore a white shirt, sleeves rolled up and top two buttons undone, and white linen pants that fit him like the ocean surf fits the shore. His smile was easier than I'd ever seen it, and by softening those one or two muscles, he was able to let even more happiness flow forth. Only this wasn't happiness; this was exuberance. The waves of primal energy rolling from him would have had pallbearers forming conga lines. In a word, Chase Becker was transfigured.

"Oh, good!" he said, his voice ringing through the apartment. "You're both here!" He breezed past me—I couldn't not step back—

and spun around, raising two indigo gift bags in his right hand. "I have presents!" he said.

You certainly do, I thought, a moment before realizing that he hadn't just said *presence*.

"One for you and one for you," he went on, pressing bag handles into each of our hands. Nadine and I exchanged *I-have-no-idea-do-you?* looks, not so much wondering about our gifts as about Chase's behavior. Then I rummaged around in the sparkly tissue paper and pulled out—

Oh, no way.

"The Motorola Razr V3," said Chase. "Color screen, camera, all the bells and whistles. Best cell phone on the market. There's a two-year contract, but it's fair. They're all set to go. The numbers are in the bag somewhere. And I've already programmed you both into my phone. I hope this is an upgrade for you," he added, looking at Nadine. He may well have been talking about the Razr V3.

"Chase," said Nadine, not so much happy as bowled over. She stared at the silver phone in her hand as though it were a pulsing, living thing. "I can't believe you did this."

"You needed it," he said simply. "Both of you," he added, turning to include me. "And I know how much you guys believe in family taking care of family."

But I knew he hadn't bought them for us. He'd bought them for her. I was merely the instrument that allowed him to do so. It was a masterstroke—he'd demonstrated his respect for our blood bond while at the same time giving himself a way to access Nadine (and her a way to access him) that they hadn't had before. I didn't begrudge him at all for using me to help him make this connection. Not at all. Anything that brought Chase and Nadine closer together was fine with me.

"Thank you," I said, holding up my own black model. "This is amazing."

"Yeah," said Nadine, still staring at her phone. "Thank you."

"My pleasure," said Chase, and he clapped his hands once. "Okay! Anything special you guys want to do tonight?"

"I want to get a new pair of shoes," I said. I held out my right foot and briefly explained why Tedd's Weejun was on it.

"I've never seen him wear those," said Nadine.

"They were way in the back of the closet," I said.

"Shouldn't you walk a mile in them first?" asked Chase, and then he burst out laughing. This wasn't the warm chuckle that I'd heard from him before; this was bigger. This was a laugh that embraced everything it touched and raised it to the skies. Behind it, his big face lit up like a full moon. My heart swelled to witness this. It just wasn't possible to be in that room and not love everyone in it.

"Okay, then," said Chase. "That's on the list. But first, we're going to get something to eat. And we're going to do that in Koreatown."

***

Chase took us to Kang Suh, a restaurant in the Koreatown district, which had the best barbecue anything I've ever tasted. He listened to me and Nadine tell stories about other restaurants we'd been to or worked at, and the waitstaffs therein. Nadine outdid us all with one story involving a customer from hell, a waiter with a malicious streak, and a plate of frog legs; when she reached the punch line, I came very close to needing a Heimlich. We were the most boisterous table in the place, and that's saying something.

From there we went to a music room for karaoke. These were heavily carpeted rooms with plush couches and a table loaded down with three-ring binders full of song titles. Punch the number of an old fave into a machine, pick up the microphone, and sing to the piped-in music, with lyrics projected on a wall if needed. The rooms were full, but Chase smiled and said a few words in Korean. Before we knew it, we had a room that was intended for six people, not just three.

"I don't really speak Korean," Chase told us. "But I know how to get in good with people in Korean."

Chase had a rich crooning voice, and his song choices played to that; he did "Unchained Melody," "That's Amore," and "Don't You Forget About Me," knowing every word of that last one—"Oh, I was a huge *Breakfast Club* fan." I'm not much of a singer, so I did a lot of hamming it up, with bad imitations of Elvis, Mick Jagger, and the girls in ABBA. Nadine's tastes were more traditional than I expected— "You've Got a Friend," "The Tide is High," and "Respect" were some of her choices. She'd fluff a few words and cover her mouth every now and then, in a sweet way, and we'd cheer her on and she'd laugh.

The unquestioned highlight came at the end, when Chase and Nadine duetted on "You're the One That I Want." It was my idea. I'd known *Grease* was Nadine's big guilty pleasure from a previous movie night, and I took a shot in the dark that Chase would know his way around the song. So I suggested they do it, as I don't know the words (no, really). Nadine jumped at the chance, and Chase wasn't about to let her down. Together they primped and preened like their on-screen alter egos, belting out the words with gusto, strutting around each other with a combination of toughness and grace that was thrilling to watch. I kept a lookout for any soulful, smoky glances between them, but there weren't any; both of them were too involved with their own singing and dancing to get caught up in each other's psyches.

The song ended, and they gave each other a one-armed hug. "That was really fun!" Nadine said.

"Yeah!" said Chase. A moment later he said it again, with an awed sense of wonder. "Yeah!"

* * *

When we left, Chase's smile was bigger and easier than ever, and the smile combined with the white clothes and the post-exercise buzz to give him a remarkable glow. As we went on down the sidewalk, I kept expecting squadrons of moths to attack him.

"I have to confess something," Chase said. "I am really enjoying myself."

"Oh, so am I!" said Nadine, giving him another one-armed squeeze. "This is a blast!"

"Me too," I said. "But you guys, I gotta get going. I got a dog to take care of."

I'd been planning on saying this all night. It was a perfectly valid excuse, and it would give the two of them the time alone they'd both tried to prevent by inviting me to join them. I had even insisted on bringing my new phone with me, along with the gift bag of information about it, to give them one less reason to stop me from going off on my own.

"No, don't go!" they both said at once.

"I gotta," I repeated.

"But we haven't found you your new shoes yet!" said Chase, pointing at my feet.

"It's almost ten," I said. "It's too late to buy shoes. And I still have a third of a mile or so to walk in these ones."

"Neds, we're having so much fun!" Nadine protested.

"I know," I said. "So go and have some more. Thank you very much for all this, Chase. I had a great night. Take care."

I turned and crossed the street to the subway stop I'd seen there; I wouldn't have said my goodbyes if I hadn't had an escape route in my proximity. When I reached it, I turned to them and waved. Neither one waved back. They stood there and watched me descend the stairs, and just before I lost sight of them, I saw Nadine take Chase's hand.

9.

"You know what this place needs?" Siege asked. "A bleach bomb."

He was looking around the house, deriving no small satisfaction from its uncleanliness. I was pouring us each a glass of Zinfandel. I'd picked out both glasses and wine from the liquor cabinet I'd discovered that morning; I'd had to wash the glasses first. It's not like I wouldn't have anyway, but the fact that I'd *had* to wasn't any fun.

"I'm going to do some major cleaning today," I told Siege, bringing him his glass.

"Aw, dude, come on—what are you, his personal janitor?"

"No, it's okay; it's purely for selfish reasons," I assured him. "I'm going to ask Alexa over, and I don't want her looking forward to leaving the minute she walks in."

"Ah, well, in that case—hey, hold on," he said, stopping me from taking a drink. Raising his glass, he said, "Here's to you for being Mister Matchmaker Guy last night. And here's to me for hooking up with a non-paper product."

My glass stopped halfway to my lips. "Siege?"

"Drink, drink."

I took a quick sip and swallow. "Why didn't you say something?"

He finished his extended quaff. "Because you were too busy yappin' about last night for me to get a word in edgewise." He grimaced. "What is this shit? Whoever stomped these grapes, I can taste their bunions."

"It's Zinfandel and it's not that bad."

"Well, that's one of us who thinks so." He emptied the rest of his glass in a cactus pot. "So you want to know what happened," he said, putting down his glass. "How did old Cameron Joyce Brandenburg break a twenty-six-month loser streak?"

"Yeah, how?" I echoed, following him to the den. "C'mon, tell all."

He flopped down on the couch. "I'm glad you asked me. While you were out caterwauling in K-Town, I was on the prowl at Bar Sinister. And I saw someone who looked to be both very sweet and right-handed."

"Doubly ironic," I said, taking a sip.

"I thought you'd appreciate that. And I wouldn't be being honest if I didn't say she was just my type. Female, heartbeat, awake—you know the drill. Now in the old days I'd go up, buy her a drink maybe, talk about how great I am, watch her figure out for herself that I'm not, and once I figure out that I'm the one breaking all the silences, I take off. But this time, I centered myself, I didn't judge, I went up and smiled and said hi. She smiled back. And then I said, 'I was sitting over there and I couldn't help noticing you. You look like you've got something on your mind.' Turns out I was right."

"She tell you about it?"

"She had to tell somebody—why not a complete stranger in a bar who's all about listening? So it seems she has a coworker who's a stealth bomber. The coworker's a great person to work with, and then one day she'll cut you down. Behind your back, in front of you and your colleagues, just the two of you in the bathroom—you never know where or when. She said she felt like a step on a ladder, and that she hated what this stealth bomber was making everyone think.

"So I go, 'What do you care what other people think?' She should just keep being herself and the truth would out, like it always does. 'Oh, and that coworker? Fuck her,' I said. I said if someone comes up to you and says, 'Hey, you want a shit sandwich?', there's no law that requires you to say 'Yes, please.'"

"But not in so many words."

"Those were my words exactly," he corrected me. "And she got it; she totally understood. I told her that some people have to make others feel worse so they can feel better, and this coworker was threatened by someone this smart and attractive, and feels the need to make these put-downs a regular thing, and what she had to do was ... disengage." He fairly sang the last word. "Ya like that?"

"Yes, very good."

"Well, she was liking all of this. So I said, 'You know what, it's getting too noisy in here. Let's go somewhere we can talk.' She said yes. Boom! Instant date. She takes me to a place called Tuffy's, and I listen and she talks and I ask questions and she talks some more. Then I take her somewhere else, little coffee bistro called The First Cup. Now we're on our second instant date and she's feeling closer to me. She asks about me and I paint a pretty good picture. Meanwhile, I'm keeping myself open, smiling, feeding her all this positive energy like you're s'posed to.

"Gets to be ten o'clock, and she says, 'Would you walk me home?' I say, 'You know, I would, but I got this little rock in my shoe.' Just joking, right? And she goes, 'Shake it out.' No nonsense. I am coming home with her. We both know what we're talking about. Turns out we're both right. And there it is," he concluded, spreading his arms. "Vidi, vici, veni."

"I think you mean 'veni, vidi, vici.'"

He gave me a rakish grin. "No, I don't."

"Ahhh. Okay. Well, congratulations," I said, reaching out with my fist.

"Thanks, man," he said, bumping mine with his. "I got her number, so who knows? But I gotta say, I owe it all to the books on that list Chase gave you. And that part about telling her to disengage—that's all him."

I took another drink—as far as I could tell, there was nothing wrong with the wine at all. "You know," I said, "that's really not how you're supposed to use it."

Siege's face darkened slightly, as though a cloud of campfire smoke had passed across it.

"It's not a tool for getting girls. It's not supposed to have an on-off switch. You have to commit yourself fully to the life. I mean, I'm happy for you, don't get me wrong, but I just don't think you should use it the wrong way."

"Oh," he said, sitting up straight. "I'm sorry. Next time I'll make sure and charge her a few hundred dollars, so I can have a clear conscience."

"It's not about money, Siege."

"I'm thinkin' Chase's clientele would disagree."

"Chase is using his skills to make a living."

"Yeah, that's dandy. 'Just pay through the nose and I'll make you happy as a dog with two dicks.'"

Siege and I didn't have a lot of uncomfortable pauses in our talks, but we had one here. Neither of us wanted to continue down this particular avenue of conversation—he because he knew he would get all fired up and come after me, hard enough to make me feel like I was running with the bulls in Pamplona; me for pretty much the same reason. He averted his eyes to the corners of the room, and I turned away and drained my glass.

"So," he said, still not looking at me. "What do you got planned for the rest of the day?"

"Well, I gotta buy some shoes, probably a shitload of lint rollers ..."

That's when Nido trotted into the room with a stuffed animal in his mouth. It was a teddy bear, brown and beige, with a missing ear, coat button eyes, and a right angle stitched into his face in the shape of a frown.

"... Figure out my new phone," I went on. "Program some names in. Call Nadine and Chase and see if they'll tell me how last night ended ..."

Nido began swinging his head in a figure eight, slamming the teddy bear on the floor to his left and to his right. *Wham wham wham wham wham wham wham.*

"Do some housecleaning ..."

The figure eights got tighter, the whams more frequent, maybe five every two seconds. Siege got up and stood next to me, watching him go. "Shouldn't you maybe take that away from him?" he asked, the amused lilt in his voice indicating that this was the last thing he wanted me to do.

"I don't know," I said. "What if that's his toy? Or what if I try to take it away and he yanks back and it rips?"

About eight whams after I spoke, it ripped. Bits of shredded cotton floated from its chest into the air. Whether because that excited Nido or because it lightened the bear's weight, he began thrashing his head around even faster. In half a minute he looked like he was inside a snow globe.

Siege giggled. "He's really working it over."

"God, I hope this isn't some precious family heirloom or something," I said.

"Ah, he looks like he knows what he's doing."

We stood there, our hands on our hips, watching the bear's chest grow more sunken, its snout become loose and wrinkled. It wasn't something you could just turn away from. Nido's wild eyes, the bear's unchanging little frown, the cotton carnage switching about … it was compelling.

Finally, when the little cloth carcass was all but empty, Nido dropped it, shook himself, and trotted out of the room, tiny white puffs of fabric trailing behind him. "I better get a bag to save the stuffing in, just in case," I said, going to the kitchen.

"That was great," Siege said, following me. "I guess *he* didn't need two dicks to be happy. Hey, let's have ourselves a little more of this so-called wine."

10.

I sent Alexa an email on Monday telling her that after a herculean bout of cleaning, the house was almost ready for guests; if she'd like to come by on Tuesday, I'd make sure it was ready the rest of the way. As an added incentive, I told her I had spoken with Chase and he'd shared what had happened on Saturday after I'd left him and Nadine alone, and I'd share that with her when she came. She wrote back to one-up me; she'd gotten Nadine's side of the story, undoubtedly far more elaborate than Chase's, and we could piece the two of them together.

This was good, because I could barely get in touch with Nadine at all. I tried to reach her on Sunday, Monday, and Tuesday, sending her emails, calling her landline (I didn't yet know her new cell phone number), leaving messages that started out, "Hey, hope you're not mad at me," and worked their way up to "Are you mad at me?"

In those three days, I only heard from her once. She sent me an email on Tuesday morning with the subject heading "You shouldn't have bailed on us." It read, in its entirety, "But I'm glad you did."

***

"Well, he's an enthusiastic one," said Alexa, as Nido jumped and danced around her.

"This is Nido," I said, trying to calm him down. "He hasn't made a sound since I got here."

"Silent but friendly," she said, coming in and kissing me hello-how are you-by God it certainly is good to see you again.

Hey, I thought, *look who's here? My old buddy, Half-In-Love.*

I showed her around the place. She noticed how much cleaning I'd done, as well as how much I'd left undone. As a dramatic illustration of the latter, she tilted one of the glowering portraits on the wall enough to reveal the bright white rectangle of paint behind it. "Yikes," I said.

She smiled. "Don't even think about cleaning it. Tedd's floor and furniture I can understand, but I draw the line at Tedd's walls."

After the grand tour, we decided to order in pizza, then go pick up dessert at a late-night café a couple of blocks down the hill, making sure to get back before the pizza arrived. And so it was that over the remaining Zinfandel, an incredible BBQ chicken pizza, and raspberry tortes, we put together the story of Chase and Nadine's Saturday night.

***

Neither one of them had said it to be polite; they really hadn't wanted me to go.

Chase knew of a shoe store with big windows; even if they hadn't been open, we could have at least looked at some of their selection. Nadine had a greater worry—she felt that as long as I was around, things between her and Chase would stay friendly and nonphysical. With me gone, overtones would be free to creep about and entwine them. That could turn dangerous. I hadn't been the fifth wheel after all—I'd been the emergency brake. And as I went down the steps and she reached for Chase's hand, the vehicle began to roll.

"He'll be all right," Chase assured her.

"Oh, I'm not worried about him."

Chase had a good idea what she was worried about, and he made it his goal to release her of that worry. Familiarity, rapport, trust, comfort. "You're having a good time?" he asked.

"Oh, yeah. This has been a great night. Any night I get to sing *Grease* songs at the top of my lungs is a great night."

"So you want to keep it going?"

She didn't want to think about her answer, but she did. A no wouldn't have been honest. A yes might lead to more yeses, maybe one too many. Why did Tedd have to be in the picture? Why did he have to be out of it?

"Can we just walk for a while?" she asked him. "And talk?"

He liked the idea and said so. As they started off, still hand in hand, he said, "By the way, I really like your earrings."

"Thanks," she said, and she thought, *Take that, Neds*.

They went up Fifth Avenue, neither one in any hurry. People around them would be planning where to go, or arguing in Spanish, or swearing at all the taxis flying by, and it seemed to both of them that the people grew quiet as they passed. Strangers turned to watch them, offered them expressions of respect and goodwill, murmured in their wake.

It was like nothing Nadine had ever experienced before. She thought it was because of Chase, all in white, all aglow, his own special electricity coursing through him, giving him power. But he was sure it was because of Nadine, a vision in pink and white, gentle and graceful as a fawn, a sight nobody in New York could help being moved by.

As they reached Central Park, with its brick wall separating the grass from the street, with tree branches reaching over that wall with promise, Chase turned to Nadine and said, "I have to confess something."

"Something else?" she asked.

"Something else." He paused, not knowing why he was telling her this, only that it was important he do so. "I said I was enjoying myself, and that was true. But I think you should know that that's not something I do."

She was confused, didn't understand. "What do you mean?"

A runner approaching them veered off the sidewalk and onto the street, running next to the curb, giving them their space until he had passed them and could go back on the sidewalk again. The sound of his sneakers slapping the concrete faded as Chase struggled to find the right words. "I don't," he said. He stopped, sighed, and tried again.

"My job is to make others happy. Others, not myself. Any happiness I have, I have to pass on. It's not mine to keep."

Nadine didn't understand. I'd told her I thought she'd broken Chase out of this prison of misplaced belief, and the last few hours had seemed to confirm that; now he was telling her this wasn't true at all. "Wait," she said. "Don't you even feel happiness when you see other people you've made happy?"

"Not happiness," Chase said. "Satisfaction at a job well done. See, I can feel good. I can feel pleased. I can laugh at comedies. I'm just not a guy who ever knew how to feel happy."

This hurt Nadine. She felt betrayed, like he'd spent the whole night lying to her. "So all this 'oh, this is fun, la-di-da,' this was all an act?"

"No!" said Chase, leaping to correct her, knowing he didn't have much time to steer them both away from this cliff. "That's just it! I spent the day getting ready, thinking, it's about her, it's all for her. But I couldn't stop feeling excited for me. And that got me even more excited. Thinking about where we'd go, going out and getting you and Ned your phones—it just kept building up. I can only imagine what I looked like when I came through your door."

"You were pretty geared up, all right," she agreed, smiling a little at the thought. He had that look on his face now, as he recounted this; she marveled that his walking pace remained slow and steady.

"And then our night began," he continued, "and I couldn't believe it, but I was *staying* excited. I was feeding off of you guys as much as you were feeding off of me. I was letting go of all my little rules; I was doing stuff I never do—I am *not* a karaoke kind of guy—and it was fun. And it was good to *have* the fun, instead of just watching it. It wasn't selfish at all. You laugh, but that's a revelation to me."

"I'm not laughing," said Nadine, trying not to laugh. "I'm just amazed."

"I'm amazed too," said Chase. "And you're the one who's amazing me."

The laughs she'd been suppressing dissolved in her throat. Her head went light. It had taken Tedd four months before he had told her, "I find you to be very special." Chase's admission had taken four hours, and she felt it so much deeper for its unguardedness, its directness, maybe even its truth.

"When I first saw you," he said, "you took me out of my world. The world of the familiar, where I have control—the only world I knew. You showed me another world, one with you in it, and I wanted to learn about that world. Then you emailed me, and over the course of a month, I got the chance to learn about this world. And I learned that any world with someone as smart, as warm, as energetic, as powerful, and as attractive—*completely* attractive—as you living in it was a world I wanted to be a part of. To be a part of me. Now I think it is. And I hope I am."

They'd come to a stop under a streetlight. They leaned on opposite sides of it. Both of them needed to recover some of their strength: Chase, from loosing such a torrent of words he didn't know had been stored inside him under that much pressure; Nadine, who hadn't known how much to brace herself, from taking the full force of those words deep in her chest. They continued to hold hands; they had relaxed but not released their grip since they'd begun their walk. They breathed lightly, looking in different directions.

The lights turned green, and hundreds of vehicles passed them at high speeds. The lights turned red, and soon their road was clear again.

Then Nadine said, "What about Tedd?"

Chase bumped his heel against the light post. "Tedd lives in this world too," he said. "Tedd has a solid place in this world."

She left her side of the post to walk in front of Chase and face him directly. "Tell me what you're going to do," she said.

Chase didn't say anything.

"I have to know what's coming," Nadine said. "I have to know if I can handle this. Tell me."

Chase held out his other hand, the empty one. He looked at Nadine, at his hand, at Nadine. She looked down and put her hand in his, and as he enfolded her in his fingers, she gripped him, hard, like she was nine years old again and gripping the handlebars of her bike, gunning full speed toward a ramp her second cousin had built, out to prove to him that she was not afraid.

"I'm going to get as close to you as I can," Chase said. "At some point you might stop me. Or I might stop you. Or we might never stop. But that's what I'm going to do." He squeezed her hands. "And whatever happens, I can tell you right now that you'll handle it just fine."

She closed her eyes, opened them. Talia Shire did that in the first *Rocky*, when she was watching him box. Why did she have to think of that? She thought instead of Chase, standing before her, all in white, his smile gone, but only for this moment. She knew she could bring it back.

"All right, Chase," she said. "All right."

"All right then," he said, and here it came, breaking across his face like a new dawn. She returned his smile with one of her own. Each of them thought the other's to be beautiful.

"Come on," she said, and they continued their walk. Neither of them said anything for block after block, sharing nothing but their time and their comfort with each other, until Nadine said, "That's my street. Let's cross here." They crossed, away from the Central Park branches, away from Fifth Avenue's lights, past the rows of parked cars, some of their tires pressing against the curb, some of them a foot away. The silence between them was losing its comfort; now it jammed up their questions as it drew toward its conclusion, at the front steps of her apartment.

"Home sweet home," she said, getting on the first step.

"Apartment sweet apartment," he said.

"Building sweet building," she said, in a sure-why-not tone.

"Nadine sweet Nadine," he said, soft as fresh snow.

"Chase sweet Chase," she said, even softer. "Sweet, sweet Chase." She put her hands on his shoulders, so broad and full, and she looked him in the face, so broad and full, and she didn't want the night to end. "Come on up," she said.

"No."

It was the only thing she didn't expect him to say. She grabbed at the only reason she could think that he would say it. "Ned's not here, remember. He's in Brooklyn. Come on up."

"No," he repeated. For the first time all evening, he looked less than happy.

"Chase," she said. "Why?"

He took a moment to formulate his answer. Then he stepped up, put his arms around her and began to lean closer. She felt her body go rigid, her hands push, her head turn to offer him her cheek. She was shocked. She couldn't believe her body could betray her like this—go stiff as a surfboard, rejecting less than she was offering. But it was just what Chase had suspected would happen. He released her, stepped back, and quietly said, "Now you know why."

She looked down. She understood. "Okay."

"This has been a wonderful night, Nadine," he said. "I'll call you tomorrow." He brought two fingers to his lips, touched them to her cheek. "Take care," he said.

"You too," she said. Then, as he turned to go: "Chase?"

He turned back. "Yes?"

"You know, just because that's as close as we got tonight doesn't mean we can't get closer."

He smiled at that, one last beam of midnight sun. "I know," he said. "But it makes me glad to hear you say it. Thank you. Goodnight."

"Goodnight, Chase," said Nadine, and she trotted up the steps as he headed back to Fifth Avenue to find out which cab driver would be lucky enough to spot him first.

**

"She definitely told you a lot more than he told me," I said, picking over the last of my raspberry torte.

"Well, that's what girls do," said Alexa. "We share every little detail. We spot the things that get past guys. Your gender can be oblivious, you know."

"I suppose."

"Suppose nothing. You have to be flat-out told things that are obvious to every girl in the place. Like that bit of sauce on your face there," she said, pointing.

"Yeah, but that's different," I said, rubbing a folded paper towel around my mouth. "Girls expect guys to be mind readers, and we're not."

"You don't have to be." She sat up straight in her chair. "Okay, here's an example. If you were to ask me to spend the night here, what would I say and why?"

I tried to look her in the eyes, but they distracted me from the question, so I took on a general, mock-pensive gaze and stroked my chin. "You'd say no," I said. "Not because of me, but because staying in Tedd Long's place overnight would creep you out. Plus you don't have any of your overnight things."

She shook her head. "Wrong on so many levels," she said. "The location's owner makes no difference, especially if they aren't around. And here's a little known fact: it's possible to spend the night somewhere without a change of clothes. Or even a toothbrush."

"Right, check, okay," I said. "I get it."

"You almost get it." She stood and picked up a few things to bring to the kitchen. Our wine glasses, our dessert plates. "One more level you're wrong on—if you were to ask me to spend the night, don't be so sure I wouldn't say yes." She scootched down, pecked my cheek, and went off to the kitchen, humming some Disney music.

I sat there, feeling like an absolute moron. Not for being unable to pass Alexa's little test, but for what I was about to do. "Alexa?" I called to her.

"Yeees?" she trilled back.

"I can't ask you to spend the night tonight."

The humming stopped. A few moments later she was in front of me, looking down. "Why not?" she asked.

"It's complicated."

She folded her arms. "Are you trying to be like Chase?"

"That's not why," I said, shaking my head. "I don't feel ready right now, is what it comes down to. Believe me, I look at you and I would love to feel ready. But if I've still got some doubts, I have to respect that. I want to be one hundred percent here for you." A sudden thought occurred to me, and I couldn't help cringing. "Unless I'm being oblivious again and you only wanted to sleep on the couch," I said.

She laughed—a small laugh, but pure. "No, you weren't," she said. "Not that time." She pulled out the chair next to me and sat down. "Something you'd care to talk about?" she asked.

"Not tonight. Eventually, yes, but not tonight."

She nodded, a nod that encompassed her whole upper torso, bobbing up and down. "Care to pick a day?"

I summoned up all my conviction. "Saturday," I said. "When Saturday comes around, I'll be able to talk about it. We'll make a night of it—order Chinese, watch a movie, put on some music ... more maybe ..."

"More maybe?" Her eyebrows went all sly on me again.

"Maybe."

"All right," she said. "I'll be the one with the overnight bag." And she stood up and kissed the top of my head.

11.

The next morning, I arrived at the conference room before anyone else and took my usual seat over toward the corner. Then Maylene came in and, as usual, sat next to me, touching my shoulder as she did so. Being the interns, we had settled in off to the side, out of the line of action.

"Hey, May, what do you say?" I said, turning up my good vibes.

"Hey, Ned. I like your shoes."

"Oh, thanks. I just got these."

She smiled and glanced out the door. "Do you know if we're going to be talking about something special this morning?"

"Nothing I'm aware of," I said, flipping open my notepad. "Why?"

"Because I just saw Chase Becker come in."

My head jerked around to face her, like a pigeon's. "Chase is here?"

"Yeah, and he looks *strange*."

I was about to ask how, but Chase saved me the trouble by walking in at just that moment. One look at him and my entire face went slack. Maylene wasn't kidding—this was a Chase I'd never seen before. He had on a wrinkled denim shirt and ketchup-stained chinos. He hadn't shaved in a couple of days, and his hair was a pillow-tousled mess. But what stood out the most was the expression on his face. His laser focus was nowhere to be seen; in its place was a serene detachment. He sat down and tipped back in his chair, directing his eyes at the ceiling as he whistled the theme to *Grease*. That did it—I didn't know where the rest of him was, but I had a pretty good idea who he was with.

"Chase?" I asked.

He dropped the front two legs of his chair back on the floor. "Ned? Hey! I didn't see you there."

I gave him a Chase-encompassing wave. "That's a new look for you, isn't it?"

He shrugged. "No different than Jamie's."

He wasn't wrong about that. A moment later, his point was driven home when Jamie Engel entered the room wearing almost the exact same outfit, only the stain on his chinos looked more like mustard. "Alley oop!" he said, dropping into his chair. "Happy seven-two-seven! Oh, wait—I should wait for more people. Too good a line to blow it all on the interns—no offense. We'll be getting more ..."

As he trailed off into self-directed mumbling, the other Peppercorn folk started coming in, in ones and twos. I usually did the hail-fellow-well-met routine, but with Chase in the room, I figured I'd step back and leave it to him. But he didn't greet anyone. He sat there and studied his nails, or wrote something on the back of his hand, or stared at his own corneas. A couple of staffers said "Hi, Chase!" when they spotted him, and he'd say, "Oh, hi, hi," and nothing more.

When everyone was in, Jamie lifted his arms to salute us, revealing a patch of armpit sweat in the shape of Australia. "Alley oop!" he re-proclaimed. "Happy seven-two-seven! July twenty-seventh. Good to see you all here. Woke up, it was a Chase-y morning, so he's here too! Joni Mitchell. Okay!"

Of course, we all knew Chase wasn't there because of one of Jamie's whims. He was there because there was potential for an uncomfortable situation, and he could be counted on to keep that from happening. Last time Chase was here, I hadn't felt that knowledge troubling anyone. This time, I did. People traded anxious looks. Bill's shoulders were hunched up tight. Andie chewed her thumbnail. Chase took out a tube of lip balm and applied it.

We came to find out that the big issue up for debate was whether or not we should publish a certain manuscript. It was called *Little Miss Mafia*, and it was the memoir of a woman who had gradually come to realize that her loving father was involved in organized crime. She had to endure the taunts of her classmates and the self-doubt of whether she deserved those good grades or that prom queen crown, or whether she was given them out of fear for what might happen if she weren't.

Wyatt, the staff's true crime connoisseur, had read the manuscript, and it was his considered opinion that it would be a mistake for Peppercorn to publish it. Lee, being the staff memoir person, had also gotten her hands on it, and she was vehement in her belief that this should be Peppercorn's lead title for the following summer. Each of them got five minutes to present their own case, and then they could rebut the other's case. It was during the rebuttals that things got contentious.

"It's not a well-written book," said Wyatt. "It's competently written, but I like to think Peppercorn aims for higher than that."

"It's a compelling story," countered Lee. "People who read true crime books read them for the thrills, and this book is packed with them."

"We don't publish true crime books. It's a niche market—"

"But we do publish memoirs, and a woman's look at the Mafia from the inside—"

"—will elicit next to no interest for the male readers of true crime."

"The reader's gender isn't relevant, and if it were—"

"—which it is—"

"—then it pays to remember that women buy more books than men," Lee interrupted once more. "Women kept Workman Books solvent by buying *What to Expect When You're Expecting*, women saved HCI's skin by buying *Chicken Soup for the Soul* books, and women will buy *Little Miss Mafia* in droves—"

"That's a specious argument. There'll always be pregnant women needing advice, there'll always be a need for feel-good stories under five pages, but the market for Don Daddy's little girl—"

"—is something you can't recognize if you're stuck thinking what these sorts of books *are*, not what they have the potential *to be*—"

"—or would have the potential to be if they were better written."

Lee grimaced. "Are you saying I can't recognize good writing when—"

"You're letting what you think it is blind you to what it really is—"

"Look who's talking, Mister Kettle—"

"You're the kettle—you can't even get that right!"

We were skating dangerously close to personal insults. A rapid glance around the table showed almost everyone to be either completely still, like frightened rabbits trying to avoid detection, or completely fascinated, like ringside spectators watching a cobra fight a mongoose. The lone exception was Chase, who was busy checking his watch.

Well, I thought. *If he's not going to use his training, I will.*

"Hello!" I said, standing up. (A friendly opening, and my rising to my feet would draw and hold the audience's attention.) Within a second, all eyes were on me. "I want to make sure I have this right," I said. "Lee, what I hear you saying is that this is an interesting story told from a unique vantage point, and that those two factors will combine to bring this book the sizable audience it deserves."

"That's what I've been trying to tell you for ten minutes!"

"And Wyatt," I continued, turning to him. "Correct me if I'm wrong, but your position is that the subpar writing and Peppercorn's inexperience in the true crime genre make this a book that will neither find nor deserve an audience." (Restate the argument clearly.)

"That's the long and the short of it." (Make sure both participants agree with the restatement.)

"So what we have are two opinions, one pro and one con. Now, has anyone else here read the book? Anyone?" Of course, they hadn't—it was still just a manuscript, after all. (Know the answers to any questions you may want to ask.)

"All right," I said. "Now if this *is* a new voice, saying something in a new way, then it would be an immeasurable help if we could say how enthusiastic Peppercorn was about this title. So here's a suggestion." (Not "Here's what we should do." or "Here's what I suggest."—know your place in the chain.)

"Have a number of people here—five, say—read it over the next week. During the week, we'll express interest to the agent and gauge their desire to publish with us and their asking price. By next

Wednesday, the panel of readers will have emailed their thoughts to Jamie—no presentations necessary." (Don't force anyone into a discomfort zone.)

"Then we'll know if *Little Miss Mafia* is worth the investment of time and money that we would be ready to give." I sat down and gestured to Jamie. (Recognize who has authority; if it's not you, and you borrow it, be sure you return it.)

At first, nobody followed my gesture. They stared at me in surprise, either bewildered (*Who is this guy?*) or pleased (*I had no idea*). Lee looked confused. Maylene winked at me. As for Chase, he was giving me not only his full attention but a smile of great pride. I hadn't just done well; I had done well in the eyes of the master. What a good feeling that gave me; it was no trouble converting his approval into positive energy and sending it back out to everybody.

"This guy's amazing!" shouted Jamie, lifting his arms and revealing that Australia had become Africa. "What's Ned short for, anyway— Solomon? All right, cut the kid in half! Ha! Any Bible readers here? Seriously, what am I even doing here? We oughta let Ned run the joint! Wait, wait, I know why I'm here—I'll pick out this reading committee. Let's see, every third person, that'd be Maylene, not Chase but Peter, Other Joe, not Wyatt but Caroline, and I'll be Mister Tiebreaker."

"Three men and two women?" said a dubious-looking Lee. "That's not exactly fair, is it?"

"You said gender was irrelevant, Lee," I pointed out. "This'll prove you're right."

She couldn't very well argue with that. She also had Maylene on the committee, which was likely as not a vote for her camp. So she was pacified enough to retreat into silence. (A positive can turn a negative into a neutral.)

"Well, the old clock on the wall is saying 'That's all,'" said Jamie, popping out of his chair. "Chase, come with me, and the rest of you do that voodoo that you do so well! All right!"

**

I hung around the door by Louise the receptionist's desk so I could catch Chase on his way out. It took a couple of minutes, but he did emerge from Jamie's office, tucking away his wallet and smiling to himself. I blocked the door so he wouldn't sail by me. He looked up as he approached; I think he saw me before he recognized me.

"Ned. Boy, weren't you something to see in action. Everything I would have done, you did."

"Why weren't you doing it?" I asked.

He blinked. "Because you were doing it," he said, as though it were the most obvious thing in the world. "I wasn't about to take that away from you."

"I was only doing it because you weren't." I was trying not to sound as put out as I felt. My training helped me considerably. "I didn't expect to have to cover for you, Chase."

"Hey," he said. "It's okay. Everything turned out fine. You got to prove your mettle. And I got paid."

"He *paid* you?"

"Believe it or not." He patted his hip pocket. "He was writing the check and saying, 'I shouldn't be doing this. I don't know why I'm doing this.' But he did it."

He was like a soldier who knew he'd just cheated death but didn't comprehend what that meant because he was so caught up thinking about his gal back home. I flashed a glance at Louise. She was talking on the phone, but if her expression were anything to go by, she dearly wished she wasn't. Chase and I were far more interesting.

"Hey!" said Chase. "Lesson day today, right? We're talking about passion?"

"Compassion," I corrected him.

"Compassion. So close. Well, I know you deserve a lot of this fee here—how about dinner on me tonight as a thank-you? When do you get out, five? I'll meet you out front."

"I ..."

"Only don't be surprised if I'd rather talk about something else. See you tonight!" He flipped a little wave at me, changed the angle of the wave to direct it at Louise, and then he was gone.

12.

"I get it now!"

I hadn't gotten a yard out of the building before Chase swooped up alongside me with those words. I took an involuntary leap—a genuine attempt to jump out of my skin, I suspect—and yelped something that sounded like *Djyte!*

"Ho! I'm sorry."

"Don't *do* that!" I said, taking care not to accept his apology. Thinking about his actions, or lack of actions, throughout the workday hadn't put me in much of a forgiving mood.

"Listen," he said, as we walked past some smokers and a fat guy selling an assortment of wallets, "there's something I understand now that I didn't used to, and it's important. You remember that night when I told you how I didn't feel? Well, I can feel now! Do you have any idea what a difference that can make in a guy?"

"I can imagine."

"See, it's like this." He neatly dodged a bicyclist. "You know why the sky's blue? Technically? It absorbs all the colors in the spectrum, and then it reflects blue. Well, I need to absorb the full range of the emotional spectrum before I can reflect pure joy. And how can I do that if I can't absorb joy?"

"So what have you been giving off all this time?"

"Synthetic joy. Ersatz joy. My interpretation of it. Not the real thing. I know the real thing now. These last few nights, I've felt it with your cousin."

"Second cousin," I said. Then I stopped. "What?"

"Yeah, we've seen—" He realized I'd stopped walking and doubled back to me. "We've seen each other every night for the past four nights," he said. "The only reason I'm not seeing her tonight is because of my previous engagement with you. She said to say hi."

I stood there, flummoxed. I couldn't believe that these two had been on multiple dates and I was only finding out about it now. I also thought of Tedd ordering me to keep an eye on things, and what his reaction might be when he discovered the degree to which I hadn't been.

"Did Nadine not tell you about this?" Chase asked. "I suppose she couldn't have called you, because I was around the whole time, just about. But I'm surprised she didn't email you."

So was I. But maybe that was for the best. The less I knew, the less Tedd could drag out of me. *Maybe*, I thought, *I should keep myself as much in the dark about their last few nights as possible.* But there was one question I couldn't quite keep down.

"Did she …" No, that wasn't right. "Did you guys …." No, I wasn't going to finish that question. I'd just let the unasked part hang between us and hope Chase would address it without me having to speak the words.

Thank Christ, he did. He shook his head. "I won't talk about that, Ned. Whether we did or didn't isn't up for discussion. I may be off my head with joy, but I'm also a gentleman." He waved his hand to dismiss the half-question. "Besides, it's not relevant to the point I'm trying to make."

"Which is what?" I said, walking again.

"My knowing what real joy is. I'm a changed man, Ned. This is going to change the way I do everything."

We joined a small mob of people at the curb. Some of them were watching the DON'T WALK sign on the other side of the street. The rest of us were looking any which way. I was looking at Chase. "You know what you sound like?" I asked him.

"What?"

"A man in love."

He didn't even have to think about it. "I can live with that," he said, and then he was dancing. He stepped away from me and did a little twirl. His ankles twitched and he was in the air. If it had been autumn instead of summer, he could have jumped from leaf to leaf as they fell; that's how weightless he was. He landed and bounced, his feet a blur as he did a quick sprint without moving forward an inch. All the while he dee-da-dee'd and dah-dee-dah'd, breathy syllables of elation. He may have been on a sidewalk on Sixty-Second Street physically, but in Chase's world, he was soaring above it all, in the thrall of his own exuberance.

WALK, the sign said, and most of us did so. Chase stayed a dance step ahead of me, still doing free spins and feather steps. People walked ahead of him, or they turned sideways as they passed him coming the other way. Nobody looked at him. They all held on to their pinched determination or their half-lidded torpor.

This wasn't right. I had seen him walk on busy streets before, and people were always getting a sense of him, turning to watch him go past. Now here he was, just about ready to bounce out of his socks, and he wasn't even worth a second glance.

It took me a minute, but I figured out why. I knew I had to tell him. In fact, there was a dark part of me that was looking forward to the job.

**

I let him dance and hum to himself until we got to the A train stairs, where I turned to say goodbye. But he was already on his way down, his feet sparkling along as he slalomed around the people trudging in front of him.

"Chase!" I said, hustling to catch up. "Where are you going?"

"I'm taking you out to dinner," he said. "Remember?"

"You know I'm not going uptown, right? I've got to walk Tedd's dog in Brooklyn."

"Well, I'm willing to bet there are restaurants out there too."

"Chase," I said, "this is the subway. I thought—"

"Oh, I can ride 'em now," he said. "No problem. Nadine took me. Check it out, I've got a MetroCard and everything!" He showed me his card, then turned and whistled his way to the turnstile.

"That's it," I muttered to myself, following him. "That clinches it. That's it, all right."

***

I waited until we had both taken seats in the subway. I waited until the car had filled up with all its glum folk. I waited until the doors had closed and the train was in motion. Only then did I turn to Chase, sitting next to me, eyes closed, humming, letting his head sway with the rocking rhythms all around us.

"Chase?"

"Mmm?"

"Do you have your notepad with you?"

"Sure do."

"Mind if I take a look?"

He reached down into his pocket to pull it out and pass it over. "Any helpful commentary I can offer, just ask," he said, and he closed his eyes again.

I flipped to the last few entries and found what I was looking for. "July twenty-seventh," I read aloud. "Eight forty-five a.m. Staff meeting with Peppercorn Pub. Should've done better."

"Yep," he said, slow and languid.

"July twenty-third," I went on. "Ten a.m. Intervention for Harris. Should've paid better attention."

He sighed. "It's true."

"July twentieth. Two p.m. Salary negotiation with New York Giants. Should've figured out what the guy wanted."

"That would've been a big help."

I closed the notepad. "You know, Chase," I said. "Earlier this summer you told me that if you could get those entries down to one line, you would be doing something right. Do these sound like the words of somebody doing something right?"

His eyelids eased open, and he looked sideways at me. "Go on," he said, without any inflection.

"You've been getting really involved with Nadine over the past week or so. More involved than just emailing and phone calling—you've made plans around her. And your work has been suffering. Did this intervention guy pay you?"

He shook his head. His eyebrows were tilted downward, and his eyes seemed to set themselves deeper.

"So that's two guys who didn't pay you and a third who said he shouldn't. You're screwing up and you aren't even aware of it. Are you?"

The train slowed down, stopped. People got off, climbed on. I wondered if Chase would get off too, but he didn't. Maybe because I still had his notepad. I resolved right then to keep it out of his hands for as long as I could.

Chase didn't say anything during the stop, which answered my question pretty well. When we started rolling again, I continued. "You know," I said, "nobody was looking at you during our walk to the station. You were tripping the light fantastic, and nobody turned a hair. Now I know you see it when people react to you and your energy as you go by them. So you must know on some level that they're not reacting now. I'm not reacting, and I'm a friend of yours who's sitting right next to you."

"They still react to me," he said. It was the first time I ever heard him sound defensive. "When Nadine and I went out, they were reacting to me everywhere," he said, snapping his fingers left and right for emphasis.

"Because you were reacting to Nadine," I said. "You were feeding off her energy, and people fed off that. But when you're alone—"

"You think I'm hoarding my joy," he said, low and strident. "Is that it?"

"No. I think the joy you're feeling is all selfish joy. It's useless to share it because it's one hundred percent about you and how you're feeling. Other people may try to give you some of their joy, but you're not about to take it—you're too caught up in your own. This morning, people were happy to see you, and you didn't have a clue. For someone who calls himself a joy facilitator, you're not doing a very good job of facilitating it."

Another stop, another shift of passengers starting their ride, another shift finishing theirs. Chase sat like a stone throughout.

"It's interesting," I said as we started moving again. "Your self-involvement is giving you that layer of protection you need to ride the subway. It's your shield. Nothing comes out and nothing comes in. Which may be fine for the subway, but it's no way to go through life, and for you especially, it's no way to do your job."

He started shaking his head. "This is just a slump," he said. "That's all it is. A slump. I'll figure out what's wrong and I'll fix it."

"Or," I said, "someone will figure it out for you. And they'll tell you about it while you're riding the subway."

He looked over at me, wounded. In his big, wide face I thought I could see the boy he once was, shut out from his parents' house parties, staring down at them from the upstairs landing.

"I thought you'd be happy for me," he said.

Part of me wanted to tell him I was, slap him on the back, and leave all this behind. But not the honest part of me. That part still had a few things to say.

"In the abstract, yes. I'm glad you make each other happy, and I think you're way better for her than Tedd is. But if it's going to turn you into some kind of an apathetic narcissist who can't do his job anymore, then no, I don't see any reason to celebrate."

That was the one time all summer I saw Chase Becker get angry, and it's a sight I never want to see again. I could sense the molecules in his body shaking as a dark force gathered within him. His muscles constricted, stretching his neck and turning his hands into fists. His body seemed to inflate several sizes. His face got red and twisted, like a peeled tomato skin. The hint of cinnamon around him seemed sharper, designed to burn. And I know that what I saw must have been his pupils dilating, but so help me, just before his hazel eyes snapped shut, they looked like they had turned black.

He shifted toward me, and I raised my hands to defend myself, knowing they'd be useless. But then he blew out a lungful of air, hard, and this forced leak pushed him back into his seat. He blew out a couple more times, and in a moment, the redness in his face was the only sign of what he'd been not ten seconds before. Then he breathed more slowly, long deep breaths, never opening his eyes. I sat back and felt lucky indeed.

We didn't say anything until the conductor announced that we were approaching the Broadway-Nassau stop, the last stop before leaving Manhattan for Brooklyn. When the intercom clicked off, I finally spoke. "Look, Chase, maybe we ought to forget about the lesson for tonight. Dinner too. I don't think either one of us is in the right mood."

All he did was nod. The train whined to a stop and the doors screeched open.

"Here's your notepad," I said, offering it to him.

He put out his hand; I placed it there and he tucked it away. Never even opened his eyes.

"Chase, this is the last—"

He held up his hand; he knew.

The passengers finished loading and unloading themselves; the high-low chime sounded, and the doors slid shut. We were on our way to Brooklyn. I shifted around a little, trying not to bump the woman next to me. I hated jarring people out of their own worlds.

"Uhh ..." he began.

I looked over at Chase. "Mmm?"

"May ..."

"May? Maylene? What about her?"

"Zee-hing grace ..." His voice doubled in volume, rose above our heads. "How sweet ... the-uh sound." His eyes were still closed. His head eased back until he faced the ceiling. "Tha-hat saved." His brow was smooth, the skin on his face soft. "A-uh wretch." His voice was bigger now, effortless, rolling through the car, floating up to meet the notes to the words, "Li-hike meee."

I took a cautious look around. Some people were making a point of not looking at him, or of looking away. Others were giving him the old hairy eyeball. The lady sitting next to Chase was looking at him like she was wondering if he were contaminated. But I did spot one or two who were watching him with interest. Maybe even a little pleasure.

"I-I wah-unce wah-uzz lost," he sang, "but now-how a-am found." A long, golden smile opened across his face, revealing his glue-white teeth. "Wah-uzz blind," he sang, opening his eyes on us all at last, "bu-ut now. I see."

He began tapping out a beat on the dirty tile floor. Not a basic thing where the toes of one foot go up and down, but something more complicated. He used his heels to make a percolating rhythm track, and he'd stomp down with his toes on top of that, or with it, or around it. Over this backing, he sang the opening verse again, a little faster now, a little more of a pulse, stopping and starting the beats for emphasis. And for the first time all day, I felt the buzzing warmth of good feelings emanating from Chase, just as powerful as they'd ever been.

I'm not going to try and tell you that every person in the car was singing along with him by the end of the ride—this is New York City we're talking about, after all, and some of these riders had spent half a century or more building their shields and toughening their hides. This much I will say: there were people up and down the length of the car who Chase affected. Men nodded along to the beat, patting their knees. Women hummed and swayed, deep within the song and the memories it brought. Young people stopped texting to watch. Old people moved down the car to get closer to the source. A couple of people were wiping tears from their eyes, trying to swallow lumps that wouldn't stay down. One woman was holding up her phone and filming him with it, something I'd never seen before. And yes, singers did start to join in. Some whispered, some belted. Their voices were clear and cragged, simple and strong. Chase led them into more verses, calling out opening lines—"T'was grace that taught!" "The Lord has promised!" "Through many dangers!"—without ever losing track of the beat. His eyes were shining, his face radiant, his voice triumphant. "That's it!" he shouted. "One more time!"

When we reached the station halfway through a final reprise of the opening verse, the joy in that car was set to blow the roof off. If someone had come through just then to ask for money, he would've walked out with tens and twenties. Chase stomped out a shave-and-a-haircut beat to wrap it all up, and as the train doors opened and we got up to go, almost everyone in the car applauded, even the people who hadn't been singing or tapping along. He ducked his head and waved, if you can call raising your hand to hip level a wave, and we joined the crowd of people filing out. A couple of them murmured praise to Chase, and one even reached out and touched the back of his wrinkled denim shirt, just to touch it. I trailed alongside, feeling like a reporter walking next to a rock star—complete access, zero adulation.

As the crowd thinned out, the subway going back into Manhattan pulled in. Chase cocked an eyebrow at me. "So how about that?" he said.

"That was ..." I stopped. The doors on the uptown train thudded open, and he went to climb aboard.

"Hold it a second," I called after him. "Did you do that just for my benefit? Or for theirs?"

He didn't turn to respond until he was already on the train. One side of his smile was higher than the other, and his eyebrows went up a hair. The energy that had been rolling off him minutes ago, like the crowd of worshipful passengers, had dissipated into nothing.

"What matters is that I did it," he said. "I hope you and the dog have a nice walk. Take care." And the subway doors closed between us.

13.

Nadine and I finally touched base the next day. I emailed her to say it must have been tough trying to call me when she didn't even have my number, which I then provided. She wrote back with her own new number and a promise to call me that night, as there was much to talk about. She called while I was out walking Nido; I called back while I fed Tristan and Esau.

"Neds!"

"Nades! Love that caller ID. Is this a good time?"

"Oh, it's perfect. I mean, all I'd normally be doing now is watching a movie with you."

"No date?"

Her laugh was embarrassed, maybe a little scared. "We're taking the night off from each other tonight. Chase said we both had some thinking to do."

"I guess you do," I said, recapping the fish food. "Speaking of thinking, what are you thinking? I don't mean that in a 'what the hell are you thinking' way," I hastened to add.

"No, I know." A fast sigh. "Oh, boy. Chase is incredible, Ned. I've never met anyone like him in my life. He pays attention. You know? Sometimes I catch myself talking to him just so I can watch him listening to me. I mean, I love to hear him talk, too, but the first time he said, 'Tell me everything,' I just about melted right there.

It's the perfect thing to say to a girl, Neds, should the opportunity present itself."

"I oughta write this down," I said, only half joking.

"I think you'll remember it when you need to."

"Yeah. Anyway—never met anyone like him, huh?"

"Well, it's not just him; it's the way he affects me. Sometimes he'll say or do something, and it'll feel like something big, like a big piece of machinery just locked into place and fit me perfectly. And other times it feels like something big just unlocked. I feel like he's recalibrating me?" Her voice went up, uncertain if the sentiment was the right one. "Like I'm turning into a better person? I don't understand it, but I want to. It's scary in a way, but it's thrilling too. I think everyone should discover how much joy they can receive. And give."

I tried to say what was on my mind as delicately as I could. "No guilt, I hope."

She sighed, a slower one this time. "About Tedd, you mean."

"Yeah."

"Let me see if I can say this right. When Chase and I are together, we're the only two people in the world. Then he leaves me and number three shows up. But only in my thoughts. You know, he hasn't called or emailed me once since we had that fight? Why would somebody do that?"

"Maybe he's dead," I offered cheerily.

"Shut up, Ned, that isn't even funny."

Whoops.

"Look, I know he rubs you the wrong way, and I respect that. There's a lot of people who don't like a lot of his personality traits. But I've known him for a long time, and I've seen more sides of him than anybody outside his family. I know who he is, and I've loved him for who he is for years. That's all there is to it."

"Okay," I said. "All I'm saying is that just because someone's known you longer shouldn't give them the inside track."

"Oh, it doesn't," she assured me. "There are other factors in play here."

"So the jury's still out."

"Neds! God, no! The plaintiff is still making his case, if you're going to use that analogy. Now let's talk about you a little." Her voice changed from girl-gruff to slinky. "Planning something special with Alexa, I hear."

"Ah, yeah, this coming Saturday. It's supposed to rain, did you hear that?"

She wouldn't be thrown off the trail that easily. "You know, she likes you."

"Cool."

"I think she's going to fall in love with you if she's not more careful."

"*Is* she."

"Well, she might."

Instant backtrack. Nothing to gather up my hopes for. Ease up on the anticipation. Easy. Easy.

"Well, let's hope for a few more good times for both of us before I move back to the couch."

"Nothing but the best, Neds."

"You too, Nades."

I hung up with a strange sense of disquiet. I had never been more uncertain of my immediate future than I was that night. I didn't know what would happen with me and Alexa on Saturday, despite my assuring her that I'd be ready to talk. I didn't know whether Chase would continue his professional free fall, pulling Nadine down with him. I didn't know whether she would need to escape somewhere when Tedd came home. Things were about to come to a head, and all I could do about my case of nerves was release it.

Let it go, Ned. Nothing to gain by dwelling on it. Let it go.

Easy, Ned.

Easy.

PART THREE

*Lucy: I'm intrigued by this view you have on the purpose
of life, Charlie Brown .... You say we're put here
on Earth to make others happy?
Charlie Brown: That's right!
Lucy: ... What are the others put here for?*

–*Peanuts* by Charles Schulz, 8.19.1961

1.

7/28/05, 11:51 PM
To: nalderman@peppercornpub.com
From: eslong@loftoncanova.com
Subject: (No Subject)

I'm writing to ensure that I was justified in my decision to leave everything in your care.

Tedd.

7/29/05, 9:06 AM
To: eslong@loftoncanova.com
From: nalderman@peppercornpub.com
Subject: Re: (No Subject)

Tedd – Everything is still standing. This includes the house, the relationship, and the dog. It would also include the fish if they had legs. See you on the seventh – Ned

7/29/05, 9:21 AM
To: nalderman@peppercornpub.com
From: nadine@cellulab.com
Subject: Hey, 2nd Cuz!

Dear Neds,

Just wanted to apologize for kind of snapping at you on the phone yesterday. I'm still sorting a lot of things out and I didn't mean to make you feel bad (hope I didn't). It's always good to talk with you—it really means a lot to have someone I can explain myself to who won't turn around and judge me for it. So thanks for being here for me, scratch Nido behind the ears for me (he loves it, or do you already know this?), and good luck with Alexa tomorrow! (Wonder if she'll leave out all the juicy details the next time she calls me?)

Have a great one –
Nades

PS – No word from Tedd still—how about you?

7/29/05, 9:40 AM
To: nadine@cellulab.com
From: nalderman@peppercornpub.com
Subject: Re: Hey, 2nd Cuz!

Nades – I judged you a long, long time ago, and you're a good person. And Tedd sent me a one-sentence email asking how things were. So he's not dead! Hooray! – Neds

7/29/05, 10:10 AM
To: nalderman@peppercornpub.com
From: chase@joyfacilitator.com
Subject: Courage

I've been thinking a lot about what you said to me on the subway the other day. It couldn't have been easy for you, and I applaud and admire you for taking the steps to reveal an unpleasant truth to me. And it is the truth. I intend to start work on this right away. Tonight, in fact—I have a job at a wedding rehearsal dinner. Should be a good place to get back on track with; after all, it's the day before the happiest day of their life, right? Anyway, thank you for the much-needed wake-up call. Take care.

Best, Chase

7/29/05, 10:17 AM
To: chase@joyfacilitator.com
From: nalderman@peppercornpub.com
Subject: Re: Courage

Chase – You're pretty courageous yourself to listen to what I had to say and not just brush it off. Don't forget—recognizing that you have a problem is the first step to solving it. Best of luck tonight – Ned

7/29/05, 11:51 AM
To: nalderman@peppercornpub.com
From: cjbrande@loftoncanova.com
Subject: Sorry, I'm busy Saturday

Not that you wanted to do anything with me tomorrow, but if you did, forget it. I'm going to be too busy entertaining the lady in my life. You remember the girl I got together with last week? Well, I called her last night, and she couldn't resist the fabled Brandenburg charm. I don't know if this'll count as our first date or our fourth or fifth. Shouldn't make a difference—I'll do some joy facilitating, pay some compliments, use some good words, and she'll fall for me like a ton of shits. Wish me luck and wish her continued bad judgment. – Siege

PS – Can you say "your eyes are like limpid pools" if their eyes are brown?

7/29/05, 1:20 PM
To: cjbrande@loftoncanova.com
From: nalderman@peppercornpub.com
Subject: Re: Sorry, I'm busy Saturday

Siege – I'm busy Saturday myself, it just so happens—Alexa's coming over to Tedd's. I think we might be having a Big Talk, but there's a chance there may be more. Rather than jinx it, I'll just tell you about it after the fact. As for you, congrats on making the move to see her again. Why not, after all? And to answer your question, "limpid" is another word for "untroubled." Not too many brown pools out there, though. "Your eyes are like limpid pools of syrup in a waffle square" might be a little too strange to count as a compliment. Anyway, good luck – Ned

7/29/05, 3:32 PM
To: nalderman@peppercornpub.com
From: mwest@peppercornpub.com
Subject: Little Miss Mafia

Hey, Ned, it's Maylene. Can I ask a favor? I really don't want to read the *Little Miss Mafia* manuscript this weekend. Not that I have anything else to do; it's just not the sort of book I think I'd enjoy. Lee keeps telling me to just give it a chance, but if I feel this negatively about it going in, I don't think I can be a fair reader. If you'd be able to do it for me, I would really appreciate it. If you can't, that's okay too, but I'm hoping you can. If you can, you could come pick it up at my apartment after work; I'm only a couple blocks away. Let me know?

Sincerely,
Maylene

7/29/05, 3:53 PM
To: mwest@peppercornpub.com
From: nalderman@peppercornpub.com
Subject: Re: Little Miss Mafia

Maylene – I'm sorry, but I've already got long-standing plans for this weekend. I'm doubly sorry it was my proposal that wound up sticking you with this. I owe you one, okay? – Ned

7/29/05, 4:41 PM
To: nalderman@peppercornpub.com
From: alpinegal@gmail.com
Subject: Want you to know

One of my friends' friends is having a bachelorette party tomorrow, one with male exotic dancers, and I was invited. I turned it down in order to spend a quiet evening with you.

Flattered? You should be.

Alexa …

7/29/05, 4:53 PM
To: alpinegal@gmail.com
From: nalderman@peppercornpub.com
Subject: Re: Want you to know

Alexa – Flattered? I'm honored. And I'm looking forward to tomorrow night. By the way, I like how you sign off with an ellipsis now. It holds promise for good things yet to come. See you soon – Ned …

2.

Saturday started off sunny, but by noon, some serious clouds had rolled in and the wind was picking up. I was glad not to have to be outdoors; I was locked into cleaning mode again. Everything that got mopped, scrubbed, vacuumed, dusted, lint-rolled, and bleach-bombed last week got it again, as did a lot of other things I'd missed. I cleaned the glass on the portraits. I polished the banisters. I took cushions off their chairs to beat the dust out of them, finding a wishing well's worth of loose change underneath. (Of course I kept it—my momma didn't raise no fool.) I cleaned the refrigerator top to bottom, getting rid of all the food that had passed its expiration date—the green chicken and furry rice came so close to making me throw up. I got rid of the shower curtain too, replacing it with a navy blue one I'd picked up the night before at Choose the Right Bath. I opened all the windows; the wind did a great job shaking out the curtains for me. I even cleaned up Nido's dog bed. He jumped and ran around and did everything he could (short of barking, which he still hadn't done) to take me away from the job, but once I turned on the vacuum cleaner, he fled. It was a revelation to see that the bed's original color was cocoa brown.

Once I finished, I took Nido out for his evening walk. He wasn't quite his usual frenzied self; I suspected that running around all day may have taken a little of the zip out of him. Or maybe he was stalling so I could get caught in the rain. It didn't work; the rain didn't start to fall until just after we got back to the house. By the time I got the leash unhooked and had filled the (nice clean) dog dish, it was coming down hard. Now it was my turn to race around the house, shutting all the windows I'd left open. Then it was finally time for me to get cleaned up, shaved, and primped. My clothes were all new, purchased the night before at a Gap store, right after I got the shower curtain. By the time six thirty rolled around, neither the house nor I could have looked any better.

Alexa showed up a few minutes after that. She was quite wet, even though she'd only just come from the taxi, and she was towing a giant suitcase behind her, more than half as big again as she was. "Where can I leave my overnight bag?" she asked, grinning.

Before I could acknowledge the no-doubt-hilarious joke at my expense, Nido came bounding out to leap all around her. "Oh," I said, "you'll want to put that in the guest room."

"That's a little presumptuous of you."

But once I reminded her of what Nido could do to shoes and stuffed animals, she saw the wisdom in my suggestion.

* * *

"Tell me something," Alexa said.

She was sitting next to me on the couch, in blue jeans and a light green cashmere sweater; the rain had turned her hair a darker blonde, and tendrils of it framed her face. Exactly one tendril hung in front of her eye, swaying incrementally, too pretty to be nudged aside. We both had gin and tonics in our hands; I had more left in my glass than she did.

"I could tell you lots of things," I said. "Narrow it down a little."

"All right," she said, smiling. "If you weren't related to Nadine, who would you say is a better catch—her or Chase?"

"Oh," I said, putting my glass down, "that's a tough one."

She cocked her head. "You think?"

"You don't?"

"No, of course not. Nadine's such a better catch."

"Well, hold on," I said. "I'm not saying I disagree, but why? Chase is smart, he's good-looking, he makes good money, he pays attention—you know all this."

"Yeah, but …" She squinted and pursed her lips. "Nadine's real. I like Chase, but I sometimes think he's just a construct. I mean, think about it—what's something you remember him saying or doing that wasn't designed to get some kind of positive reaction?"

I squirmed a little, trying to get comfortable. I summoned up all the Chase moments I could, and there were plenty, but these moments that had once seemed inspired now came across to me as artificial. The subway singing, the date with Nadine, the things he did on my first day at Peppercorn, even the way he shut down Tedd at the benefit dinner—all of them put into action by the push of a mental button, the pull of a mental lever. My training had given me too good a look at the man behind the curtain—no, not that so much as the knowledge that there was in fact a curtain, and Chase was in fact the man behind it.

I tried to think of Chase the human being, everything I truly knew about him, and I discovered how little there was to come to mind. Only the idea of Chase, or the reaction of people to Chase. Chase himself? Smoke. Fog. Wind. Easy to be aware of, but impossible to grasp, even as it sinks into your clothes.

"It's tough, isn't it?" said Alexa, moving her rogue lock back into place. "I mean, I'm glad he's one of the good guys, but I don't like how he's always on the job. When I talk to someone, I want to know he sees me as a person, not some kind of lab rat."

"He doesn't do that," I said, shaking my head. "He doesn't see Nadine as a lab rat."

"I hope you're right," she said, sipping her gin and tonic.

A variant on my discussion closer. I wouldn't let it end this one. "Hope," I said. "That's the key, you know."

Her eyes narrowed. "Excuse me?"

"I'll grant you all the points you've made," I said. "But I think Chase has something extra in him that makes him more man than machine, and I think that something is hope. He still has wishes and dreams. He still looks for better—not for himself, but because he wants there to be better. And I think that his hope is reason enough to believe in him. The real him."

She thought about this, rotating her glass back and forth in her palms. "You truly believe that," she said, less a question than a statement, a testing of the waters.

"Alexa," I said, "he wouldn't be building this relationship with Nadine if he didn't have hope."

Rain rattled against the window, blown there by one heavy gust of wind. Alexa looked at the window, then back at me. "Okay, then," she said, and she raised her near-empty glass. "Give it up for hope."

"To hope," I said, touching mine to hers. "May it strike us all one day."

***

One of the interesting things I'd discovered about Tedd in the past week was that he wasn't just a jazz aficionado; he was closer to a jazz fanatic, with all sorts of literature and hundreds of CDs on the subject. Having a girlfriend like Nadine meant he also had a decent collection of jazz-themed movies. There were a number of documentaries (*Jazz on a Summer's Day, Let's Get Lost, A Great Day in Harlem*) and a few movies where jazz is one of the picture's key brushstrokes (*Bird, The Man with the Golden Arm, Round Midnight*). I left it up to Alexa, and she picked *Sweet and Lowdown*, one of the better Woody Allen movies from the last half of his career. We silenced our cell phones, set out our Chinese, and pressed play.

"If he weren't such a good guitarist," said Alexa, pointing at Sean Penn's character with her forkful of beef with satay sauce, "there'd be nothing whatsoever to love about this guy."

I swallowed my moo shu pork. "Do you think that happens a lot?" I asked. "That people fall in love with people for their skills and talents, and they ignore their personalities?"

"Oh, all the time. Think of Nadine and Tedd. Or me and you." She smiled, very teasing.

"I love you too, Duchess," I said. Her quizzical look prompted a hasty explanation, so she would know I was just teasing too.

After the movie, I went through Tedd's jazz collection and picked out John Coltrane's album with Johnny Hartman. I was tempted to fiddle with the stereo levels a little, but I figured Tedd would realize I'd done some tampering within about four seconds, and that wouldn't be good. Besides, he did indeed already have them at the ideal setting; the two artists sounded first-rate as they worked their magic, and the low, warm static of the rain falling outside accompanied them beautifully.

"This is perfect," said Alexa, putting her dessert spoon down. "Dinner and a movie. Strawberries and sorbet. Good music. You know, you might be the first guy who didn't do everything he could to keep his energy as high as mine."

"I always knew you had a quiet side." (Universal truths can sound like hard-won pearls of wisdom.)

"Well, you're the first."

"The second, after you." (Recognize them for what they know about themselves.)

"Well, you might as well be the first." She moved closer to me by the length of a couch cushion. "What tipped you off?" she asked me.

I'd been thinking this over since Tuesday night, thinking over Alexa, caring for her in the back of my mind. I knew it would help me to tell her tonight. Outside, a faint flash of distant lightning, and the soft rumble of thunder making its way down the sky's alleys.

"I've thought about you a lot since we met, Alexa," I said. "I can honestly say I've never known anyone quite like you. But it wasn't your differences that made me stop and notice you. It was the idea that the two of us could have similarities as well. Not in the stuff we liked, so much as the kind of people we were. I thought that if someone who's not gregarious is drawn to someone who is, maybe someone who is will be drawn to someone who isn't. You with me so far?"

She nodded. "Opposites attract, sure."

"Well, that and the strength we draw from being opposite. Like, I like having control over my environment. I get a sense of security from that. Which is a good part of why I spent the whole day cleaning this place. The more responsible I became for its presentation, the greater the comfort I gained and the more I could feel like I knew what I was doing when I talked with you tonight."

She seemed uncertain of what I was saying. I was losing her. "You didn't have to do that for me," she said.

"But I wanted to. I—"

"Ned." She moved over again, close enough that our legs nearly touched. "You know it's okay to be quiet," she said. "You know you don't have to justify anything. You know there's nothing wrong with letting things happen."

(Hold the space. Smile and eye contact. Stop trying. Let it all flow. Simplify. A peaceful mind generates power. Analysis can ossify. Less from the head, more from the—)

She stood. "Shut up and dance with me, Ned."

I stood. "Lush Life" was playing; the wire whisks had just started brushing the drums. My hands reached out on their own accord, found her shoulder, her waist. The song doesn't have the cheeriest lyrics in the world, but the music makes perfect sense for taking someone into your arms. I didn't have to dance as well as Chase; I only needed to slowly turn as I swayed.

Alexa pressed her ear to my chest. I kept swaying, kept turning. All the men in the portraits on the wall regarded me with impatience. The boy in the derby was afraid for me. I mouthed something to them all—it could have been *what next*, it could have been *watch this*—and in moments her lips met mine, and we shared the sweet chill of sorbet.

The song ended. Miles away, lightning struck somewhere—the ocean, maybe—and the sound waves from the thunder took forever to reach us, barely registering above the rain's patter. Alexa pulled away. "I want you," she said. "Do you know how much I want you?"

"Tell me," I said. I flashed on Nadine's words. "Tell me everything."

She shook her head. "I," she said, "am going to *show* you everything." And she took me through the half-light, and as the storm played itself out, we merged together like two raindrops on the window.

3.

Okay, Ned, I thought to myself. *If you're not more than half in love with her now, you're never going to be.*

I was lying on my side, watching Alexa sleep next to me, her hair uncoiled across the pillow, her eyes shut, her face tranquil (limpid, in fact). One of her breasts was exposed; the other, covered by the loose, thin folds of the sheet. I put my hand under the covers and sent it gliding just over her body, like I was playing a theremin; the sheet shifted down to reveal her other breast. They were equally lovely.

I propped my head up with my hand and watched the morning light spill across her chest, her skin growing warmer as it rose and fell with her breathing. All her kinetic energetic ways were banked deep inside her, leaving her quiet self in charge. Her mouth was closed, her nostrils flaring ever so slightly with each deep breath. Her cheeks had such a sweet soft curve to them; if I could have found a way to touch them without disturbing her, I would have done it. She was untroubled and so alive, a long tongue of flame at rest. I lay there, memorizing every last detail—the two moles on her clavicle, the freckle just under her lower lip—and I awaited the inevitable.

Finally, it came: Nido scratching at the door, wanting to walk. The final moments ran out. She blinked her eyes once, then closed them tight, squeezing out the last bits of sleep like a sponge. She took a deep loud breath and opened her eyes for good, startling dashes of blue that completed her portrait, a perfect finishing touch.

"Hi," she said, her voice matching her slow smile. She did that eyebrow thing, making no move to cover herself.

"Good morning," I said. "It's nice to see you."

"You too." She had a touch of hoarseness that would be gone by breakfast, I was sure.

Nido scratched again. He could wait.

Alexa turned on her side, her back to me, and arched a full-body stretch. Her arms extended out over her head; her heels bumped my shins. She made no apology. When she rolled back to face me, the covers had climbed to shoulder level.

"I have to say something," she said.

I nodded. I had to say it too. She was saying it first. She had more courage than I did.

"I really like being with you, Ned. Last night was one of my best nights with a guy ever, and I'm not just saying that. I think we connect on an emotional level, and I know now that we do on a physical one."

More scratching. I tossed an annoyed glance at the door, next to which one of my chewed-up shoes sat. I'd saved those shoes for Nido; he liked a little tug-of-warring action while I hooked him to his leash.

"But," said Alexa, bringing me back, "but it's not enough, Ned. I need someone on my level spiritually. And you're not. I'd know if you were, and you never have been. I know that sounds flaky and I don't care—it's important to me."

"It doesn't sound flaky," I said. My voice was quiet and encouraging, but big as well, somehow, bigger than I ever knew I could make it. I knew what she meant. She was talking about the other half in love that I had never felt.

"I'm sorry," she said. "I thought I should tell you now before you start losing your heart to me. It's happened before, and I hate to see it. So I hope you weren't thinking one thing all this time I was thinking the other."

Her brow was knitted tight, so different from how it had been just minutes before.

I pressed my palm against it, to soothe the anxious ripples. "It's okay," I said. "I understand."

"You do?"

"I do."

"Really?" Her voice was a disbelieving squeak.

"Yeah," I said. "Maybe we can't be a couple, but we can still be an us. I don't see the problem with that."

Relief swept across her face, and I kissed the curve in her cheek as it relaxed. She kissed my cheek, a nervous giggle breaking loose the seal between her lips and my skin. I brought my right hand to the back of her neck and let it play down the length of her spine. "Thank God for the physical connection," I said, as it kept on playing.

Her laugh was near breathless, her kisses growing hungry. "Thank God," she repeated.

Nido scratched away. He scratched until we couldn't hear him anymore. Eventually he stopped scratching.

***

When Nido and I finally did get outside, we barely made it to the sidewalk before he was squatting, giving me a reproachful stare. "My bad," I told him, taking out a bag that had once held a loaf of rye bread. To make up for it, I took us a couple blocks farther than we usually went, allowing him to zing around and sniff and pee on a whole new set of trees and hydrants. By the time we got back to the house, I think we were square again.

Alexa was waiting for me. She had showered and dressed, and her expression was grave. "I think you better check your messages," she said, handing me my cell phone. "I need to call a cab."

I opened my mouth to ask her what was going on, but she had already turned away, her phone up to her ear, listening hard, shutting me out. I turned to my own phone, hitting all the necessary buttons to access my voice mail. "One new message," I told Alexa, but she paid me no mind.

I heard one breath, which kept catching on itself as it descended. "Ned, this is Chase." Another raggedy breath. "It's Saturday night, I think it's about a quarter to ten. Yeah, quarter to ten." Five second pause. "I have to say, you were right. I can't do my job if I'm happy.

It went horrible. Horrible. So I just now got back from telling your cousin I can never see her again."

Another pause. Alexa, to my right, was holding one of Tedd's *Wired* magazines, reading the address on it to the dispatcher at the other end.

"Second cousin," said Chase. "Sorry. It's the only thing to do. But it hurts. And I'm dry. And you gave me good advice before. So call me when you get this. No, better—come over when you get this." He gave me the address, an apartment in the East Sixties. "I'll be here," he said, his voice bland and crumpled, an old piece of corrugated cardboard. "I'm not going anywhere."

END OF MESSAGE. TO HEAR THIS MESSAGE AGAIN—

I hung up and looked at Alexa, who was waiting for me. "That was Chase," I said.

"Chase? Not Nadine?"

"Is that who called you?"

"Yeah." She became all business. "She must want to talk to me first. There's a cab coming to get me in a few minutes. I'm going right to her place."

"Chase asked me over to his."

"Okay, you go see him and I'll go see her. We'll hear them out. Call me tonight and we'll go over what they said."

"I'm going to call her too."

"Oh, do, do. But don't come over—this could be an all-day girl thing."

"Okay. But we should both go over tomorrow. We'll go together, after I get out of work."

"Great. We'll coordinate all that when you call tonight. Okay, I gotta get my shit together."

"I'll wait at the curb with you."

"No, you go get cleaned up, get right over there."

"Okay. Give her my love."

"I will. Bye."

"Bye."

We hurried a kiss and she headed for the door while I went for the bathroom. The mirror was still fogged up, with the letters "XOXO" written in the steam. A bead of moisture rolled down from the second X. I looked at the letters as I undressed and thought how professionally Alexa and I had just behaved, how swift we were in coordinating our plans, how brief but sincere our affection was as we parted. If somebody had been watching, they might have thought we'd been married for years. That's how well we understood each other.

Nido was waiting as I emerged, the leash still attached to his collar. I unhooked it, gave him his breakfast, and went to throw on some clothes.

4.

"The bride had three fathers," Chase said.

He sat in the corner and drank from the carton of orange juice I'd bought at the corner bodega. The box of crackers and the aerosol cheese I'd also picked up remained in the bag, untouched. The only light in the room was whatever light managed to sneak in the two small windows. It landed on Chase slumped in a recliner, wearing red gym shorts and a white T-shirt, freshly stained with orange juice. One eye had a dark smudged circle under it, from lack of sleep. The other had a darker circle, with tinges of lavender, from being punched. The eyes themselves, the color of crispy, dried-up moss, were muddled and spent. There wasn't a trace of cinnamon in the air. Everything I knew about Chase Becker was gone.

"One was the birth father," he said in a gray monotone. "One raised her from age two to about nine. And one was there from eleven on. They were all at the dinner last night. And they all wanted to be the one to walk her down the aisle."

"She hadn't decided yet?" I asked, leaning against the wall by the door.

"No, she had. She went with dad number two because he had formed her the most. Dad number one didn't like that—he said if it weren't for him, she wouldn't exist. Dad number three thought he deserved the honor because he had steered her through adolescence to adulthood, and he was the reigning dad still." Another swig of orange juice. "That's how he put it—'the reigning dad.'"

"Did you know any of this coming in?"

"Yeah, the bridegroom gave me the whole story when I took the job. So I had my goal right from the start: keep the peace and talk about the bride so much that they came to realize it's all about her and it's not about them."

I shifted to my other foot. "That's a good goal."

"Mmm. Too bad I didn't reach it." He waggled the carton; judging by the pitch of the splashing sounds, he had half-emptied it. "They sat me next to the birth dad, I guess because he needed the most help. I gave him my attention and he liked that, and for a while everything was okay. Then he asked me if I didn't think the bride-to-be was an absolute honey. I said she was a beautiful bride. He said that was all genetics, and where did I think she got those great genes. He must have liked that question, because he asked it a couple more times, a little bit louder."

"Oh, boy," I muttered, touching my forehead and closing my eyes.

"The other two dads took the bait. They said things like, let's see … 'just accept it,' 'we should flip a coin,' 'I got something else to flip,' 'rich prick,' 'sperm donor.' I think it was after 'sperm donor' that the three of them stood up and started to converge. I got in somebody's way, and the next thing I know I've got a bag of ice on my head, another one on my eye, and a big grease stain on my blazer from landing on a plateful of butter pats." He made a slashing movement with his hand. "End of dinner."

It was hard to know what to say after that. I decided to be gauche. "I'm guessing you didn't get paid."

He pulled the carton away from his lips with a smack. "I didn't want to be," he said. "Believe me. But the bridegroom pointed out that nobody in either family got hurt—only me. After they saw they'd knocked me out cold, that was the end of it. I think the bridegroom thought a fight of some kind was inevitable, and he felt bad that I'd used my face to stop it." He pressed the bottom part of the carton against his bruised eye and held it there. "He was a good guy," he said. "I hope the marriage lasts."

I gave him a minute to rest, helping myself to the cheese and crackers. He watched me with one unblinking eye as I chewed and looked around. The apartment's décor was a lot sparser than I would have expected it to be. The walls had recessed shelves crammed with books, many of which I recognized from my own reading. But there was no artwork on the walls—no paintings, no posters, not even a calendar. And aside from the chair Chase was sitting in and the floor lamp watching over it, there wasn't a stick of furniture in sight. He didn't have a dining table, let alone a coffee table. He didn't have another chair, let alone a sofa. The bare wood floor had no rugs or carpets. This, I thought, was not an apartment designed to be shared with people. But it wasn't grim in there; the walls were white, the floors were swept, and the kitchen just around the corner was well-maintained. It was much more a lair than a cell. Again, though, it was a lair for one.

"Then what?" I asked, spritzing a dollop of cheese on my finger.

"Then I spent Saturday in this chair. I thought about how my work has been suffering, to the point that I set out to do better and ended up doing worse. I thought about how I couldn't focus anymore, how I'd lost my sense of purpose, my sense of self. That's death for a joy facilitator, Ned. If you can't give people an undiluted shot of who you are, then you shouldn't be giving them anything."

"You can't give that pure a shot to everyone, though," I said.

"You have to."

"You shouldn't."

"Ned," said Chase. "Do you think I'd be so good at my job if I didn't?"

The answer was no, of course, but I wouldn't say it. Chase finished the carton of juice and dropped it on the floor, where it made a hollow, dead *ka-lunk-a* for an eternal moment. He dropped both his arms on the arms of the chair and breathed several deep sighs. He didn't want to go on, it was clear, but it was just as clear that he knew he had to.

"So you broke it off with Nadine," I said, helping him along.

"So I went to Nadine's," he said. I'm not entirely sure he'd heard me prompt him. "We'd planned to go to the movies. I had to tell her why we couldn't. What I was going to say, I couldn't say over the phone. It was raining pretty hard by the time I got there, and I stood around on the sidewalk for a while before I could climb the stairs. I probably looked like some kind of drowned animal when she opened the door. I told her what I had to tell her, told her what I had to do, and why. I told her I had gotten as close to her as I could and that I couldn't stay that close. 'Remember Icarus,' I said."

"And what did she say?"

He shook his head. "Not a word, Ned. She didn't say a thing. All she did was stand there. I mean, I'm sure her mind was tearing through any number of obstacle courses, but she didn't fight me, didn't disagree or anything. She didn't even fold her arms. So I just left. I walked back here, through that rain—a cab just would've been wrong. I got home, I called you, I sat down, and I've stayed sitting down pretty much ever since."

"Did you sleep?" I asked.

He made a phlegmy snort. "Too busy entertaining my thoughts. And none of them were leaving. It was like one of those parties I get stuck at sometimes, only nobody's paying me to stay."

Someone outside laid on their horn, followed by a fast volley of obscenities and the scream of tires.

"I've got a fundraiser to go to tomorrow night," Chase said. "This is the first time in years that I haven't been sure I can do my job. I need your help, Ned. I need you to walk me through the basics. Get me on my feet again."

I felt like Einstein had just asked me to give him a hand with his long division. Me help out Chase? What could I tell him that he didn't already know, that he hadn't field-tested again and again? Nothing, that's what.

"Chase," I said. "Maybe I could just talk about Nadine with you. Help you put those thoughts to bed. That might help."

He shook his head again. I didn't think he could move anything from the neck down at this point. The rest of him was smaller, sunken, even his hands. There was darkness inside him, feasting on the light, and the early results were unsettling. If this kept up, they could turn downright scary.

"I've been thinking about Nadine for the past twenty-four hours, Ned," he said. "What I need to do now is think of something else. Help me with that."

I bit my lip and tried to remember. "Okay," I said. "Step one. Smile. Let's see those pearly whites."

He bared his teeth at me.

"Maybe a Mona Lisa kind of thing would be better," I suggested. "Yeah, like that, that's good. Uh, use names, listen with your body— okay, let's playact a conversation. Pretend I'm one of the guys you'll be meeting at this fundraiser tomorrow. Okay, ready? Go."

He held up a limp dishrag of a hand and bobbed it up and down, two halfhearted karate chops. "Chase Becker," he sludged.

"Hi, Chase. I'm Pete Chambers." Pete was a guy I'd known in high school.

"Nice to meet you."

A pause the size of a gymnasium.

"Pete."

"You too."

"So what brings you here tonight … Pete?"

Not certain what this fundraiser was going to be for, I faked the best answer I could. "Oh, good cause, good food. You?"

"Much the same, much the same." He boosted himself up in his chair. Something inside him had begun stirring. "Any chance I get to give back to nature, I do. It's given me so much, you know?"

"Oh, me too. Do you ever go camping?"

"Oh, *absolutely*." There was a pinch of feeling in the way he said *ab*, the first I'd heard him use since my arrival. His smile had outgrown its Mona Lisa size, and there was a small spark in each eye. "Back when I was a kid," he said, his voice picking up speed. "Let me tell you, Pete, some of my best—"

That was when Chase's phone went off behind me. It marked the first time I'd ever heard Frank Sinatra's recording of "Come On, Get Happy" used as a ring tone.

"Oh, hold on," said Chase, pushing himself out of his chair. He went to the kitchen counter where the phone sat and picked it up. For a second he statued on me, staring down at the device, and then he turned and sent it my way, three-quarter underhand with a little zip to it. I caught it against my stomach. Frank got muffled as he sang to me.

"You get it," he said. "I can't answer that." His voice sounded waterlogged, like a campfire that had just been doused. I didn't have to look at the name on the display to know who it was.

"Hello?"

"Chase, this is Nadine."

"Hey, Nades."

"I wanted to—wait. Ned?"

"Yeah."

"How did I get you? I thought I was calling Chase—what the hell?"

At least she still sounded like herself. "This is Chase's phone," I said. "Chase is indisposed at the moment."

Suspicious. "Is he really?"

I looked over at him, his back to me, one hand on his hip, the other sunk deep into his hair. "I can't think of a better word," I told her. "Listen, how are you doing?"

"I'm fine. Really. Alexa's here and she's been great. She says you guys had quite a night too."

I was walking through the apartment as she spoke, leaving Chase alone in the kitchen, finding the bathroom. "Yeah, we did," I said, shutting the door behind me. "Listen, Nadine, promise me something, okay?"

"Sure, what?"

"Don't give up on Chase just yet."

She didn't say anything.

"I don't know everything he told you last night," I said, keeping my voice down. "But I know when people have a real connection. You guys have one, Nades, and you know it's a rare thing. You gotta protect it, keep it alive. That's all I'm asking. Just—just don't give up yet."

She made a little clicking noise. "You've been talking with Alexa, haven't you?"

"This is all coming from me," I said. "Why, did she say the same thing?"

"He sounded pretty definite when he—"

"Please, Nadine. Promise me."

She was quiet. I looked at my reflection in the mirror. I felt like I should have looked more different than I did, considering how much things had changed from two days ago. Outside, I heard music, some classical piano.

"There's a lot going on that you don't know, Ned," Nadine said.

"Negative stuff? Wait, he's not—"

"No no no, nothing like that. It's just … I've got a lot to think about these days."

"Okay, keep thinking. Don't stop. Don't give up on Chase."

She sighed. "The powers of persuasion. Look, just tell him I called and he can call me back if he wants. I'll talk to you later."

"'Kay, bye," I said, right before she hung up, so it would feel like the call had come to a natural conclusion.

I went back into the living room and looked around a little. I hadn't noticed the speakers posted on the support beams before; they were not only unobtrusive, their sound was amazingly pure. Or maybe the artist's playing was.

"Wireless technology," said Chase, coming out of another room. "You press play in the bedroom, and you can hear it all through the place."

"Who's this playing?"

"Glenn Gould. You like it?"

"I'm pretty ignorant about classical, but yeah."

He made an affirmative grunt and sat back down. He had moved with a little more vim than he had before our playacting—maybe he was encouraged to learn that he could still give and take. Or maybe he was glad Nadine would still call, even if he wasn't ready to answer.

"Nadine said for you to call back if you wanted."

"I don't." The consonants were hard, cutting to the bone. His eyebrows came down low over his eyes. Then, as I watched, they rose up and came apart, like a drawbridge. "I can't," he said, and now the consonants turned to fight the vowels, pulling them apart until they were ready to break. He swiped at his eyes with one hand.

"Chase," I said. "You can't give up—"

"Ned, don't take this the wrong way," said Chase, his voice a cement whisper. "Thank you for the juice, for the cheese and crackers, for role playing, and for answering the phone. It all helped, and I really do appreciate it. But I have to ask you to please get out."

No amount of couching could dull the impact of those last two words. In less than half a minute, and without another word from either one of us, I got out. I watched him watch me close the door, his face a mask of tension. I could almost see Glenn Gould's piano notes bouncing off him, unable to penetrate. Then the door was shut, and I got outside and walked away, fast, so I wouldn't hear Chase if he started to yell, or scream, or cry.

**

I had a new voice message on my phone from Siege: "Hey. Congratulate me. I'm two for two. Later." I didn't think that one needed immediate attention, so instead I called up Alexa. We talked for a couple hours, right through my walking Nido. I told her all about Chase, and she told me about Nadine. (I hesitate to say "all about" because I'm sure they discussed any number of things I'll never know.)

"Honestly, she wasn't as bad as I thought she'd be," Alexa said. "If she did feel anything, she put the feeling on hold. I'm starting to think that she's got less invested in this than any of the rest of us."

"Has she heard anything from Tedd yet?" I asked.

"Still no. She's called and emailed, and he hasn't answered once. As long as he keeps himself out of the picture, I think Chase has a chance."

"You think she still likes Chase?"

"She still 'feels' him, she says. Even when he was breaking off with her, she got that buzz off of him. You know that buzz."

"I know that buzz. Is that why she called him?"

"Ummm." She packed a lot of embarrassment into the one syllable. "Actually, I made a bet with her that Chase'd talk to her and Tedd wouldn't. But you'll like the stakes—whoever lost had to cook dinner for the three of us tomorrow at her place."

"Say, those are good stakes. Either way, I would've won."

"Uh-uh. Either way, you're washing the dishes."

5.

It started out as such a nice, fun evening.

I got permission from Jamie to get out of work a little early ("What, you think we can't hold the fort down without you? Ha! You know I'm kidding!") so I could feed the fish, take out the trash and recycling, and give Nido a good walk—better early than late, I figured. Then I phoned a cab to pick me up and bring me to Alexa's. We picked her up there, went to Nadine's, and Alexa, as prearranged, paid for the entire fare. (It must be nice to be rich.) In exchange, I got to lug three bags of groceries up four flights of stairs. It was a fair trade, and I'd gladly do it again. The handles made it a snap, anyway.

It was great seeing Nadine; neither of us could believe it had been over a week. She peppered us with lots of questions and practically ordered us to become boyfriend and girlfriend—"You guys look so good together, you're both awesome, and it would make me happy. You want to make me happy, don't you?" Both Alexa and I did our best to explain why we were content to remain at the friends-with-benefits level; it wasn't easy to avoid sounding ridiculous—neither one of us could say the word "spiritual" without harebrained or pompous tinges coming into play—but our insistence and sincerity did end up carrying the day.

Over paella, corn, and the inevitable pasta salad, Alexa and I took turns talking to Nadine about Chase. Alexa said that Nadine had had a glow to her last week that she'd never had before, like a beautiful stained-glass window that had just been cleaned for the first time in a hundred years. "You can't just let that go," she insisted. I took the angle of Chase being a better catch than Tedd—less staid, freer, more ideally suited to Nadine. "The way you fit together is an inspiration to me," I said. "You've got to know that."

"Guys," said Nadine, holding up her hands. "I'm not saying you're wrong. But I'm not the one who broke up with Chase. He broke up with me. And you can't even call it breaking up—we were never officially a couple."

"Of course you were!" I said, appalled.

"You gotta fight for him, honey," said Alexa, raising a go-get-'em fist. "Fight for your man!"

"My man is Tedd," Nadine reminded us. "Say what you will about him, he would never carry me up to the stratosphere and then drop me."

"That's because Tedd would never carry you up to the stratosphere in the first place," Alexa said. "He'd ridicule it and refuse to learn a thing about it."

"That's right," I said. "And if you tried to make him understand, you'd just make him want to stop talking to you for two weeks."

If I could have tied a string to those words and yanked them back down my throat, I would have. But it was too late; they were out there now, torturing the silence that had fallen across the table like a giant redwood. Alexa was glaring daggers at me, while Nadine's eyes had been stunned empty. She was like a soldier trying to comprehend that she'd been hit by friendly fire. Her pupils moved in millimeters—up, down, up. I stared into them, gestured, trying to express how bad I felt without having to resort to near-meaningless words.

The knock on the door made us all jump. Five knocks, loud ones, stinging hard against the wood. "I'll get that," I said, and I left the table before anyone could tell me I didn't have to. They traded murmurs as I went to the door, grasped the knob, and turned it.

There stood a bolt of lightning wearing a Chase Becker costume. Honestly, I can't think of a better way to put it; that night, at that moment, he was electricity personified.

"I need to talk to Nadine," he said.

His face was fierce with light; I could sense the dangerous current pounding beneath it. He wore a flawless black suit that didn't seem to belong to him. For that matter, neither did his body. Really, now— how do you dress a bolt of lightning?

"Chase," I said, taking two involuntary steps back. "We were just talking about you. How's your eye?"

"I need to talk to Nadine," he repeated, sparks flying from every T in the sentence.

I glanced over my shoulder. Nadine and Alexa had followed me and were a safe distance back. They both looked aware that they were approaching trouble.

"Think that's a good idea?" I asked, turning back.

"Yes," said Chase. Nothing else. Bolts of lightning do not elaborate.

"Shouldn't you be somewhere?" I asked. "Don't you have a fundraiser?"

"I canceled. They'll be fine without me. This was more important." His words came at me hard and fast as a jai alai ball. Then he turned his body to line up with Nadine's. "It's good to see you, Kay," he said.

"*Godfather*," she whispered, unable to hold back a smile.

He didn't offer her a smile of his own; instead, he just nodded. "May I come in?"

Alexa and I turned to Nadine. I don't know about Alexa, but I was struck by how tranquil Nadine's face had become. It was as though she was witnessing a vision, and the vision was telling her to come into the light, and she had accepted that that was what she had to do.

But then she said, "I have guests, Chase."

Alexa and I both sighed with relief.

"I need to see them off."

"See them off?" we echoed, as a surge of Chase power went through me. Of course it did—she'd just made him happy.

"We're not going anywhere!" said Alexa, reaching down to grab Nadine's hand.

"Right!" I said.

"You guys," said Nadine. "Why not? It's just Chase."

I don't think it occurred to us until that moment that Nadine might actually want to be alone with Chase. Either she couldn't see the danger we saw, or she thought she was safer than we did. As I looked at her calm posture and her relaxed expression—very sure of herself and what she knew—I started to have an inkling that maybe she was right. What Alexa and I were seeing and fearing was a stranger, someone we didn't recognize. But Nadine recognized him. She could see behind the magnesium brilliance, and what she found there was, as she said, just Chase.

"Why not?" she repeated, looking from me to Alexa.

"Because … because Ned has to do the dishes!" The vehemence with which she made this point was so absurdly out of place that I almost burst into laughter.

"I'll take care of the dishes," said Chase. He seemed unconcerned about putting his high-voltage hands in her dishwater. Apparently, he was willing to face electrocution for the chance to be alone with Nadine.

I had to think fast. I rifled through all the newly learned techniques in my mind and found the one that I thought might work. It had to work. *Please.*

"Chase," I said. He turned back to me, and I struggled to look into his eyes. "Quid pro quo," I said. "Meet me at Sweethaven tomorrow at seven, and I'll leave you guys alone tonight."

"Done."

"And I have the option to bring Siege," I added. Who knows—I might wind up needing an eyewitness.

"Done and done."

"All right. We'll be out of here in ten minutes."

He didn't seem to like that. His mouth twitched a little, and he brought his finger up to point it.

"We need ten minutes, Chase," Nadine said.

The finger went down, the mouth smoothed out. "Okay," he said. "I'll be back shortly. Thank you." He reached in, grabbed the top of the door, and pulled it shut in front of him.

I stood there, staring at the door, feeling the hair on the back of my neck return to its straggly coils. The room's tone went back to normal. The smell of paella resumed its drifting through the air. And Alexa was finally able to explode at Nadine and me. "What is the matter with you two?" she demanded. "You want to talk to this guy? Did you see him? He's crazy! And you—making deals he's never going to keep? Whatever happened to family taking care of family? What if she gets hurt?"

"He's not going to hurt me, Alexa," said Nadine. There was a special note of confidence and assurance in her voice; it was the sound of confidence being well-placed.

She knew she was safe with Chase and—perhaps more important tonight—safe from him. I don't know how she knew it, but I knew that she did. And now I did too. "It's okay, Alexa," I said. "She's going to be fine."

She didn't look like she believed us, but she also didn't look like she could beat us both in the same argument. "Next time I'm going to be more careful what I wish for," she said. She told Nadine she would call in an hour to say she'd left a spoon or something in the kitchen, "and you'd damn well better answer."

I told Nadine we should get together for a movie night on Thursday (she loved the idea) and begged her pardon for my faux pas at the table.

"You're fine," she told me and gave me a hug. "Thank you both for coming over," she said, hugging Alexa. "Take care."

* * *

Alexa was quite cross. All the way to her apartment, she kept trying to pick a fight. Her comments ranged from "I thought you would care what happens to her." all the way down to "You just didn't want to do the dishes."

I didn't respond to any of them. I was busy thinking about how much calmness I got from Nadine, how much surety. She never gave me this feeling before that first date with Chase, and now here it was coming off her in waves. Something had happened deep inside her in the past week and a half. Something had changed her enough that even a man leaving her was nothing to get worked up about, and neither was a man coming back.

My theory, developed over the subway ride home: Nadine had taken, or been given, a sense of how to tap into her own ability to facilitate joy. But instead, she chose to facilitate peace. Not world peace, nothing that grand, but just the influence of clear heads and placid hearts brought to bear, both for herself and those around her.

Like all theories, it was probably false. But it gave me a lot to dwell on as we rumbled toward Brooklyn. It made me wonder if Chase, even at his most electric, had any sense of what he was getting into. Better yet, it made me wonder what would go through Tedd's mind when he returned from the West Coast to find his girlfriend transformed. That brought a smile to my face that lasted all the way home.

6.

"So where is he?" asked Siege, looking around.

"He'll be here," I said, checking my watch.

I actually wasn't expecting Chase for a bit longer. I'd asked him to come to Sweethaven at seven; I'd invited Siege to join me there at six. I figured I could fill Siege in on me and Alexa, as well as hear him expound on his own romantic success.

"Her name is Lindsay and she's a peach," he said over his second beer. "Funny, nice, easy to get along with, and a sweet little can. Plus the fact that she gets a charge out of me. Don't know what she'll think of me once the novelty wears off, but until then, we're gonna have us some fun."

"And the joy facilitating still works?"

He held up his hands in amazement. "Dude, it's like I'm a whole other guy. I'm kicking ass at work and at play. I may have to take a closer look at this."

I still wasn't comfortable with Siege cherry-picking the whole concept and then using it like a faucet, turning it on and off, rather than making it an ongoing part of his life. But it wasn't going to go anywhere if I started harping on it now, so I just raised my glass and said, "More power to you."

"Yeah, cheers. Hey, catch up with me, you wuss." He pointed at my glass; I was still only halfway through my first beer.

I couldn't catch up just then—I had to tell him everything about the weekend with Alexa, do my best to explain what our relationship was. As that proved too hard for either one of us to grasp ("What are you talking about? Of course you're fuck buddies. Sorry, I'll be quiet."), I segued to the story of what had happened the night before, with Chase's fire and Nadine's flow.

"What happened?" he asked, genuine concern making a special guest appearance on his face. "Is she okay?"

"I got an email from Alexa this morning. She called Nadine, and Nadine said they'd talked and everything was fine."

"Meaning what, they're a couple now? They're going to try and get Tedd to buy a load of life insurance?"

"She wouldn't say."

"Who wouldn't say?"

"Alexa said Nadine wouldn't say," I clarified. "I'm hoping I can find out from Chase. Who is officially late," I added, checking my watch—7:05 p.m. "I hope he hurries—I still have to walk Nido."

"Hope all the stuffed animals are out of reach," said Siege. "Hate to see you go home and find a mess like that."

"A mess like what?" said Chase, pulling out a chair.

I think Siege and I both jumped. Speaking for myself, I hadn't seen, heard, or felt Chase come in. He was no longer a bolt of lightning; maybe now he was a painting of a bolt of lightning. There was still energy and power to him, but a much different kind, not lethal at all. If anything, he looked frazzled, a touch out of sorts. At any rate, he was not traveling the same road he'd been on some twenty-three hours ago.

"Chase, I'm glad you could make it," I said.

"I told you I would." He looked around the place as he sat down. "Not the busiest night," he said. This was true—I think the number of people may have reached the teens—but it wasn't like him to comment on it.

Siege put his hand out and imitated me, saying, "Siege, this is my friend Chase." Then he imitated Chase: "Uh yeah, we met, how's it going?"

"Yeah, hey," said Chase, shaking Siege's hand while barely looking at him.

"Hmph," said Siege. "Pleasure's all mine, apparently."

I got to the point quick. "Chase, how did last night go?"

"Last night? Yeah, we talked. She said a few things, I said a few things. You know."

"Uh, no," I said. "I can't say as I do." I wanted to try matching my energy level to his; what would have been impossible last night now seemed to be an attainable goal. "I'm just looking after the both of you, making sure—"

"Everything's fine," said Chase, either finishing my sentence or making a statement. He made an effort to lock in on me. It took an extra moment for the distraction to clear away so his eyes could meet mine. It was not his usual look; in fact, it reminded me a lot of the way Tedd first looked at me back in May. That visual pithing wasn't much fun then and it wasn't any better now, coming from one of the good guys.

"Hey, Chase," said Siege, and Chase released me from his sights and turned to fix on him. "Just want to say thank you," Siege went on. "Ned sent me your reading list, and I've gotten enough from it that I got a commendation at work and I met a girl. It's been great, and I just …"

He trailed off when he saw that Chase wasn't looking at him anymore. In fact, he was glaring full throttle at me. "You sent him the list?" he asked.

"Uh," I said. "Was I not supposed to?"

"That list was for you!" Chase said. He said it loud. The bartender, wiping down a glass, shot a glare at us. Chase didn't see it. "People like him don't understand how to use that list!" he said. "That list is—"

"People like *me*?"

Oh my God. Siege was using That Tone.

Back in college there'd be times when someone would make a hackle-raising statement of some sort, and Siege would look at them and you could almost hear him shifting into a more powerful gear. His speech became more deliberate, more forceful, and it also took on an oddly playful shade. *I am really going to enjoy teaching you this lesson*, was the underlying message of That Tone, and it was more dangerous to hear Siege speaking like this than it was to hear most people shouting.

One night Anton Percival, whose father had prepped with the president of the college, made the statement that elite schools were for elite Americans and that the common herd belonged at state universities, which would provide an education more suitable to their needs. Siege, who was fiercely proud of his lower-middle-class heritage, said, "Well, *there's* an interesting theory" in That Tone and went to work. Twenty excruciating minutes later, Anton was a self-confessed xenophobic segregationist with no grasp of history and an overrealiance on Big Daddy. Watching Siege turn that pompous clown into a worthless sinkhole was one of the high points of my junior year. I didn't know what he could do against a champion joy facilitator, even one who was off his game, but if That Tone was coming into play, I had to like his chances.

"People like *me*?" he repeated. "You trying to tell me I have to have a special mindset before I can bring out the sunshine?"

"You have to respect your source material," Chase parried. "It's not an aspirin you take to make you feel better; it's a way of life. And you're not going to better yourself if you don't recognize that." He said the words by rote, his delivery more about logic than feeling.

"So according to you, a guy can't make people happy if he's only applying a few lessons to a few points in his life."

"I'm saying you don't use those lessons for selfish purposes, is what I'm saying."

"Well, I got a question for you," said Siege. "You ever volunteered at a soup kitchen?"

Chase was not expecting that one. If he'd been standing, he would have stumbled backward a couple of steps. "That's not what I do," he said.

"Why not? I bet they could use some joy there."

"There's not enough time—"

"How about going to an old folks' home? Talk with someone there, brighten up their day. You ever do that?"

"Yes!" Chase said through gritted teeth, pointing at Siege as though his finger were a switchblade. "Yes, I have, thank you very much!"

"Somebody had to pay you good money to do it, though, didn't they?"

Whatever words Chase was going to say, Siege's knowing question shoved them back down his throat. There they burned, sending their angry heat into his eyes and face.

"Doing all these good deeds for money is a pretty selfish purpose," said Siege. "Don't you think?" He had a glint in his eye and the smile of a cobra.

"Look," said Chase, holding out his hands. "Let's just drop it, huh?"

"No, let's not," said Siege, pointing at me. "You're trying to get together with his cousin."

"Second cousin," I said, out of pure reflex.

"Yeah, get your facts straight," said Chase. There was a note of desperation in his voice. He could have started talking in a French accent and it wouldn't have been as out of place as that desperation.

Siege swatted the comment aside. "And in the process you've used your skills to manipulate her into a 'happy-happy-joy-joy' outcome. How's that for a selfish purpose?"

"Well, you're doing the same thing, only worse!"

"Oh," said Siege. "When I do it, it's selfish. When you do it, it's respecting the source material. I get it."

"You're not listening!" said Chase. The bartender shot another glare our way. If Chase had had anything to drink, they would have cut him off. "This isn't a lark for me—this is my job! This is my life you're talking about here! You don't know what my relationship to Nadine is. You have no idea what I've had to go through to get to this point in my life—"

His words were covered in thick coats of pain, making them bigger, harder to expel. He rose to his feet, fingertips pressing down into the table. Siege, who'd readied his next hard serve, wasn't expecting Chase to go physical; he tensed himself, ready for anything. All I could do was watch.

"Siege ..." Chase's voice was so desolate, so full of despair. "Don't ..."

Then he turned away so we couldn't see his face, and without another word, he walked out the door, smacking the top of the frame with both hands as he passed beneath it. "Hey!" the bartender barked, but Chase didn't turn around.

"Geez," said Siege, mortified. "I didn't think he was going to get all bent out of shape like that."

"It wasn't your fault, Siege," I said.

"No, I know, but that was the last thing I expected. I was trying to pay the guy a compliment and he insults me. I fire back and he goes to pieces. Dude, I'm starting to feel bad."

"Don't," I said. "I don't think that was the real Chase Becker."

Siege lowered his head, the better to cast a look of suspicion at me. "Care to tell me who it was?"

I took a drink. "Remember that time I had to study all night and Harry Tatelbaum gave me some uppers and you started fucking with me?"

He chuckled. "Yeah." Then he stopped chuckling. "Oh."

I'd never taken anything more potent than ibuprofen, so when Siege found out that I'd, as he put it, "scarfed a couple study buddies," he razzed me for such a long time that I finally went ballistic on him, shouting and swearing and even punching him a couple of times. It was so out of character for me that Siege spent my entire tirade giggling.

"I'm not saying he's on medication," I said. "Just that he's been acting like he is. Or at least he's not acting like he does when he isn't."

"I follow," said Siege. "Hey, how long before Tedd's in town again?"

I counted the days out on my fingers. "Wednesday, Thursday, Friday, Saturday, Sunday. Five days."

"And what happens then?"

That was the big question, one I couldn't begin to answer. "I don't know. Everything goes back to how it was, maybe?"

Siege finished his second beer. "You know," he said, "I never thought I'd even think this, let alone say it, but all of a sudden I'm really looking forward to Tedd coming home." He belched. "Life makes sense when he's around."

7.

The next morning, I called in sick. "I threw up the minute I got out of bed," I told Louise. "It kind of shimmied in the bowl there—"

"No need to draw me a picture, hon," she said. "Hope you feel better."

Of course, I hadn't actually thrown up, nor did I feel any urge to. This was just me taking what my mother used to call a sick-of-it day. Over the years, I'd found it beneficial to take my brain and squeeze out the tar and the mud of the responsibilities of life. Nothing organic in this world can't be improved with a good rinsing every now and then.

So, after I walked Nido and fed him and Tristan and Esau (all three still equally silent), I set myself up for a day of idle action. I put on a Charlie Christian CD, took out my composition notebook, and started studying Stephen Covey's paradigms and principles. When the CD ended, I took a break and had a nice long soak in the tub (something I'd never have done if I hadn't just taken the Clorox to it a few days earlier).

By the time I put on my shoes, shorts, and shirt, I could not have reached a clearer or more relaxed state of mind. It was a day for me to be at my best and brightest. The sun was shining, the birds were singing, and I felt like I could tap-dance the length of the Promenade.

Instead, I decided to drop in on Chase.

We hadn't parted on good terms the night before, and I wanted to remedy that. I also felt I was so full of positive energy, it would be a good thing to let some flow his way. Last of all, I thought that if he'd want anyone to help him pick up the pieces from any fallout with Nadine or Siege, it would be someone who was close to them both. And so it was that I stepped back out into the beautiful sunshine and made my way to the Upper East Side.

Sometimes I wonder how I'd feel about Chase today if I'd stuck with that dancing-down-the-Promenade idea.

***

I buzzed. "Chase?"

No answer.

I peered through the door's windows, but they revealed nothing beyond the lobby and the stairwell. I tapped the shale steps and thought. A floor or two above me, someone opened their own window, offering the breeze somewhere to go.

Inside, a noise.

I buzzed again. "Chase, are you home?"

Silence.

I turned the doorknob, expecting nothing, like when you turn the crank on a gumball machine without putting any money in, just on the off chance—

The door fell open.

I stared at the seven-foot-high, two-inch-wide pillar of dark space I'd just created. By rights it shouldn't have been there—someone should have locked this door, I should have given up, maybe left a message with my regards. But that's not what happened. Now I had this space. I'll never know how I got it, but I had it.

I pulled on the door, and the pillar of space grew thicker, wider, until there was room enough for me to pass through it. Down the hall, another door, not as strong and sturdy as the first; it didn't need to keep the weather out. I reached for it, sure that this one had to be locked, I couldn't be lucky twice—

Click.

Behind the click, a ripping sound, mixed with a rattle.

"Chase?" I said, and I pushed the door open.

The floor was covered in two layers of white. One layer was made up of goose down, and lots of it—if Nido had assaulted two dozen teddy bears stuffed with feathers instead of cotton, he might have reached this level of destruction. The other layer was notebook paper. Most of it was crumpled into balls the size of small apples, but there were also some paper airplanes perched atop the white wads, and a few sheets had been twisted together into foot-long origami javelins. Between the two layers, I couldn't see any of the living room floor.

It took a moment for me to gather up the wherewithal to move my eyes to the recliner where I knew Chase would be sitting. He was wearing a blue flannel bathrobe, a few feathers in his hair, a few traces of down lodged in his stubble, and a heavy-lidded expression that conveyed no feeling at all. Whatever energy he'd had last night, artificial or otherwise, had run its course and left him far behind. He was burned. His eyes were spent flashbulbs; his body, snapped filaments beneath powdered white glass.

There was a cardboard box on the left side of his chair, half-filled with notebooks. To his right, a few wire coils poked through torn notebook covers whose heavy creases and thick angles only partially concealed the papers beneath. There was a notebook in Chase's lap and a piece of paper in his hand. As I watched, he smacked his other hand into the notebook, making a *whock-crrr* sound as the white-lined paper contorted to fit against his flesh. He crumpled it further, turning it in his long slim fingers as he did. When he was done, he held up the wad between his thumb and two fingers and lobbed it at me, making the whistle and dull explosion sounds of an approaching bomb. It landed near my feet, kicking up a few light tufts that drifted an inch or two before settling.

"The door was open," I said.

Without looking directly at me, he bobbed his head forward and back a couple of times—it looked like he'd forgotten how to nod. He ripped a page from his notebook and sent it spinning onto the downy floor.

"Jesus Christ, Chase," I murmured, closing the door behind me. "You want to tell me what happened here?"

He raised his horribly dead eyes to meet mine. "No," he said. His voice was a charred husk, soaked in vinegar, stinging me even as it crumbled. "Figure it out for yourself," he said, and he tore out another page.

"At least tell me where all these feathers—"

"Few pillows."

I looked around the room. Over in the corner, under one of the windows, I saw the remains of the outsides of the pillows. Two were crumpled in the corner; a third dangled from the radiator, a skin hung up to dry.

I walked a little farther into the room, as gingerly as I could, unsteady on the wads of paper, feathers kicking up in front of my every step. I felt like an angel walking on clouds. I wasn't sure what I would do once I reached him, so I stopped well before that. I bent down, picked up one of the crumpled wads, and read what words I could without actually uncrumpling it.

12 midni
Never ask whe
polit
of dis-ease

"You know," said Chase, flipping another wad onto the floor, "at first I was going to try rereading all these. But it got depressing. I never wrote down any of the good things I did. Just the mistakes I made, the things I needed to work on. There's a decade's worth of failure in that box."

My knees felt weak, like they were made of shivering rubber. I needed to rest them, but sitting down in this scattershot mess of white was out of the question. So I approached him in his chair and hunkered down in front of his knees. Looking up at him as he pulled out page after page, too focused to stop and too weak to yank, I knew there would be no way for me to facilitate joy. Not here, not now. The best I could do would be to facilitate peace. I would have to get Chase to wash away the soot and ashes in his psyche, to ease open his mental doors and windows, to clear the way for his thoughts to stop stumbling and start flowing. And I could only do that by bringing him peace.

By bringing peace to a man who was in the middle of a personal and professional death spiral—unless he was closer to the end of it.

I had to try.

"Chase," I said. "You've got to listen to me."

He stopped crumpling the page he'd just torn out and dropped it on his lap. "I'm listening," he said, studying the smudges of blue and black ink in front of him. "But you know I know what you're going to say."

I didn't doubt it. But I had to try.

"Then you know you've got to let go of your pain," I said. "You know you can't destroy it; it's not like one of these notebooks, or one of those pillows. You've got to let it go, release it. You've got to disengage, Chase. You said it yourself—there's no shame in walking away."

He raised his head, and I willed myself not to look away from his eyes, thin and black as candle wicks. I could only guess at the pain shielded behind them, but I knew I had to get that pain out of his head. My mind scrambled for a way to get through to him.

"Chase," I said, "do you remember when you asked me to believe in love for you?"

His eyes flicked up and to the left, then returned to mine.

"You do," I said. "Good. Because now it's time for you to believe in it for yourself. I don't know that you've ever had a love to believe in before, but—"

"Astrid," he said.

That annoyed me for a second—I was trying to give him a shot of redemption, and I didn't need him slapping the needle away. Then I got it. "Astrid who?" I said.

He took a breath. "Astrid Tyler."

I nodded. "Tell me about her."

"She was a theater student at NYU. Very pretty. Sharp as a tack. Gorgeous singing voice. When it rained, she'd sit on her windowsill and sing torch songs. I'd be in another room and I wouldn't move, because if I went to where she was, she'd stop singing and talk to me. Not that she wasn't a great talker, because she was. We'd go see plays off Broadway, and then we'd talk about them until sunrise. I mean, we'd digress every now and then …."

He stopped, his strength expired for a few moments. His words had turned from ashes to clay; they were still lumps of lifeless matter, but given the proper care, they could now be made to form something beautiful. I had to encourage the process some more. "And then she broke your heart," I prompted him.

"No," he said, shifting in his chair. His voice was beginning to gain strength, even as his body kept threatening to drop parts, like an old jalopy. "What she did was break my heart open. She's why I got into the joy facilitation business."

"How'd she do that?"

"We were at the West Fourth station," he said. "She told me we were done. We were complete. I thought being complete was good, but for her, it was time for another project. She wrecked me. Then the train pulled in, she got on board, and just like that, she was gone. I never saw her again.

"Right there and then I made two vows: One was to never set foot in another subway station. The other was to never invest myself in feeling happy. I didn't think it was worth the pain. In fact, I knew it wasn't. Any good feelings I would get, I'd redirect them, without hesitation. Better to give those feelings to people who could use them than to waste them on me.

"Well, I was already making the rounds as an excellent party guest, but this vow of mine kicked me up another couple echelons. One night I was in great form, slinging back all the good vibes like they were jai alai balls. A friend of mine said, 'Goddamn, Becker, you could make a living doing this. A professional life of the party.' And that's more or less just what I decided to do."

He crumpled up three or four more pages, his hands moving with heavy, lethargic grace. I waited, knowing he wasn't done. I'd found the right rocks to dislodge, and this landslide I'd started was only going to gain momentum.

He sighed. "Fast forward to the start of summer this year. You introduced me to Nadine. And like I told you the next day, she stopped me. I think she's got a spirit to her that a part of me deep down recognized and truly understood. If that makes sense," he said, his eyebrows rising.

I thought of Alexa and me, our two ships destined to pass. "It does," I said. "That's a rare thing."

"I know. That's just what she said when she emailed me—this is a rare thing, and I have to know where it can take me, she said. So over the next five or six weeks, we wrote and we called and we talked and we did things together, and she did something I'd come to believe was impossible."

"She became your girlfriend," I murmured.

He closed his eyes and bumped the back of his head against his chair in gentle exasperation. "No, Ned," he said. "She healed my heart. It wasn't broken open anymore. It was whole; it was in one piece. She made it okay for me to go to the theater. She made it okay for me to sing in public. She made it okay to take the subway again. Oh, hey—guess what Astrid's favorite song was."

"It was 'Amazing Grace,'" I said. It wasn't a guess.

He nodded. "Point is, I was feeling again. Feeling, Ned. Me. Think about that for a minute."

He lapsed into silence again, a longer silence than his last one. I gave him time to pull the loosened pieces of his psyche back together, and I honored Chase's request and thought about him regaining that sensation of emotional touch. It was a good thought to have. Chase deserved to simply remember his favorite things—and then feel.

"Then you pointed out how my work was suffering," Chase said. Strain was beginning to show in his voice, making it tighter, less supple, but he couldn't stop this flood of words any more than he could stop the sun from going down. "And you were right; it was. I thought that once I realized this, my work would recover, but instead it suffered all the more. I decided the only thing left to do was to break my heart open again. So last Saturday I told her no more. And it didn't work. My heart was still there, still whole. I'm sorry to keep saying 'heart,'" he added. "I have an idea how it sounds."

"It sounds fine," I said. "Go on." I shifted my weight, putting down my hand to steady myself and sending up a few feathers.

"Well, I couldn't focus on my job without her any better than I could focus on my job with her. So I said to hell with the job and went to her place. I was never more sure of anything in my life than I was in the two of us, right then. I got there, I made you and Alexa leave"— he grimaced a *sorry*— "and I told her what she'd done for me and what I could do for her and how much the world had to gain by our never leaving our path again. I held nothing back. She listened to it all. And then you know what she did?"

"What?"

"She said it didn't matter. 'It doesn't matter,' she said. Well, I took that to mean it didn't matter what I thought. I held it together long enough to get out the door, and then ..."

Another silence. I had to be careful here. I couldn't allow him to stop, but I ran the risk of driving him back over the brink if I pushed him too hard. I couldn't yank the words from him; I had to keep encouraging them to come out on their own.

I went to the kitchen (which was relatively spotless) and fixed us each a tumbler of water. When I walked back, I kicked some of the paper and feathers ahead of me; they skittered and floated into Chase, bumping into his feet, sticking to his robe. He took the water from me, then sucked it down in four swallows. He dropped the tumbler down on the right side of the chair; it landed in the row of coils and tipped over with a *clink*, sending a thin stream of water to bead up on a violently creased notebook cover. I got back in my crouch in front of him and waited. I didn't have to wait long.

"I spent the next thirty-six hours going through Pandora's box," he said. "Pain. Jealousy. Rage. It got really ugly. Fortunately, I kept my human contact to a bare minimum. You and your friend Siege were the only ones who interacted with me for any extended length of time, and you saw how well that turned out."

"What did you do?" I asked.

"Most of the time I was here," he said. "Hit all the emotions. Busted up some plates. I swept up the glass that was too dangerous to leave lying around. Everything else, you see." He gestured at the paper and feathers. They seemed wholly apart from him now, another man's refuse illustrating another man's tale. The man before me was a waning disaster, a tornado that had returned to the skies and seen its gusts turn to fading zephyrs.

"Finally," he said, "I was sitting here, tearing out page after page, and I got into a pretty good rhythm, and doing it kind of drained all the irrationality out of me after a while. And then, right in the middle of a rip, a thought occurred to me. I thought, you know, Astrid Tyler never made me act quite like this." He coughed a weak smile up to his lips. "And that made me laugh, right out loud. And I thought, that's it. I've reached the last item in Pandora's box. You remember what that was?"

I nodded. "Hope," I said.

"Hope is right. I laughed. If I can laugh, then I'm going to be okay. I have no idea what I'm going to do, but I know I'm going to be okay. Right now, that's good enough for me." With that, he tore out the final page from the notebook carcass in his lap, pushed both the paper and the cardboard onto the floor. His task and his story were both done, and he could finally let his traces of power go out. "Ned," he said, "I'm kind of beat. I'm going to get some shut-eye."

I stood to go. "Help you up?" I asked, offering a hand.

"No, no, I'm going to sleep right here," he said. "I haven't done this for a while."

"Well," I said, going for the joke, "that's one way to make sure the bedbugs won't bite."

"Just the demons, Ned," said Chase. "Just the demons." He tipped his chair back into full reclining mode. "But do me a favor, Ned?"

"Of course."

"Don't go away until I'm asleep," he said. "I'd appreciate that."

I saw at once that this wouldn't keep me for very long. "I'd be glad to, Chase," I said.

"Thank you." He closed his eyes. "Leave everything the way it is," he said. "I want to clean all this by myself." His voice betrayed his weakness, cracking a couple of times and dying out with a whisper. The flood had spent its force at last.

I didn't think cleaning the place would take long, certainly not as long as Tedd's—all it needed was a good sweeping. Then I remembered something. "Hey, Chase," I said.

"Mmm?"

"You know what Emily Dickinson said hope was?"

"Mm-mm."

"The thing with feathers."

His eyes remained closed, but he smiled and laughed, a laugh that turned into a cough and then back again. "The thing with feathers," he said. "How about that." And by the time the smile had faded from his face, he was sound asleep.

***

Walking back to the subway, I thought of what a paradox I'd witnessed. Chase, at first, had seemed to be weaker than I'd ever seen him before—his body next to useless, his nerves not jangled so much as unraveled. But to me, he was actually at his strongest when he was at his weakest. He wasn't putting up a front of cheer or following any preplanned diagrams designed to generate enjoyment. He was showing his vulnerability, perhaps the most honest thing he could have done. And that refusal to cover for himself was a declaration: he didn't need to pretend. He wasn't going to say everything was fine when it wasn't, and that fact made everything fine. He'd torn down his tower, and now he lay asleep above the rubble, broken in many respects but very much engaged in the healing process.

Still, I didn't want to see him go back out on the playing field for a while. Just because he'd come to grips with so much didn't mean he was ready to start facilitating joy with complete strangers again. It would take him a while to adjust his game to his hard-won knowledge, and he couldn't even start that course of action until he was better. I'm no expert on breakdowns, but I felt that Chase had just had a textbook example of one, and the man simply had to have time to recuperate.

It was a lot to think about. I was glad I had the rest of the day off. I was glad, too, that I'd get the chance to talk about this with Nadine tomorrow night.

8.

"Oh, you brought crumb cake!" said Nadine, patting her hands together in a brief flurry of golf claps.

"It's just your basic crumb cake," I said, coming in. "But it looked pretty good to me."

"It's perfect. I was just fixing us some mint tea."

In a few minutes, we were clinking cups on saucers and forks on dishes. The window was open, and the August night breezes were finding their way past the curtains. Neither of us wanted to leap into the movie watching just yet; there was more interesting stuff to discuss.

"I saw Chase yesterday," I said.

"Oh, tell me." She put her plate on the coffee table. "How'd he look?"

I spent the next twenty minutes answering that question, telling all about my visit and folding in the story of Siege bringing out the knives in Sweethaven. Nadine listened, making little noises of sympathy or appreciation, but saying nothing until I'd finished. She was listening with her whole body, but not as any kind of tactic; every part of her being just Had To Know. I kept the story as real as I could, exaggerating nothing; the feathers and paper didn't go flying in every direction with each step I took, but they really did cover the entire living room floor. By the time I'd finished, I was so caught up in what I'd said that it took half a minute of silence to realize I needed to use the bathroom quite badly. "I'll be right back," I said, and I hastened off.

When I returned, Nadine was still sitting there, nibbling at her cake. She was dressed for comfort in her shiny black pajama pants (they were cool enough that she'd once gone clubbing in them and raked in the compliments all night) and oversize T-shirt, and that colored the way I saw her a bit. Had she been in nicer clothes, she'd have been thoughtful. In a nice dress? Pensive. In the dress she wore on the night she met Chase? Lost In Her Own World. But here, with me, dressed like that, she was Just Kinda Sitting There.

"I talked to him on the phone yesterday," she said. "You're right; he sounded like he was a wreck. Actually, I woke him up, and he asked me to call him in the morning."

"When was this?"

"Maybe eight o'clock last night. So I called again at lunchtime today; he denied it, but I think I woke him up again. I was really glad I got the chance to clear something up with him. Remember when I said, 'It doesn't matter'? That didn't have anything to do with him. What I meant was, it didn't make any difference what we thought or did, because now it's all up to Tedd."

I about dropped my plate. "What's all up to Tedd?"

She put her cup and saucer on the table. "He still hasn't been in touch with me, you know," she said. "Not once. And now it's been more than two weeks."

She bunched up a napkin and threw it at me. She meant it to be playful, but it just served to remind me of what I'd said and left me mortified. "Nades, you have no idea how—"

"Oh, please don't apologize. It would have only hurt if I hadn't agreed with the point you were making. I'm not happy with him right now. But I'm taking the position that there's some kind of reason he hasn't been in touch. I just don't know what it is. So I'll meet his plane, I'll give him the chance to explain himself, and then I'll know what to do about me and Chase."

"Do you know his flight?"

"American Airlines 24, four forty-five. That was the last thing he said, remember?"

This was way more interesting than any movie would have been. "So what did Chase do when you explained all this?"

She took another bite out of her cake. "This is really good," she said.

"It is," I agreed, and I waited.

"Hm." She smiled as she chewed. Finally she swallowed. "He didn't turn cartwheels or anything. He just said, 'Thank you very much for clearing that up, that's good news.' All in one breath. Then we said we loved each other and hung up."

"You said you loved each other?"

"Well, we do," she said, like it was the most natural thing in the world. I don't think she thought of it the same way I did. "Anyway, he still sounded pretty bad to me, worse than I hoped. That's why I asked you how he looked, to see if the visual was better than the voice. Not so much, huh?"

"Not so much," I agreed. "So there's a chance you and Chase—"

"Neds," she said, "let's not follow that yellow brick road quite yet. Besides, I'd way rather hear about you and Alexa."

Once again, I found myself trying to explain to a disbeliever why somebody I was so well matched up with couldn't be my girlfriend. Was this something that only made sense when discussed by the relevant parties themselves, naked on a Sunday morning? I asked Nadine what Alexa had told her, and she said, "Pretty much the same thing. You want my opinion? I think you're both wrong, and you're both trying to talk yourself into believing you aren't, and you can't understand why you're failing."

"Well, you may be right," I shrugged. Really, I've stopped more arguments that way.

We finished our cake, watched *Before Sunrise*, and made plans to watch something else in a few days when Tedd came home and I could move back in. "And two weeks after that, I'm gone," I told her.

"Two weeks? Oh, that's too soon."

"Well, maybe nothing will happen and it'll seem like a long time."

She rolled her eyes. "I doubt that. But listen, do me a favor."

"Sure."

"Don't try to get in touch with me over the next few days. I've got a lot to think about, and I've got to do it by myself. Nobody's input. It's got to be just me. Can you do that?"

She said it with warmth and a very strong sense of resolve, strong enough that I knew that the only answer I could give her was yes.

"Hey," I said, spreading my hands. "Anything for a second cousin."

"Anything?"

"Anything."

"In that case," she said, pointing to the coffee table, "wash those dishes. You're not sticking me with them twice in four days."

9.

We spent the next few days holding our breath, waiting for Tedd to come back. I tried to get in touch with Chase, but he wasn't responding to messages any more than Nadine would have been. Siege bemoaned the reintroduction of Tedd into his life. "It's like I'm the guy who cleans the toilets at Fred's Tacos," he said. "I got the place spotless, you could eat off the floor, and this sweaty fat guy comes trottin' in—"

"You can stop right there."

"Oh, Analogy-monger can't take it, huh?"

Alexa and I talked on the phone Friday, and I spent a good part of Saturday afternoon over at her place. We talked about our spiritual sides and how we couldn't force them to do what we wanted. We also spent some more time exploring our physical connections and finding them to be as strong as ever. In the end, we reaffirmed that the world would be okay without two good singles patching together to make one slightly irregular couple. Either we were mature beyond our years, or we were too scared to make any serious commitment and had to grab for any excuse we could. That's one I don't think I'll ever figure out.

***

August in New York City gets hot like few other places get hot. The sun comes down headlong and takes hard bounces off the streets and buildings, hitting you from all sides. The collective misery of eight million New Yorkers serves to push the mercury even higher. I've never been in Florida or Arizona or anywhere in between, and I know their record highs are nothing to sneeze at. But I'm also willing to bet that they have "nice hot days." In New York City? No such thing.

My last night at Tedd's, I had to sleep on top of the covers in my underwear, lying as flat as I could, not wanting any part of my flesh to come in contact with any other part. Sunday, I showered after walking Nido and then again after lunch. Nido drank his entire bowl of water before noon, a first for him; aside from that, he spent the day lying on the floor, not moving and, of course, not barking. As for me, I did nothing but read and take notes on Stephen Covey. I thought about giving the place one last cleaning, but I decided I'd done more than enough, so all the polishes and powders stayed right where they were.

It was about half past five when the cab pulled up to the curb. I watched from the office window as Tedd climbed out, wearing a white dress shirt and suit pants (but no tie), and went to the trunk to get his luggage. Nadine got out behind him; she wore a white summer dress and a straw hat with a black band. Both of them looked clean, crisp, and cool. She stood by him as he hefted his suitcases out onto the pavement.

I went downstairs. Nido met me at the base of the stairs and tracked me to the door, tail perked up and wagging; he sensed something special was up, or maybe he sniffed Tedd's cologne. I looped a couple of fingers under his collar and opened the door.

There was Tedd, hauling his suitcases up the last couple of steps. His hair had grown out a little, and he looked rested and relaxed. He even had a new pair of glasses, rounder with gold rims. The severe edge was nowhere to be seen; two weeks on the West Coast had really agreed with him, I have to admit.

"Hey!" he said, crouching down in front of Nido. "How's the boy? How's the boy?" Patting Nido's flank, he looked up at me. "You can let go now," he said.

"Oh." I released my hold on the collar, and Nido popped up and gave Tedd's face a couple of licks. Dogs are so nonjudgmental; a guy could learn a lot from them.

"Hey, Ned," said Nadine, moving past both of us. "I have to use the bathroom; I'll be right back." Her sandals smacked her heels as she went by.

"You know," said Tedd, "the whole way from the airport, she practically never let go of my hand."

"Huh."

He pointed, and Nido turned and went inside. Then he stood up and fixed his eyes on me. "So," he said. "Anything to report? Any appraisals on our situation?"

I knew what he meant. I looked right back at him and delivered the line I'd been planning for days. "Nothing untoward happened," I said.

Tedd took this in, considered it. Then he said, "You should know that we had a long talk on our way over here. We talked about a lot of things. If you want to change your answer, now's the time."

"Nothing untoward happened," I said again.

"Nothing untoward happened, or you *think* nothing untoward happened?"

"I won't speculate. Nothing untoward happened."

"Nothing untoward happened," repeated Tedd. He was working up a head of glowering steam. "What's that supposed to mean?"

"You don't know what 'untoward' means?"

"I know what it means," he said. I had a hunch that that wasn't true, but I kept my mouth shut. He still hadn't paid me, after all.

After a few seconds of silence, Tedd figured out that I wasn't going to be changing my story. "New topic," he went on. "The warmer, Becker. You know how much he charges?"

"It all depends on how long he works and how big the crowd is."

"Say, forty-five minutes, twenty-one people."

"That'd be three hundred dollars," I said.

"Well, I need to get in touch with him," he said. "I've got some news to deliver in the office tomorrow, and I'd like the best 'joy facilitator' in the business to be there." He didn't draw quotation marks in the air when he said "joy facilitator," but he might as well have.

"I don't know if he's accepting any new clients right now," I said.

"I think he'll accept six hundred dollars up front," said Tedd, taking his wallet from his front pocket. "Don't you?"

The word *no* withered and died on my tongue. Twice his going rate, guaranteed, after his string of failed gigs would be a big help. But … for Tedd?

"He gave me this the night we met," said Tedd, pulling Chase's business card out with a snap. "Is the information on here still correct?"

"Yeah, as far as I—"

"Fine." He was looking past me, returning the card to the wallet, the wallet to the pocket. I turned and saw Nadine coming back to us, barefoot now, smiling. "Ned, did you clean?" she asked.

"Some," I admitted.

"Tedd, it's like a whole new bathroom," she said, touching his arm. "You've got to go check it out."

"All right," he said, and he reached down and hefted his suitcases.

Nadine and I moved out of the way so he could get inside, and once he'd gone around the corner, I turned to her. "How are you?" I asked, trying to freight it with meaning.

"Good," she said, in a way that told me nothing.

I tried again. "How is everything?"

She nodded. "It's good." Then she asked, "Has he paid you yet?"

And so the conversation turned. "Not yet," I said.

"He made out the check in the cab, so you are getting paid," she declared. "Not to worry."

"Oh, I'm not worried. You know, I should probably get my stuff. What movie are we—"

That's when Tedd yelled from the kitchen, a yell that was equal parts horror, dismay, and anger. "Hey!" he yelled. "What happened to Big Bear?"

***

It took a full minute for Siege to stop giggling.

"I thought you'd appreciate that," I said, switching my phone to the other ear, "but I didn't think you'd like it that much. Come on, you're about to get an aneurysm."

"Oh, that is the best," he managed to say. "Big Bear. Oh God."

"Yeah, it turns out it wasn't Nido's chew toy after all. Tedd's had it since he was about—"

"Fifteen?" Siege suggested.

"Four." I began unpacking my duffel bag with one hand; my composition notebook was right on top.

"So did he stiff you or what?"

"I think he wanted to, but Nadine was right there. She pointed out that I'd saved the stuffing and she had a friend who could fix it, and I'd more than made up for it by cleaning the place. So he gave me the check and I pretty much took off."

"Smart."

"But that's not all that happened." I told him about Tedd looking to hire Chase.

"You think Chase'll do it?"

"I really don't know. Never mind that it's for Tedd; I don't know if he even wants to do the job anymore. But six hundred bucks for an hour's work ..."

"I smell me a rat," said Siege. "He doesn't want Chase's help. He's doing this for some other reason."

"Tell you what," I said, tucking my empty duffel bag back under the couch. "Give me a full report tomorrow. Let me know the minute he shows up, first of all, if he even does. Then let me know later on about the meeting."

"Okay, Chief." There was a pause, and then he said "Hm" a couple of times, his smile embedded in the syllables. "Big Bear," he said. "Chortle, chortle."

**

I called Alexa, and we had one of those forty-minute talks where nothing really gets said. She was peppy but distant; I was kind of the same, but not quite as peppy. Eventually she had to go; Nadine was on the other line. It wasn't a bad phone call or anything; it was just unfulfilling. Then I tried Chase again—still no answer.

I fixed myself a couple grilled cheese sandwiches; there weren't any tomatoes in the fridge, but there was Pepper Jack cheese, which more than made up for it. I finally finished with my Stephen Covey, and I celebrated by watching *City Lights*, one of my favorites, while waiting for Nadine to come home. It was about ten thirty before I figured out that that wasn't going to happen tonight. It was just as well; I always cry a little at that last scene, where the girl who used to be blind realizes who the Little Tramp is, and I still get embarrassed about doing that in front of anybody.

10.

8/8/05, 8:54 AM
To: nalderman@peppercornpub.com
From: cjbrande@loftoncanova.com
Subject: Elvis is in the building

Saw Chase come in. He's not looking like Mr. Happy-Happy Joy-Joy, I gotta say. Tedd, by contrast, looks like the cat that ate the boneless canary. Meeting's about to start – more later.
– Siege

"Mister Alderman, a moment of your time!"

Jamie Engel was across the room, waving me toward him like a cop directing a driver. I closed my email, got up, and followed him to his office. Behind me, Bill hummed some funeral march music. Without looking back, I flashed him the devil's-horns gesture. I'm sure we both smiled at what the other did.

"Grab yourself a seat," said Jamie, plopping down in his chair. He had a somewhat cluttered desk, neither a disaster nor neat as a pin, and a few gadgets—an eraser the length of a hand, a pencil sharpener shaped like a nose. A humidifier churned away in the corner behind him. It kept his office cooler, and it also kept all his office paperwork on the clammy side.

"Nice to have that today," I said, pointing at the humidifier.

"Oh, yeah. Hot as all get-out, right? Coming to work, saw a tree chasing a dog. Not really. So I noticed you and Maylene are leaving in two weeks. Two weeks notice! Ha! And an exit interview seemed appropriate to me. This a good time? Probably should've asked that before I called you in, huh. File under Good Ideas I Almost Had."

"It's a fine time," I assured him.

"Right, great. Break out the crayons and color me relieved. Cough drop? Some days I pop these babies like candy. Some of 'em you gotta watch out for, though. They got an anesthetic in 'em. There's one brand, when I use it, my tongue goes numb. Can't feel a blessed thing with it. Clears my head out beautiful, though." He took a deep satisfied sniff. "Ahh. Feel the burn. So what's your plan, Ned?"

"My plan ... for ... the rest of the summer?"

"Naw, your basic future, you know. Back to school, graduate, then what?" He dropped his elbows on his desk and put his chin in his hands. "Give. Spill. It's your uncle Jamie."

"Uh ... Jamie, I graduated last year."

Now his hands dropped to the desk, and his mouth fell open; I saw more of his tongue than his teeth. "Bullshit! Scuse. I mean—really?"

"Yeah, Maylene's the one who's still in college."

"But you look so young! How often do you shave? No, dumb question, skip that." He started swiveling in his chair, back and forth, his feet banging on the desk to stop him from spinning too far either way. "Adopt, adapt, improve," he said. "Monty Python. Know something? This might not be an exit interview after all. Howzat grab ya?"

Now it was my turn to be perplexed. "I'm not sure I follow."

"Here's the story, Ned. You've made a real impression here. Everybody here loves you. From Maylene right up to me. You got a moxie thing going on that works great here. You chip in, you help out anywhere. You're great on your own too. Your *Little Miss Mafia* idea? Killer. Killer!"

"Hey, how'd that turn out, anyway?"

"Oh, you were sick that day, weren't you? The vote was four to one against. Off the record? Piece of shit. No, that's not fair. Not my cup of tea, put it that way. But off the record."

"Who was the one?" I asked, though I had a pretty good idea.

"Confidential. Really shouldn't say. Turned out to be Peter. I wouldn't have guessed, would you?"

I not only wouldn't have guessed, I didn't even suspect. "Not Maylene?"

"I know! But hold on a second here, I'm trying to pay you some compliments. Take 'em, they're free. What I want to say is, you're a good guy to be around. Always smiling, always glad. Don't know how you do it, but it's great. You realize the entire summer I only called Chase Becker to come in once? That's hundreds of dollars saved, and it's on account of you. You out-Beckered Becker. Is Becker a verb? Should be. Becker. Beckon. Beck and call. To Becker. Toooo Becker. Tobacco. Now I wanna smoke! Ha!"

I know he meant it as a compliment, but it still felt strange to me to be compared to Chase and come out ahead. I wasn't sure I liked it. Chase was the standard for me, something to strive after, reach for—attainment was out of the question, and superseding not even in the realm of possibility. It was a hollow chocolate egg of a victory, sweet but so empty.

"No, I don't smoke really," said Jamie. "What it comes to is this. I want you on my staff. About fifteen grand more than you're making now. Some extra responsibilities. Nothing you can't handle. Room for advancement. Greatest city in the world. You cannot say no, you understand."

I didn't say anything.

"Money? Is that it? Okay, eighteen grand more. Does get expensive around here, I'll give you that."

I just sat there, my thoughts Tilt-A-Whirling through my head. *Work? Stay? Go? Life?* I couldn't comprehend any of this. I'll be honest—if I'd known this was coming, I might not have entered the office.

"Are you thinking, or is this strategy? Thinking, right? Because I'm not going above eighteen. Twenty maybe."

"No, it's just—this is something I can't answer right on the spot."

"Oh," he said, chagrined at having tipped his hand. "Well yeah, think on it. Talk to your mom. Ask anybody here. Forty-eight hours be enough time?"

***

After I left Jamie's office, two cough drops in my pocket ("You might meet a girl and she'll have a cold! Who can tell? Or a guy."), I went back to my desk and sat down. For want of something menial to do, I untied and retied my shoelaces.

"So," said Bill, looking over from his computer. "Been nice working with you. Who gets your stapler?"

"Bill," I said, "what would you say to the idea of me sticking around here for a while?"

He understood at once. "Yeah?" he said, mild even in his surprise. "Well, congratula—"

"No no, it's something … it's something Jamie asked me to think about."

He nodded. "Hope you do," he said. "Hate to lose you."

***

"He asked you to stay on?" asked Lee over her turkey and sprouts on a pita. "Here? With us?"

"Only because I'm not going back to school in the fall," I said, looking over at Maylene.

"Oh, you'd be way better here than I would," said Maylene, waving her hand fast, like a child saying goodbye. A bike messenger whooshing past spotted this and raised two fingers back at her.

"You'd be terrific here, May," said Lee.

"You think?"

"You'd be great anywhere, Maylene," I said.

"Yeah, anywhere," said Lee. She didn't like getting trumped.

"Well, so would you, Ned," Maylene said. "You should think about it, definitely. I mean, I know you're thinking; you should definitely say yes. I think."

Lee got deeply involved with her pita. She studied it as she chewed, and the silence grew until she looked up and saw Maylene and me watching her, waiting. She took a drink of her flavored water, swallowed, and said, "If you think you should, Ned, you should," before taking another giant bite.

Coming from Lee, that was a big stamp of approval.

* * *

When I walked back in, Louise whispered, "Take it," and winked. So five out of five coworkers felt I should take the job, more or less. I figured Nadine would be happy if I stuck around, though I wouldn't want to stay on her couch forever. Alexa might be glad to see more of me, and I knew Siege would—

Siege!

I got back to my desk as fast as I could and brought up my email, and sure enough.

8/8/05, 10:15 AM
To: nalderman@peppercornpub.com
From: cjbrande@loftoncanova.com
Subject: (No Subject)

We. Have. *Got* to meet for drinks. Sweethaven at six. And since I'm the one with the story, and you're the one with three hundred smacks, you're buying. – Siege

11.

I've seen Siege getting ready to go out on blind dates. I've seen him get pulled over for going eighty-six in a fifty-five. I've even seen him on the witness stand in a courtroom for his older sister's custody hearing. But I have never seen him antsier than he was that night at Sweethaven. His leg was jiggling up and down, and he couldn't keep his face still—he bit his lips, licked them, puffed out his cheeks. And yet, for all that, he had a laser focus. He had a story, and by God he was going to tell it.

"This is gonna go on for a while," he said, "so if you gotta take a piss, do it now."

"I went before I came," I said, setting down two glasses of Belgian white on the coasters. "Okay, now tell me everything."

Which he did. And it sounded something like this.

***

Okay, so I just get into work, and I see old man Winters there, the CEO. He never closes the closet door, even though there's signs everywhere saying Don't Forget—it's a real pain in the ass. Anyway, he tells me there's going to be a West Coast strategy meeting for selected members of the trading desk, and will I be one of them. I say sure. "Great," he says, "see you at nine in the conference room."

I start working, and a little later Tedd comes in. Now, Winters is the CEO, but all that really makes him is a glorified office manager with a desk in the back corner. Tedd's far and away our best sales trader, so he's got the most power. Someone could replace Winters and you wouldn't notice; if someone replaced Tedd, you would.

So anyway, Tedd comes in, holding his briefcase and his coffee, and I'm making ready to say something like, "Hey, the big bear is back!" But then he comes over, and he's got a look to him. Kind of a dangerous glow, like they dipped him in nuclear waste or something. Has a smile on him that'll knock you over. Not a good day to mess with Tedd, is what I'm trying to say here.

He says, "Brandenburg, I want you at the meeting today." I tell him I'll be there, but I don't think he even heard me. Or maybe he just went back to ignoring me. Anyway, he walks off, drinking his coffee, and goes to his seat and talks all friendly to the guys over there. They're all buddies, and they're all laughing, pointing at his glasses. He's got new glasses.

I go back to work, and I'm trying to get the best price on a thousand shares of—oh, wait, yeah, you're not interested in that. Skip ahead to about quarter of nine. Chase walks in. He's got something funny going on with him. He's got a nice suit, close shave, perfect haircut— he should fit right in, right? But it's weird; it's like he was wearing a costume, playing dress-up. First time I met him, he seemed like he owned the room. Here, he didn't even own himself. If that makes any kind of sense.

I say, "Chase," and he sees me. Now usually he hits you with that smile, right? Well, this time the smile kinda comes walking up from a ways away. I mean, it's there, but you can see it coming for a while, like it's taking him some time to get it together. Sort of takes away the impact. Still a nice smile, just not much behind it.

He comes over and I start apologizing for how I acted last time we got to talking. 'Cause I was still feeling kinda bad about that. He says it's no problem, and he's about to say more when Tedd calls out to him. He says "excuse me" and goes over. Tedd gives him a big handshake, takes out an envelope and hands it to him, and then steers him over to where Winters is. Tedd's got a few inches on Chase, and he was holding them up high. Chase wasn't exactly slumping, but let's just say his head and shoulders looked like they were feeling gravity's pull a little more, you know what I mean?

I send you that email, and then it's time for the meeting. Winters is at the head of the table, Tedd's next to him, and Chase is sitting behind them in the corner, facing all of us. I thought it was a little weird he wasn't sitting with the rest of us, but that's where they set him up, so okay.

Winters says we're all going to listen to what Tedd learned out in San Francisco and San Jose, and Tedd starts his presentation. I'll skip what he was saying 'cause it's all financial stuff and I don't care to watch you pretend you're interested, because you're so bad at it. No, dude, seriously. Anyway, I'm listening to him talk, and I'm thinking, hey, this isn't such terrible news. Things sound like they're going pretty good. What did he need to bring in a joy facilitator for?

I look over at Chase, all by himself up there, him and his thoughts, and he's looking a little listless. Not bored, just doing his own thing, not really a part of the pack, but he's still got something going on. It was like watching a bowling pin wobble around. It's not doing much, but you keep watching, 'cause you know it's about to do something really soon.

So Tedd looks like he's winding up, and everything still sounds great. Then he nods to one of his buddies, who gets up and leaves. He looks out at all of us and says, "I'd like to wrap this up on a personal note. It's rather unusual, I know, but this is important to me, and I wanted to share it with all of you. As of approximately nine p.m. last night, I'm engaged to be married."

I know, right?

Well, I'm guessing she wanted to tell you in person. Guess I just blew *that* little surprise.

Anyway, a bunch of Tedd's flunkies start clapping. I'm too surprised to. And Chase looks like a ghost just passed through him. He's sitting there getting paler and paler.

Tedd goes on, he says, "Now as some of you know, this has been a long time coming. I bought the ring back in May, and I've been trying to get everything to be perfect for the proposal, and I couldn't quite get it. I made a reservation at Whittaker's. That didn't work out. I was going to take her to that new restaurant Hamilton invested in, on the Fourth of July. That didn't work out. I was going to bring her with me to California—not on the company dime, of course—and take her onto the beach at sunset. And that didn't work out.

"By now I'm starting to wonder if it's ever going to happen, or if it's ever even supposed to happen. Then I remembered that old saying—if you love something, set it free. If it comes back to you, it's yours. If it doesn't, it never was. So, I decided to set her free. I left her to do whatever she wanted. I didn't call, I didn't write—for two weeks I was incommunicado. I was up nights wondering what she was up to, but I'd made a resolution and I let her be.

"Yesterday I came back to New York. I get off the plane, walk into the terminal, and there she is, waiting for me. That confirmed it. I knew she was mine. I mean, I knew it. So I said to hell with the special occasion or fancy atmosphere, and that night, back at my place, I proposed and she of course said yes."

More clapping from the sycophants. The guy who'd left comes back with some paper cups and a few cold bottles of sparkling cider. Not champagne—a couple of the guys who work there are hardcore alcoholics. He starts pouring cups for all of us, and Tedd says, "Now you may have noticed this man sitting behind me. His name is Chase Becker, and he makes a living as a joy facilitator." And the way he said "joy facilitator," he sounded like one of those inspirational speakers who says, "Even if you're a *janitor*, make a decision to be the best *janitor* you can be." You know what I mean? "I have no contempt whatsoever for *janitors*." Yeah. Sure you don't. Well, that's how he said "joy facilitator."

He goes on, he says, "Chase is the best in the business. And I may be being a little selfish here, but I want nobody but the best to give the first toast to Nadine's and my future." He takes a cup of the cider and brings it to Chase, who's still just sitting there. This is the first time Tedd has even looked at Chase since the meeting started. He hands him the cup, he says, "Mr. Becker?" and he steps back, and he's as happy as a pig in shit. Everyone thinks it's 'cause he just got engaged, right? And it's not. It is not.

All I could think of was that time when Chase told me that there was nothing wrong with walking away if your opponent was superior to you. And there was no question in my mind—today, at this specific moment, Tedd was superior. He took his engagement and twisted it into a guy who's all but burned out, and then told him, "Tell everyone here how great I am." I couldn't do that, could you? No, not even on a good day. So I'm sitting there holding my cup and waiting for Chase to walk out the door.

He gets up. He looks over at Tedd, who's standing there blocking the door, I don't know if on purpose or not. He gives him a nod. He looks out at all of us, makes sure we've all got our drinks. And he starts talking.

12.

"I met Tedd and Nadine a couple of months ago at a benefit dinner. I met her first, so I guess I've known her about thirty seconds longer than I've known Tedd. In my line of business, you train yourself to learn a lot about someone within the first thirty seconds of meeting them. So by the time I met Tedd, I knew that Nadine was beautiful, that she was a *Godfather* fan—always a plus, right?—and that she had an amazing soul.

"Let me explain how I think of a soul, because that's a word that gets bandied about enough that it's lost a lot of its meaning. Here's what I think: The human body changes over time—unfortunately. The human mind is constantly absorbing and discarding information. But there's a part of you that stays the same, isn't there? A way of seeing the world. A knowledge of what's right and what's true, one that didn't come from people or from books. An essence. A spirit. Well, to me, that's the soul.

"Nadine's soul is flourishing. It's always reaching out. It's generous. It's loving and kind. It's full of grace. Above all else, it's compassionate. I've been preparing a talk about compassion, so I know the dictionary definition: a profound, strong feeling of sharing the suffering of others and having the desire to help them. Now, I never bought into this definition. I always thought, shouldn't you feel compassion for all people, not just for people who are suffering? Wasn't my modified definition the superior one?

"Then I met Nadine, and she made me see how wrong I was. Because we're all suffering, to some degree, at some level. Nobody's immune. Whether we share the world's troubles, or whether the troubles belong to us and us alone, we all have them, and they all affect us. But then comes Nadine, with her compassion, and she eases our pain. Her soul is a balm to the souls of others. Simply put, she is a joy to be around. Not because she makes a point of being that way, like I do, but because that's who she is.

"Tedd, you've known Nadine for a long time. More than six years, right? Which is, let me do the math, don't forget the two leap years, ah, more than six years longer than I've known her. There's a part of me that wants to envy you for all that time you've had the privilege of knowing her. But I can't. I can't feel any jealousy, any hint of 'how'd he get so lucky.' All I can feel is happiness. I'm so happy for you, Tedd. I think of how I knew her for those thirty extra seconds, and I think of her knowing you that way for thirty minutes, hours, days, years, longer. And I'm so happy, so grateful that she found someone she can bring her joy to, her compassion to, her soul to, every day. Someone who can receive it, who can give it back and watch it being treasured.

"So, I'd like to raise my cup to Tedd and Nadine. May they always love each other. And may they always set each other free."

***

Not a dry eye in the house, man, I'm telling you. People stand up, clapping harder than anybody ever claps in that room. Old man Winters is clapping so much he forgets to take a drink. I do one of my two-finger whistles. And this is nonstop clapping—I keep thinking it's going to slow down, and it's not slowing down. Everybody's just feeling so goddamn happy.

Chase is standing there, holding his drink, smiling at everybody. It's a different smile than his other one. I like his other smile fine, don't get me wrong, but it always had kind of a purpose to it. This is a smile that just is. It's there because it's there. Anyway, I like it a lot better.

Tedd's standing there, and nobody's paying any attention to him, not even his toadies. He's got this look on his face like somebody's just asked him to solve a problem on the board and he has no idea how to do it. Chase goes over to him, puts a hand on his shoulder, and whispers something in his ear. The applause finally dies out, and people are going up to Chase, just to be close to him, going past Tedd like he isn't even there. So Tedd turns and goes out the door. And as he's going, you know what he does?

He zips up his fly.

* * *

"Oh my God," I said. "That's fantastic. Well told, Siege."

He took a long drink. "Just trying to capture the spirit of the thing."

"Did you get to talk to him after?"

"Oh yeah, dude. I almost forgot the best part."

"Wait, it gets better?"

"It does," he said. "After everyone's done practically carrying Chase around on their shoulders, we're all going back to work. I go up, and I'm in the middle of telling him how awesome he is when old man Winters comes up. 'Young man,' he says. He calls everybody that. Rumor is he once called Betty Ford that by mistake. So he says, 'Young man, my niece is getting married at the end of the month, and it would gladden my heart if you would come to the reception and tell everyone there what you just told us here. Whatever Mister Long paid you, I'll double that.'

"Chase says, 'I'd like that,' and he hands Winters one of his cards.

"'Will you join me for lunch, Mister ...'" Siege mimed peering at the fine print of a business card. "'... Becker?'

"Chase says, 'I'd like to, Mister Winters, but I already have an appointment for lunch at Twenty-Eighth and Ninth. I really can't miss it.' And a minute later, he was gone."

Siege sat back and looked at me.

It took a few moments for me to realize that I was supposed to react to something. "What?" I said.

"Twenty-Eighth and Ninth," Siege repeated. "You know what that is?"

I shook my head. "Should I?"

"That's the address for the Church of the Holy Apostles."

I blinked. "He's going to church during the week now?"

Now Siege shook his head. He had a natural smile of his own, much along the lines of how he'd described Chase's. "No, dude," he said. "That's where the biggest soup kitchen in New York City is."

13.

Nadine was in the apartment when I got back, around eight thirty. She was adding a banana to a blender concoction that was whirring away at full blast; her back was to me and she didn't hear me come in. I waited for her to turn the blender off so she could hear the door close and not be startled by my sudden presence.

"Oh hey, Neds. You're just in time for a Sweet Muddy." She opened the cupboard and took out a coffee mug shaped like a monkey, with his arm serving as the handle. It was one of a set; other handles consisted of an elephant's trunk, a giraffe's neck, and the one she was using, a tiger's tail.

"Heavenly hash ice cream," she said as she poured. "Chocolate syrup. A banana. And skim milk. Defeats the whole purpose of skim milk, right? Really, I should never make these. But this is a special occasion." She brought the mugs over, smiling at them, at me as she handed mine over. I have to say, she looked more radiant now than I'd ever seen her look before. Being engaged agreed with her.

I raised my mug. "To Mrs. Nadine Long."

Her smile became an open-mouthed smile. "How—"

"Siege told me."

"Oh, of course." She clinked my mug with hers, and we drank. "Aw," she said once she'd swallowed. "I wanted to be the one to tell you. Hey, check it out." She showed me her ring, and I made a few admiring noises. It was tasteful, not at all gaudy, and it didn't look like it would snap apart with one good pinch. Definitely worth two months' salary.

"Are you going to be changing your name?" I asked.

"You bet I am. Nobody's ever going to say 'Whatchoo talkin' 'bout, Willis?' to me ever again."

"People still say that?"

"People still say that. Believe me."

We drank some more. I knew the sugar and caffeine would mean a late night, but the taste was worth it. It was sweet the way the sun is warm, or water is damp. "Good stuff," I said, pointing at my mug, touching the monkey's face.

"It's going to keep me wide awake," she said, "but I figured I was going to be wide awake anyway. I wasn't last night, but I am today for some reason. I guess it just took a while to hit me."

"Siege told me that Chase gave you and Tedd an incredible toast," I said.

She nodded. "He called me at work to congratulate me. I was a little afraid he might be upset, but he wasn't at all. He was genuinely glad for me, deep down. He had every reason not to be, or to pretend he was. But that was no front. I think he might have been even more excited about it than I was."

"Maybe he made you more excited," I suggested. "Maybe that's why you're more wound up today than you were yesterday."

"Could be," she said. "I guess." She looked down at her Sweet Muddy, staring into it like a gypsy waiting for her crystal ball to clear. The idea of Chase still touched off something strong inside her. It made me wonder how honest I'd been with Tedd. It made me want to have been honest. I had to ask her.

"Nades," I said. "Did anything untoward ever happen between you and Chase?"

She looked up at me, smiling faintly. "Untoward?"

"Yeah," I said. "You know."

I could see her weighing the decision of how to answer me. I was about to apologize for asking such a personal question when she shook her head. "No, Neds," she said. "We never even kissed. We never got past long hugs." She leaned closer. "Is that what you wanted to hear?"

I found myself shrugging and saying, "I don't know. I guess anything you said would've answered some questions and raised others."

"Yeah," she said. "You know, it's funny you use the word 'untoward.' Yesterday Tedd was asking me what that word meant."

I smiled. "That *is* funny."

She didn't smile back. "Neds," she said, "remember when I said that I wanted the right man, not the perfect man? I know you don't think Tedd is perfect. I don't think he's perfect. But I do think he's the right man for me. I like what we have to offer each other. I like what we can bring to the world. Now I know you just want to keep an eye out for me and save me from any more harm. Well, I want you to know that as long as I'm with Tedd, I am safe. Nothing can hurt me in this relationship. Nothing. I'm not asking you to understand it, but I do hope you can look at me and believe, truly believe, that I'm not making a mistake."

I wished she had told me this yesterday, so I would've been able to try one last time to steer her out of the Tedd Seas and into Chase Harbor. But Chase's toast had banished that kind of attitude from me. Besides, the good ship Nadine was never meant for harbors.

"Here's what I know," I told her. "You're the best thing that ever happened to Tedd. If he didn't know that before, he knows it now. And now that he knows it, he might turn out to be the best thing that ever happened to you."

"Aw," she said, and then she was hugging me tight, her arms quite strong, one hand still holding the tiger mug. "I'm glad we're cousins," she said.

"Me too."

I didn't correct her. We may have been second cousins in the technical sense, but this summer we had earned the right to be cousins, just like our mothers before us.

***

It was a good thing I'd had that Sweet Muddy, or I would have been sound asleep at eleven o'clock when Chase called me.

"Hello?"

"Ned? You're still up?"

"I can't sleep," I said, putting down the book I'd been trying to read. This one was all about the Myers-Briggs test.

"Neither can I," he said. "Today was a big day."

Considering Chase's state of mind the last time he wasn't able to sleep, I felt a little pang of worry. But that was washed away by the way Chase sounded. He wasn't driven or agitated like he'd been on his last restless night; instead, his words had quiet buoyancy to them, like balloons tapped back and forth between two kids. There was no distress in his life tonight, let alone his voice.

"Ned," he said, "I helped out at a soup kitchen today. It's not depressing." He said it with true wonder, like it was a stunning revelation, which it very well may have been. "Neither is the subway," he said. "It's just life. It's just people. They're not out to drain me. They don't take any more than they need. You know?"

"Sure," I said, not wanting to interrupt his flow.

"Ned," he said. "Listen to this. One last lesson, one I just learned today. Happiness is like matter. It can't be created or destroyed. What you do is, you have your own well of happiness. You go around making it available. And when people partake of the well, that makes you glad, and the well's replenished."

"So you can feel good now?"

He laughed, a laugh so free and easy, I found myself laughing listening to it. "Can you believe it?" he asked. "After all these years, I've finally realized that it's okay if bringing happiness to people makes me happy. It's not payment for a duty anymore. It's finally a reward."

"Why, do you think?" I asked.

"Nadine." He didn't even pause to think about it. He didn't elaborate any further. Really, he didn't have to.

"Siege told me about your toast," I said. "I'm impressed."

"I meant every word. That's the reason it worked."

"Truth to power," I said. "But Chase, I have to ask." I lowered my voice, in case Nadine could hear me from her room. "Wouldn't you rather it be you and her living happily ever after?"

Silence. Long enough that I was about to ask if he'd heard me. Then he said, "Happiness at everyone's expense isn't happiness, Ned. Things didn't happen because it would've been wrong if they had. I was an obstacle on her path. No, that's not true—I was a gateway. Something she passed through on her journey. And she's a gateway for me. So no, I don't wish that. This is my path, and I'm going to stay on it and see where it brings me."

I sighed. "Well," I said, "I'll let you get moving down that path again. Have a good trip."

That free and easy laugh again, only quieter. "You too. And don't forget to enjoy the view."

"I won't."

"Goodnight."

"Goodnight, Chase."

I put my phone down. After a moment of silence, I got up, went over to the recycling bin, and moved it to the entryway to the living room. Then I went back to the couch, picked up my composition notebook, and flung it. Sidearm, like a Frisbee, with plenty of spin. I didn't get it in until my third try.

14.

My last week and a half in New York couldn't help but be anticlimactic.

After getting advice from an impartial panel—"Do it! You could take over the lease on this apartment!" "Oh honey, I wish you'd come home, but that's such an opportunity." "Don't be a fuckin' idiot, Rooms."—I went to Jamie Engel and told him I was going to pass on taking a permanent position at Peppercorn. He countered with an offer of a $22,000 salary increase, but I told him it wasn't about that; I was simply more an emotional person than a driven one, and for all New York had to offer, it appealed more to my drives than to my emotions. "I've got a different path to be on," I concluded.

"Different path, okay," he said. "Different path. Well, if I can't talk you out of it, I can't talk you out of it. You do what you gotta. *Cough.* Mistake! *Cough.* Sorry, little stuffy here. Wait, sneeze coming … ah … achyoublewit! Kidding! Hate to lose a good guy, Ned. You ever need a recommendation, you come to me. Family takes care of family. Where's that from? *Godfather,* right?"

They had a little going-away thing for Maylene and me. Nothing big, just punch and cookies and good wishes. Maylene sent an email to all departments with her postal and email addresses at Yale, so I followed suit with my own contact info. I was pretty sure it wouldn't get used; interns aren't supposed to be remembered. I'm surprised "forgettable" never shows up in the job description.

***

Nadine was home less than she used to be; she was spending more time at Tedd's now. "It's because you did such a good job cleaning," she said, but I suspected there was more to it. Really, I think Chase's speech might have woken up Tedd a little, made him realize how lucky he was. When I did see Nadine, she would tell me how nice he'd been, how he was loosening up. It was a little hard to believe, but her joie de vivre convinced me as well as anything could have. Anyway, she didn't miss a movie night—our last three were *Diner*, *Gun Crazy*, and (of course) *The Godfather*. Both of us murmured lines along with the actors, but she trumped me in the parts set in Italy, where she murmured along in Italian. Back in high school, Pete Chambers could talk along with Jabba the Hutt in *Return of the Jedi*, but this was even cooler.

"You're amazing, Nades," I said.

"No, I'm not. If it weren't for the subtitles, I wouldn't have a clue what they were saying."

"You *are* amazing."

"Okay, okay, I'm amazing."

***

I also got to see Alexa a couple more times. She was busy planning Nadine's bridal shower and bachelorette party, as well as a going-away party for me. I didn't want one, but she wouldn't take no. What I wanted was to just hang out at Sweethaven and drink and talk and laugh. And since I got to do that a few more times with Siege, I was content.

Well, one more night with Alexa would've been nice too, but it didn't work out. Hey, I never said this was a perfect summer.

***

And so it was that nine o'clock on a Saturday rolled around, and the regular crowd swanned into Alexa's place to celebrate my departure. Most of them I didn't know, though many of them remembered me.

"You're the guy who made out with Alexa on the Fourth of July!" one guy said, grabbing my forearm so he could hold it up and high five me.

Alexa had burned a CD of songs with the word "Happy" somewhere in the title, and it was remarkable how many good ones there were. We heard "Love and Happiness," "Shiny Happy People," "You've Made Me So Very Happy," "Happy Together," the *Happy Days* theme song, even a version of "Happy Birthday" in honor of Aaron Brown the dentist. The best part was when "Happy" by the Stones came on. That was when I first saw Chase. He was in the middle of the living room floor, wearing a black T-shirt and jeans—the first time I'd ever seen him dressed that casual. He was dancing with his eyes closed, shaking his shoulders, punching the air and spinning around. He wasn't using any of the knowledge he'd picked up in his dance classes; he was moving from his gut, with an unselfconscious, uncontrolled exuberance that was fun to watch if you didn't know him and fascinating if you did. He was able to lose himself in the moment, to let go of any plans for the upcoming moments and just let things happen.

Judging by that unforced joy on his face, he was happy to do it.

***

Nadine and Tedd left early. They didn't come to the party so much as stop by; they were going to be at Tedd's all weekend, and since my bus out of Grand Central left at eight the next morning, this was going to be the last time we'd see each other this summer.

"Neds," she said, hugging me.

"Nades," I said, hugging back. It was all we needed to say.

Tedd wasn't much chattier. "Best of luck," he said, shaking my hand. He still hadn't had a haircut, and his new glasses softened his features further. Even his wire-thin smile wasn't as taut as it used to be. For the first time, I felt good about smiling back at him.

"You too," I said, and I meant it.

＊

"Ned," said Siege, "this is Lindsay."

"Hey," she said, shaking my hand. "How's it going?" She was on the short side, not much over five feet. When women are that short, I always expect them to be cute, but Lindsay was more than that. With her auburn hair pulled back in a ponytail, her cheekbones were free to dominate. Her eyes were narrow, catlike, and she had a sneaky smile. I liked her immediately.

"I want to congratulate you," she said. "Siege says you went the whole summer without ever partying until you puked."

"Well, it's early yet," I said.

"Listen," said Siege, holding up a narrow paper bag. "We gotcha a going-away present. I know you like the occasional potable, so I found you this."

"Thanks." I took it and pulled out a large brown bottle. I'd never seen the label before in my life.

"That's a pound and a half of the best beer the Honduras has to offer," he said. "Cost me eleven-fifty, and that's before the deposit. So you better enjoy it."

Knowing full well that this was about as sentimental as Siege was likely to get, I reached around the back of his neck with one arm and gave his back a couple of good affectionate whacks. Of course, he fake-burped.

"Thanks for a great summer, man," I said.

"Leggo of me," he said, pulling back and allowing himself to give me a chuck on the shoulder. Then he steered me toward the wall and leaned in close. "Listen," he said. "You and I are the only ones who know the whole story of how I met Lindsay. Is any of that still buggin' you?"

Maybe the drink and the girl together had brought his guard down more than usual, but he suddenly looked and sounded more apprehensive than I'd ever known him to look or sound. He knew how much it had bothered me that he'd only wanted to use the joy facilitating process to get a girl, and now he needed to know if it still bothered me. I was oddly touched by his concern. Oddly glad, too, to realize he needn't have worried.

"Siege," I said, "You used those lessons to meet a wonderful woman. I could never deny you the joy of meeting a wonderful woman. And I'm sorry if I ever tried."

He brightened. "That's the spirit!" he said, and he grabbed my shoulder again and steered us back to Lindsay, who waited for us with that smile.

"Lindsay," I said, "take care of this guy for me."

"We take care of each other," she said, hugging him. "He's just a big softie."

"She's drunk," he said. "She doesn't know what she's talking about." As she laughed at that, he gave an embarrassed little smile. "On the other hand," he said, "she may be right."

* * *

I brought my Honduran beer to the kitchen so I could put it in the fridge.

Chase was there, taking out a ginger ale. "Hey," he said, keeping the door open for me. "How you feeling?"

"Ready to go," I said. "You?"

"I don't feel so bad," he said. Two and a half months after he'd begun that line from *Sound of Music,* he'd finally finished it.

"Some summer," I said.

"Yeah." He was sweating more than I'd ever seen, with parts of his shirt a darker black than other parts. It was honest sweat, though, not produced by nerves or by just lying in the sun, but by hard play. It looked good on him.

"Listen, Ned," he said. "I need to tell you something." He went over to the sink and ran some water into a bowl that had held salsa. He turned back to me, looking serious.

"I'm not very good at staying in touch with people," he said. "If someone moves away, or I move, and we don't have the option of seeing each other, I just kind of lose contact. So if you send me something and I don't respond, don't take offense."

"Oh," I said. "Well, I'm kind of the same way, so ..."

"Okay." I think both of us were getting uncomfortable at the idea of our impending separation being a permanent one.

He took a moment to breathe, and the sense of calm came back to the room, to our mutual relief.

"Look at this," he said, turning back to the sink. He dipped a finger into the water in the salsa bowl, then pulled it out. "You see how there's a ripple when I put my finger in, and a stronger one when I take it out?" he asked, repeating the procedure for my benefit. "That's the impact you had on me when you came into my life. And that's the impact you have now that you're going out."

I stared at him. "That's all?"

"All? Ned, a splash is over in five seconds. But the ripples from that splash go on and on."

"Chase," I said. "I've learned a lot from you this summer, and you mean a lot to me. So don't take this the wrong way. But this might be the last time we see each other. So if you could drop the Zen for a minute and talk to me in your own words, I'd appreciate it."

He took my words in and thought. Then he started to do his karaoke croon. "Don't you ... forget about me ..."

"Your own words, Chase," I said, managing not to smile too much.

He was quiet again. This wasn't the same Chase I had first laid eyes on twelve weeks ago, easing into the Peppercorn conference room and projecting confidence and warmth. Now he wasn't using his positive emotions as a force field, launching them into those he met. They were staying inside him, a part of him, and those who came up to him in need of sustenance from those emotions would find it. But he was still learning how to tap into them himself.

"I'm not good at this," he said, less an apology than a pondering.

"Try," I said.

He took a long, full breath and looked deep at me. "Please take care of yourself, Ned," he said.

All summer I'd heard him say "Take care" so many times, it had faded in impact to the same intensity as "g'bye." But those extra words changed the meaning of the phrase entirely for me; now it was a wish and a command, made out of concern that I'd have to and confidence that I could. It was just what I'd been hoping for. I wanted to give him a thank-you hug, but he didn't look like he would welcome that. I settled for reaching out and grabbing his upper arm as I shook his hand, making both grips as strong as I could. "You too, Chase," I said. "Be well."

His grip was just as strong as mine. "Be well," he repeated, and he gave me one last smile, the true smile he'd just discovered this summer. I can still see it. "Take a good look," he said. "You're shaking hands with the happiest guy in the world."

**

"You're always leaving my parties early," Alexa pouted.

"Sorry," I said. "I've got an early bus—what can I tell you? I'm sure it'll go on fine without me."

"I know, but still."

I took one last look at the people dancing and eating and, in one case, making out in the corner (go, Siege!). "I did enjoy all of this," I said. "Thank you."

"You know what?" She did that thing with her eyebrows one more time. "I figured out a way to explain to people why we didn't become a couple."

"Oh, tell me," I said. "Any help you can give."

"Okay, listen. We're like the settlers in the pioneer days. We started out planning to go to California, but on the way there, we figured out that Nebraska had an awful lot going for it."

I was elated. "That's it," I said. "That's it exactly."

"People will understand that, won't they?"

"Especially the ones from Nebraska."

"I know."

I savored her eyes one more time before we went in for our goodbye kiss, deep but not hot. For someone who kissed everybody, Alexa still found ways to make each one fresh and new. It was a true talent and I God-blessed her for it.

***

As I walked down the hall, holding Siege's farewell present by its bundled-up neck, the elevator up ahead of me dinged, the doors rumbled open, and out stepped maybe the last person I expected to see here tonight.

"Maylene," I said, stopping.

"Oh, am I too late?" she said, approaching me. She had on the same gray turtleneck she wore the first day on the job. I wondered if it always fit her that closely and I was only just now noticing. She was carrying a small gift bag with rope handles.

"I was just leaving," I said. "How'd you learn about this little shindig?"

"Louise forwarded an email to everybody from Alexa Pine," she said. "Is there no one else from Peppercorn in there?"

"No, no one." Doubtless it was past their bedtime.

"Oooh," she said. "I guess I won't go in, then. But I got a couple presents for you."

"Oh, Maylene," I said, "you didn't have to do that." I meant it too—I still owed her one for not reading *Little Miss Mafia.*

"No, I really wanted to." She reached into the gift bag and pulled out a wrapped present, clearly a CD jewel case. "I hope you don't already have this."

Ten seconds later I said, "No, I don't. Is this—"

"It's a tribute album to John Denver and it's really good. I found it after you said how good his songs were, and it's a bunch of reinterpretations and it's great." Her words ran all together, not from nervousness but from excitement, getting pleasure from sharing something she enjoyed. I knew the feeling well from all the times I'd recommended arcane movies to my friends.

"May, this is great," I said. "Thank you so—"

"Oh, and here's the other one," she said, pulling out a white cardboard box.

"Oh boy," I said. "More cookies."

"No, no. Open it."

I put my CD and my Honduran beer on the carpet so I could hold the box as I opened it. I took out a clear plastic container holding Romaine lettuce, croutons, and flecks of white cheese.

"It's a Caesar salad," said Maylene. "It's kind of a joke gift. Do you remember that time we were eating with Lee and she said she was about to give birth to a salad? And what you said after? I loved that. I really wanted to laugh, but I didn't dare—I thought Lee would kill me if I did."

It had taken almost my entire stay in New York, but at that moment it finally, finally hit me. I could feel the oxygen flooding my eyes as the scales fell away. I hadn't been lunching with Lee and Maylene; Lee had been lunching with Maylene and me. Maylene hadn't been sitting next to me in the morning meetings just because we were both interns. She could've asked anyone to read that manuscript and invited them to her apartment to get it. She'd made those peanut butter cookies a second time after I'd told her how great the first batch was. And all those cookies that she'd always buy for lunch and give me most of— she wasn't buying them for herself. That first day, when she'd bumped into me. She didn't have to bump into me.

Nadine, shaking her head: *You are oblivious, aren't you?*

Alexa, smiling: *Your gender can be oblivious, you know.*

Jamie, sweating and grinning: *Everybody here loves you. From Maylene right up to me.*

"Oh my God," I said. "I'm an idiot."

She smiled. She knew my block on her had just been decimated, that I was now flying toward the half-in-love mark yet again, and I was probably a sight to see. She got up on her toes, putting her hand on my shoulder to steady herself, and gave me one soft kiss that I felt in the backs of my legs. "G'night, Ned," she said.

By the time I got my powers of speech back, she'd reached the elevator doors and was pressing the down button. "Maylene!" I shouted.

She turned to me as the doors opened. "Yes?"

What could I say? Where could I begin? This was too much to realize in too little time. I needed to tell her more, and have longer to tell it. Then I remembered—I could. "I'll write you!" I said. "I have your Yale address and your email—I promise I'll write you!"

She smiled again. "I love you too, Duchess," she said, her inflection perfect. And as she vanished into the elevator, I gripped my Caesar salad until the plastic container started crackling. I knew that Maylene didn't just appreciate me, she *got* me; she got me like nobody ever had before. With that knowledge, I caught the wavelength we shared and rode it across the threshold, arriving at last in the land of 51 percent or more in love.

15.

I kept my promise and wrote to Maylene throughout her senior year. My emails were mostly brief little notes telling her what was new with me—I got a job with Taro Books, thanks in part to a killer recommendation from Jamie Engel; the proper pronunciation of my new hometown was "Lemon-stah." I also sent her handwritten letters that went into more depth about myself, her, and us. Her responses were warm, confessional, and so inspiring.

Before Thanksgiving, we were talking on the phone once or twice a week, and I paid my first visit to Yale on Valentine's Day weekend. When I heard a position was going to open up at Taro, I told her she should apply for it; within a month, it was hers. (Like I said, 90 percent of life is who you know.) Within a week of her graduation, she had found a bigger, better apartment for the two of us to share. We lived together long enough that when I offered her the ring, it came as no surprise.

There was never a question who my best man would be; for one thing, I knew his toast would be the second-best part of the day.

"Ned," said Siege. "Can I just tell you how disappointed I am in you? That summer in New York City, you were seeing a woman. She was rich, she was funny, she was beautiful. I was making plans to visit you and the kids in your bungalow on the Saint Something Islands. Then you called me, your very best friend, to say you were seeing Maylene West. And I, with all the knowledge of you and your ways that I could muster, said, 'Who?' So yeah, I'm disappointed. You kept this amazing woman a secret from me for so long. If I knew you had a fourth for bridge, I would've learned to play the damn game. Now all I got to look forward to is shuffleboard. Maybe I'll get to play it with you both. You'll want to get away from the kids— they'll probably be off running for Senate or something.

"But Maylene, thanks to what I've come to know about you, I think I've been looking forward to this day even more than Ned has. You guys are great together, you're going to have a great life together, you're exactly what Ned has needed—a woman who understands him just as well as I do.

"So, here's to the two of you, and here's to your future, and I'll see you on the shuffleboard court, and may the best man win. Not the bride or groom—the best man." And he pointed at himself and nodded smugly, with a great big grin.

That night, in a honeymoon suite in Cape Cod, Maylene kissed me and said, "I can't wait to meet our little senators."

"We'll have to, though," I said. "Nine months, minimum."

She smiled. "Siege was right. I was a secret for too long."

"You were a secret from *me* for too long."

"You were never a secret from me."

"I'll never be a disappointment to you."

"Never," she said. "Which puts Siege one up on me."

"Let's keep it that way," I said, and we laughed and kissed again.

Now we've got an anniversary coming up, our tenth, and two little girls clamoring for us to go somewhere romantic and take them with us. While we think about it, we're reading them *The Princess Bride* and teaching them why the book is so much better.

***

I didn't stay in touch with any of the other Peppercorn coworkers, though I did have good thoughts about them whenever I saw any books with our little black logo on the spine. Interestingly, once I was at an indie bookstore and found a copy of *Little Miss Mafia* for sale on the remainder table. Turned out they found a publisher after all. The reviews I was able to track down were, shall we say, mixed.

* * *

Nadine and Tedd got married too, but I didn't attend, purely for geographic reasons. Tedd had been bitten hard by the California bug and went after a job with the LA division of Goldman Sachs. Of course, he landed it, and Nadine was able to find a lab job with little difficulty (it didn't hurt to have the award-winning *Enough* on her résumé). I still exchange Christmas cards with them; last year's included a photo of Tedd holding little Matthias ("with two Ts," Nadine wrote on the back). She told me she thinks I might actually like Tedd now. I'm prepared to give her the benefit of the doubt.

* * *

Alexa's the sort of person you can't help but stay in touch with. She sends me texts and emails regularly, and I still get the occasional phone call from her. She aged out of her carefree years with grace and spirit, and she still knows how to make a living by being Alexa. She's threatened to go hunting for a sugar daddy, but she still hasn't found the right star to hitch her wagon to. I hope she does.

Alexa tends to talk more about that summer than the present. "Ned," she once told me, "sometimes I wish you and I had made it to California." I told her I was sure she'd see the Pacific someday, and it would be a treat to watch her celebrate the view.

* * *

Siege and I visited each other a few times over the years, and he was the same as ever, with one exception—Lindsay. She stayed with him and stayed with him until it dawned on him that this was a serious relationship he was in. I think that caught him more off guard than it did anybody else.

One summer weekend he and I were walking up Broadway, and he was wondering out loud if it might be too early for him to commit, that he still had some wild oats and maybe he should get them out of his system. As he talked, about a dozen beautiful girls passed us going the other way (which doesn't take long when you're walking up Broadway). I kept turning my head to admire them, and Siege kept missing them. "How can you not notice all those gorgeous women?" I asked.

"I saw the one in red."

"That's only because she lit a cigarette just before she passed us. You never would've seen her if she hadn't done that."

"Ah, leave me alone."

Then I had an epiphany. "You know why you don't see them? Because you're not looking for them."

He stopped walking.

A year and a half later, I was wearing a tuxedo and watching Siege and Lindsay dance to "At Last" by Etta James. I wasn't best man—some Lofton-Canovan landed that gig—but I was a groomsman, seating all the guests I could, and that was all right by me.

***

Chase kept his word. In all the years since I left Peppercorn, he's never written or called. I've been able to keep track of him, though; he has a high enough profile that he's easy to find on the internet. He's a motivational speaker now, and he does work for an organization called Eat to Live, coordinating benefit dinners and leading food drives.

Sometimes he'll be pictured with members of his or other organizations, and he looks just the same, only more content. It's funny—the people standing next to him are invariably smiling at him instead of the camera. I smile at him too, sending those ripples his way.

On some level, I know he gets the message.

ACKNOWLEDGMENTS

The titles and authors mentioned within all gave me a good view on the mindset and beliefs of a joy facilitator, but the two most helpful books haven't been mentioned until now—they are *Secrets of the People Whisperer* by Perry Wood and *The Game* by Neil Strauss. I can't imagine anybody who loves one will love the other, but they both played extraordinary parts in creating Chase's world.

The first draft of this book was written in a 1968 Airstream trailer. My thanks to my brother-in-law, Steve Whalen, for providing such a fine writing space, and to my parents, Jon and Judy Robbins, for providing such a fine parking space, not to mention food, shower, and unyielding support.

Thanks beyond thanks to Thom Hayes, who believed in this book when dozens and dozens let me know they didn't, and who saw the dream through to the end.

Amy Ashby's edits proved to me that books still have a long way to go even after ~~their~~ they're done. If I ~~was~~ were to have my choice of anyone to make my book better, it would be Amy.

I was lucky enough to have Jenny Boylan, Susan Kenney, Richard Russo, Tony Giardina, Sabina Murray, Brad Leithauser, Noy Holland, and Chris Bachelder for my teachers. The worthy parts of this book came through them and their lessons; the unworthy are mine alone.

Thanks to Erin Coakley, Jim Tamulis, the Goetcheus family, and especially Chris Selicious for the insight into New York City and its denizens.

Many people read early drafts of this and offered support and encouragement that were more needed than they may know. Rather than risk forgetting one name and hating myself for it, please accept this blanket appreciation as being meant for you alone.

Finally, thanks to John Purcell, Jamie Lewis, Paul Neidich, Jarrett Villines, Andrew Bird, and all the Robbins family, just for being you. And most of all, thanks to Rachel Greene for taking my own warmer life and making my own life warmer.

CPSIA information can be obtained
at www.ICGtesting.com
Printed in the USA
BVHW030903230123
656893BV00013B/501/J